Ayan, of the Lucky

Ayan, of the Lucky

FADUMO YUSUF

BEAVER'S
POND
PRESS

This is a work of fiction. Names, characters, places, and incidents are either the products of the author's imagination or are used in a fictitious manner, and any resemblance to actual persons, living or dead, businesses, events, or locales is purely coincidental.

Edited by Ben Barnhart
Cover illustration by Maggie Nancarrow
Book design and typesetting by Dan Pitts
Project manager: Laurie Buss Herrmann

ISBN 13: 978-1-64343-882-5
Library of Congress Catalog Number: 2020903388
Printed in the United States of America
First Printing: 2020
24 23 22 21 20   5 4 3 2 1

Beaver's Pond Press
939 Seventh Street West
Saint Paul, MN 55102
(952) 829-8818
www.BeaversPondPress.com

To order *Ayan, of the Lucky,* visit www.fadumoyusuf.com. Reseller discounts available.

Contact the author at www.fadumoyusuf.com for school visits, speaking engagements, book club discussions, freelance writing projects, and interviews.

*To the children of this world who
lost their homes to war and oppression.
May we all find peace and an accepting home.*

Ayan, of the Lucky

1

An eerie, unfamiliar scent filled the air. Unlike the Somali incense my room usually smelled of, now it smelled of dust and abandonment. I opened my eyes; I was imprisoned in a glass sphere. Outside of it, everyone was happy. As I walked through the crowd of people, the glass moved with me, every step and every move. The terrifying part was that I didn't know a way out.

I walked through the crowd and noticed familiar faces.

You went to high school with her. Look how happy she is! What an adorable baby she is holding. That must be her baby. As I looked at them, they smiled as if ready for the perfect family photo.

Didn't he ask you out at one point? He has a family too, and even a golden retriever. A group hug, how amazing that must feel. Aren't you feeling a little cold? My own voice mocked me.

You went to college with him, and here he is surrounded by his family. I hope you are not getting mad. I am just pointing it out, in case you didn't notice. Look, they are laughing.

I gasped for air as I walked through the never-ending crowd of people. I stopped and looked in every direction. I was surrounded by happy people who were all smiling and content with their lives.

"I will be all right," I whispered, lifting my chin up.

I couldn't join any of them. No one belonged to me, and I belonged to no one. I tried to touch the glass sphere surrounding me, but it moved away from me, keeping its distance. I looked around me, searching for something, anything that wouldn't be repelled by my touch.

The only things I could touch were papers. They lay scattered at my feet like the leaves of a maple tree on a windy autumn day in Minnesota. I picked up one of the papers, an MD certificate to me, Ayan Raage. A tear escaped from my eye and landed on my hand.

"Ayan. Ayan." The voice sounded as if it were inside the glass sphere, but I was alone.

"Ayan, wake up!" Nura, my mother-in-law, shook me by the shoulder to wake me. "Don't you have school today?"

"Oh my God, I am late!" I sat up quickly and tried to be quiet so I wouldn't disturb my sisters-in-law, Hibo, Hodan, and Haboon, with whom I shared a bedroom.

"Keep it down," Hibo said from her bed. "It's early!"

I ran to the bathroom, got ready as quickly as I could, and left the apartment.

As I walked out of the building, I was greeted by the fall wind. Our neighborhood felt windier than the rest of the city.

Maybe the buildings harness the wind and funnel it down on anyone who dares to walk its sidewalks.

My building was the M building, and from it I turned right toward the D building, where our school bus picked us up. As I walked toward D building, I wondered about the checkered walls of the Cedar-Riverside towers—pink, gray, white, blue, sometimes red and yellow.

Why did they name the buildings with letters only? Buildings B, C, D, E, F, and M. Why is there no building A? How did they go from F to M building? Why did the architect design these buildings this way? Such a unique pattern! Maybe the pattern meant something to the designer. Maybe the architect designed them with immigrants and refugees in mind—different, yet with a place in America. Maybe the architect was a refugee like I am. Stop looking at these buildings and walk faster before you miss your bus!

I made it to the bus stop with a few minutes to spare. I wondered if I would see my best friend, Nasteho, on the bus that day.

I stood there with my eyes closed and enjoyed the fall wind caressing my face. I lost myself in the music of the fallen leaves. The wind was making them dance freely, without a care in the world. There was something so beautiful about those leaves.

I was startled by a strong wind that almost knocked me over.

While I waited for my bus, I couldn't help but think about the dream that I had had this morning before Nura woke me up. It lingered in my mind. I remembered all the happy faces that I'd seen. I remembered how alone I'd felt in that glass sphere. Tears came to my eyes as I thought of the family that I had once had. A family that I might never see again.

I opened my eyes and reached into my backpack to get my black journal, one of my two most precious possessions. It was so precious that I refused to go anywhere without it, just in case I couldn't go back home. I gently touched the half rose carved into the cover and remembered my family and a time when I belonged. I remembered when I had a family to call my own.

- protoganist is a refugee, who is probably living in a house with other refugees

2

I was eleven years old, in the living room of Uncle Ali and Aunt Zainaba's house in Mogadishu. My cousins and I were watching *Willow* when Uncle Ali, my father's younger brother, called for me.

Adults sure know how to ruin a good moment, I thought and went to the yard where he was sitting with Aunt Zainaba.

They were sitting on a white swing on the yard between two big palm trees. Aunt Zainaba's bare toes played with the grass beneath them. She was sitting on the left side, close to Uncle Ali, gently moving with the swing.

Aunt Zainaba loved letting her long hair loose and sitting on the swing as the wind made her hair dance. Uncle Ali would often join her on the swing, where they would chat, smile, and laugh. Often, they would get lost in each other's gaze.

Uncle Ali was tall and big, and Aunt Zainaba was very short and petite.

How do they hug each other? I couldn't help but wonder, because their odd sizes seemed like the wrong pieces of a puzzle put together.

I am definitely going to marry a man who is my height. As I walked toward them, I made up my mind about my future husband's height.

"Yes, Uncle, did you call me?" I asked, hoping that I was not in trouble. I could never tell whether he was angry or happy. He always smiled. He was a gentle giant.

"Yes, Ayan, I just wanted to say that I am very proud of you! Your teacher called me today to say you scored the highest again. You are number one in your whole class. Well done, my daughter! Well done." Uncle Ali patted my shoulder as he praised me for working hard and doing well that year.

"Thank you, Uncle!" I smiled.

He then handed me a gift, wrapped in maroon gift wrap with beautiful white roses, my favorite flower.

"What is it?" I asked, looking at him with admiration.

"Open it, you will see," he said, smiling.

I opened it carefully. It was a thick book, with black hard covers and rough texture. In the middle of the cover, an incomplete rose was engraved deep into the cover. I thought it was a textbook that was going to help me become a doctor.

Looking for a title, I flipped the cover hastily. It was a blank book with no writing on it, except for one line on the first page that read, "To our future doctor, Dr. Ayan Raage."

Puzzled, I asked him, "What is it, Uncle?"

"Well, since you love stories so much, I figure you would like a book where you can write your own stories when you have time. Do you like it?" he asked me.

"Cool! Thank you, Uncle. Yes, I love it!" I said.

"I didn't know what to get you. I am glad you like it," Uncle Ali said.

"I love it, Uncle! Thank you."

"Ayan, don't be scared to speak your mind, and don't ever be scared to ask for what you want. In life, it's important to be honest with yourself and with others. I just wanted to see your reaction. Here is your real gift." He handed me another gift.

I opened it and found a beautiful necklace with a pendant that read *Dr. Ayan.*

"Thank you! Thank you, Uncle! I love you. You are the best." I gave him a big hug.

"You earned it! Good job! Seventh grade is tougher than sixth grade. Keep working hard and I will get you a better gift. I promise," he said as he smiled with his perfect white teeth. Now that I think about it, it might have been his thick black beard that made his teeth look extra white.

"Thank you, Uncle!" I hugged him again and ran to my bedroom, which I shared with Fathiya, Uncle Ali's oldest daughter.

❧ I swung the door open with all my strength. It hit the wall with a loud bang and swung back at me, almost hitting my face. Our steel door was decorated with golden flowers and colorful leaves that seemed like they were plucked from a steel valley filled with colorful flowers. I took off my shoes and stepped into the room where my bed and study table were on the far side of the room, below the window opposite of Fathiya's bed and study table.

I looked at my necklace, gold and beautiful. I put it on and then took it off. I decided that I was going to wear it the day that I became a doctor. I looked at the mirror and imagined myself wearing a white coat with a stethoscope and a bright smile on my face like Uncle Ali's. I put my new necklace in my collection box and closed the drawer.

I flipped my pillow and grabbed my black pen. I had hidden it there because Uncle Ali and Aunt Zainaba didn't allow anyone to use pens before high school.

Uncle Ali always said, "How are you going to learn from your mistakes if you cannot erase them to fix them? Plus, you will be wasting paper. Paper is made from trees, and trees are important."

"No one can erase their mistakes completely," Aunt Zainaba would add. "That's why smudges are left on the paper as a reminder to be careful next time. Of course, that's when you use pencil, so use pencil." My uncle and aunt sounded like a bad commercial for pencils.

On the left side of my table, the most recent books that I had read were organized neatly: *The Holy Quran, Human Anatomy, Biology, Sixth-Grade Math, Seventh-Grade Math, Ayaan Daran, Sayid Mohamed Abdille Hassan Poems,* and *World History.* I loved reading and trying to understand books that I was either too young to read or that I wasn't supposed to read. My wall wasn't yet decorated with awards as Fathiya's wall was. I used to imagine my wall filled with awards.

I straightened the only frame on the wall above my table—a handwritten quote from my mother that read:

Life is four seasons on a circular thread, until death cuts the thread and makes it a line:

The first season is the downpour season, the season of happiness. It puts a smile on our face as everything comes to life. It plants the seeds of inner peace deep in our heart.

The second season is the chilly season, the season of fear. It kills most of the grass and doesn't give a drop of rain, but it leaves just enough brown grass to feed the animals.

The third season is the season of scattered rain, the neu-

tral season. It neither makes everything perfect nor destroys anything. It's the season of hope.

The fourth season is the season of famine, the season of destruction. Everything dries, deforms, or dies, except for that which endures.

In whichever season you find yourself, prepare for the next one and you will be of the few that endure.

I sat at my study table and decided to write my own story first. I would write about my childhood in Ruuraan, living as a nomad with my parents in the outskirts of a village in Somalia.

As the Butterfly Flies Away

"Mom, why do we have a butterfly in our hut?"

"It will ward off the evil eye and keep our family safe."

"But why trap it in a bottle? Doesn't it have a family?" I remember asking her in an innocent voice.

"To keep it in its place. Everyone has to do something that they might not like to keep their place, to be respected, to be honored, to be happy, and to find a bright future, a husband, and motherhood. Sometimes we have to be strong enough to live through the darkest times and through the most excruciating pain to find ourselves. We might even have to lose a piece of ourselves to find a better future for ourselves and for our loved ones, especially we women."

"But it doesn't belong in there. What if it loses itself and becomes human? We have to let it go, Mom. Its family and loved ones are waiting for it."

"Ms. Know-It-All, don't start with me now. And yes, it does need to stay in the bottle, or else it will spread its wings and fly away. It could get hurt."

My mother twisted my hair in a bun so it would stay in place and not be buried in the sand while I slept. She kissed my forehead and stroked my bangs back gently with her long, thin fingers. I could smell the smoke from all the food that she made mixed with Somali incense, uunsi, and foox. She then blew the light out and walked out of the hut.

I untied my hair by shaking my head from side to side until I could feel my hair on my back. I laid my head on my pillow, shaped from sand, under my green mat and stared at the only light in the vast darkness—that poor butterfly—before drifting off to sleep.

Earlier that night, Grandma had told us the story of shapeshifters called Qori Ismaris.

Grandma told us that there was an ancient Somali tribe that had discovered a very special plant. This plant was so special that when someone puts its dried sticks on their skin, they could turn into any being they wanted to. One season, thousands of years ago, there was a really bad drought. A lot of animals and people died because of the drought. To survive the drought, this ancient Somali tribe became cannibals. To this day, they turn into wild animals like lions, hyenas, wolves, and foxes to hunt and eat people.

They have also developed the ability to turn into any human being they wanted to. They do this to trick kids into coming with them to far places, away from their families, so they can eat them. Sometimes they take the kids to their place to fatten them up for months. They pretend to be their family members until the kids have enough meat on their bones, and then the cannibals eat them.

Grandma told us many stories that night, and Grandma and Mom seemed very happy. They fed us well, and they let us sleep in our favorite corner of the hut, a corner that was usually reserved for older people.

I wonder why Grandma and Mom are so happy tonight? I had an uneasy feeling in my gut, but I ignored it and went to sleep.

The next morning, my father woke us by saying, "It's prayer time!" and then doing the call to the morning prayer. Everyone woke up to the prayer call and started getting ready.

Around our huts and animal pens was a fence made from thorny shrubs that my brothers, uncles, and dad put in place to protect us from wild animals. The huts were on one side, and the pens for camels, goats, and sheep were on the other side.

My dad was praying on a mat between the animal pens and our huts. My mother was starting a fire on his right side toward the entrance in the fence. It was still dark out and a little hard to make out everyone's face.

My sisters and aunts were sharing one water container for their ablution, and my brothers were sharing another water container. Grandpa, Grandma, and my uncles each had their own water containers.

Like soldiers getting ready for battle, everyone did their ablution quickly. My father started leading the morning prayer. My father never waited for anyone, so everyone got ready quickly so they did not miss the morning prayer with the family. He stood in the front, while all the men in our family lined up behind him shoulder to shoulder, and all the women lined up behind the men shoulder to shoulder.

After finishing the morning prayer, my father gave a short lecture about the hereafter and how our goal in life was to please God by doing good deeds and by helping those who are less fortunate. Once he was done, everyone went on about their duty for the day.

My younger sisters and I were to herd the goats and their kids. My older sisters Ahado and Sulekha would milk the goats, then they would let the kids feed. My sisters would put the milk in a container called a *dhiil,* and then our family would share the milk by drinking from the *haruub,* which is the lid of the dhiil. Several members would often drink from the same haruub. I liked goat's milk best.

Our family was rich in the sense that we had a lot of goats, sheep, and camels. Everyone had a chore for which they were responsible, until someone got married, ran away, died, or could not do their chores anymore. At that time, everyone's duties were reassigned to make sure all the chores were getting done.

That morning, my mother told us that we were not going to herd the kids. We were going to do something special. At first, I thought we were going to go with my mother to the nearby village. I had never been to the village, but my sisters told me about it.

They told me that they used something called *money* to buy anything they wanted. They said that I could give the people in the city one of our goats, milk, or butter and that they would give us money. They said there were a lot more people in the village and that their houses were different. I thought that maybe it was the day that we would finally go to the village with Mom.

"Ayan, take a jug of water and go wash up," my mother said. "Take your sisters Asli and Ramla with you and make sure you help them to clean up good like the big girls you are."

From the moment those words came out of her mouth, I knew what was coming. My veins shivered with fear. I had heard from my sisters and cousins about the horrors of this day. I had heard about the pain that they experienced and the weeks it took them to heal. I knew it was coming, but I didn't think it was time already.

"Mom, do I need to wash up? I washed up three days ago. I will just go help them. I don't need to wash up." My voice quivered.

"No, Ayan, today is a special day. Go clean up and help your sisters too." My mother gestured with her hand to go clean up.

I was eight, my sister Asli was six, and Ramla was just over four. Asli and Ramla were happy that they didn't have to go herd the kids with me that day.

They were playing tag around the huts, unaware of their fate. I couldn't help but feel sorry for them. I knew this day was coming; it had been my nightmare for the past four years. It was long overdue for me because my mother wanted all three of us to have it done at once. I had heard plenty of tales, tales of terror about that day from everyone for as long as I remembered. My sisters, my cousins, my mother, my grandmothers—every woman I had known had lived through it. The younger ones described its pain, and the older ones told about its glory and honor.

I remember asking her, "Mom, why do adults glorify this terrifying custom?"

"Because adults have a third eye, an eye that sees beyond pain and struggle. It's an eye that sees the good in the bad, in the ugly, and in the painful."

"Where is this third eye? I have never seen an adult with three eyes," I remember asking her.

"You won't see it, dear; it's deep within us. You will understand it when you become an adult."

"What about the fourth eye, the one you have in the back of your head? The one that lets you see us when we are playing behind you? Do all adults have that too?"

"No, dear, only mothers have that." She smiled and fixed my scarf. I looked at her shining brown eyes filled with love and care.

"Why is it that only mothers have the fourth eye?" I asked.

"Because mothers love and care about their children so much that we developed a fourth eye that enables us to keep an eye on them. So we can always protect them from harm and be there for them."

"What about when we go to pee? Do you still watch us?"

"You never run out of questions, do you?" My mother walked to her hut laughing.

My sisters and I walked away from our huts toward the largest bush we could find. We took a shower there, helping each other. Once we were done, we put on our clothes, and my sisters chased each other back to the huts. I was torn between running away to become a coward and going through it quietly like a woman. I walked behind them slowly, my heart beating faster with every step that I took toward our huts.

Then I saw her, and I knew I had made the wrong decision. The old hag that had butchered so many little girls was here, and she was ready to feast on our blood. Her eyes were red, her face was wrinkled, she had no teeth, her skin was dry and dusty, and she had cuts all over her skin. She looked like a monster. She was washing her blades, which she was going to butcher us with. Everyone was ready. It was our turn to be butchered in the name of protection, respect, and honor.

Four of my aunts, my grandmother, and my mother were in the hut chatting with her as she gave them instructions for how the job was going to be done. I tried to run back outside, but my brothers were already at the door, ready to force us back into the hut if we decided to run away. We were trapped. The old woman was waiting for us. She had no mercy in her eyes. I knew crying to her would be of no help. My sister Asli was grabbed first, and they pinned her to the ground. While two aunts held her hands to the ground, one of my aunts sat on her lightly so Asli wouldn't be able to move her little body, and my grandmother and one aunt pinned her legs to the ground.

The butcher looked at her vulva and said, "She is clean. I will start cutting her now." She said it as if my sister were a piece of lifeless meat. I knew we were in trouble, and I acted cool as I waited for an opportunity to run away.

My mother left the hut because she couldn't watch her little daughters being butchered. Her eyes were tearing up because she remembered what she had gone through. I tried to make eye contact with her to show her my pain, but she wouldn't look at me and soon was out of my sight. They put a piece of cloth in Asli's mouth so she wouldn't be able to scream with agony. The monster was ready to butcher.

She put a bagful of blades on her left side and a big bowl of warm water on the right side. I couldn't see my sister's face, but I had a perfect view to see everything else. I could hear her screaming with pain underneath the cloth as her body turned red with the struggle. Ramla started crying, and they took her out of the hut. I started crying too, but no one cared. In fact, they called my brothers to stand near the hut so they could catch me if I ran away. I was to be next after Asli.

The old monster started cutting my sister's vulva. The blood that was gushing out of Asli's body terrified me, but there was nothing that I could do. The old hag had no mercy and acted as if she was not a bit moved by the pain that my sister was going through. She sliced Asli's clitoris, then her labia, and everything that was in her vulva until there was nothing left except for a little bit of her labia majora to be sewn together.

No anesthetics, no painkillers, and nothing to ease Asli's pain were used. The old hag just continued cutting her flesh as my sister felt every bit of the cutting and the pain. I couldn't watch it anymore. I wanted to get out of there, but there was no way out. I started throwing up and crying. I faced the wall, but I could still hear Asli being butchered and felt her pain. One of my older sisters came into the hut and cleaned the vomit.

"Please, sister," I pleaded, "help me get out of here! I don't want to be circumcised! Please!"

"Stop being such a coward! You are big girl. Start acting like one and stop crying! Your younger sisters are watching you." She slapped my hand off her arm and walked out of the hut.

"Heartless! Die! Disrespect! Ugly! Monster! Monsters! Devil! Evil! Shit! Evil eye! Witch! Black magic! Urine!" I screamed every bad word that I could think of. I kept crying loudly, unsure of what to do or feel!

I got up, grabbed the bottle that contained the butterfly, and shattered the bottle. I charged toward the door with a rage like a mad bull. I ran out the door as the butterfly flew over me, but it was blinded by the sunlight and fell to the ground. I couldn't help the butterfly, so I kept running, and before I knew it, there was a whole army of family members chasing after me.

I ran as hard as I could, and our running raised the sand of the desert like horses galloping at full speed. I was running for my life, and they were running for my life.

One of my brothers was getting very close to me, but I couldn't run any faster. He then pushed me and fell right behind me as I fell on my face. My nose started bleeding and my face was scratched, but he didn't care. He was happy he had caught me. They dragged me back to the hut. I watched my brother put the butterfly in another jar. It was my turn to be butchered.

I went through the same thing that my sister had. I couldn't scream, I couldn't cry, I couldn't move—there was absolutely nothing I could do. There was nothing I could do to stop feeling the pain as my flesh was cut from my body. She then washed off the blood, spiraled down a rope from my hips to my ankles to tighten my legs together like a mermaid. I couldn't get up alone, I couldn't walk without turning my feet from one side to the other, and I couldn't urinate without help.

We were tortured for another two weeks to make sure that the wounds healed properly so we wouldn't have to go through that pain again. We were fed nothing but dry bread and no more than a cup of water for the whole day. They wanted to minimize our urine so it wouldn't open the newly sewn wound.

"Ayan, you need to drink water! Open your mouth now and drink this water," my mother insisted.

"No! I will not drink it! I would rather die of thirst than drink that water!" I cried.

"Ayan, just take a sip. You will only have to pee once for the whole day at the most. I don't want you to die. Please drink some water, and I will buy you new clothes and take you to the village once you heal. You are a woman now."

"I would rather die than go through the pain of peeing! And you can tell your friends that thanks to you, your daughter died!"

"I am your mother; I only want what's best for you. No one will respect you and no one will marry you if you are not circumcised. I went through it too. So did your older sisters and your grandmother. We did it for our future, our honor, and respect," my mother tried to comfort me.

"I hate you all! I hate everyone! I will run away to a far, far, faraway place, and you will never see me again."

"Ayan! Don't ever talk to me like that, young lady! I am your mother! And you are a girl. You should know your boundaries. Do not raise your voice again!" My mother stormed out of the room, taking the water with her.

In those two weeks, every morning, my mother would dig three holes after everyone left to fulfill their duties for the day. She would burn wood until it started smoking, and then she would put the smoking wood in the holes, and then she would help us sit over the holes until the smoke died out. She said it was to help us heal faster and keep us from becoming infected.

I started to take the butterfly out so it could get used to being outside, alone in the sun. With time, the physical wounds healed, and the old woman came back to confirm that we had healed. She removed the ropes.

Fortunately, none of us had to go thought it again. I walked freely for the first time in two weeks. I walked far from the huts to the largest bush that I could find. I took a small mirror with me.

At first it was hard for me to look at it, but I convinced myself to take a good look at it. Nothing was left but a flat surface with a small kite-shaped hole. It was nothing like what it used to be.

"I have lost my vulva!" I cried as salty tears rolled down my cheeks.

I looked around to make sure no one was around, and then I started crying out loud. I had lost a part of me, but I found a different part of me, one that I was trained not to have—my voice.

The very next morning, I broke the bottle that imprisoned the butterfly and watched it spread its wings to freedom as it flew away from the darkness and into the light.

3

I closed my new journal with my first entry about my life in Ruuraan, where I was born and had lived with my nomadic family. And then I looked at the clock and realized that I was late for my lesson with Mohamed, Uncle Ali's oldest son.

I sprinted to the study room across from our bedroom, where Mohamed was studying.

Think, think, think of a good excuse to tell him, Ayan. I urged myself to come up with a plan before going into the study room. I tried to think of an excuse to tell him, but nothing came to my mind.

Why can I not think of anything when I need it? I went into the study room.

"You are late! You are late *again!*" Mohamed said, shaking his head.

"Sorry, Mohamed. I was doing something important."

"No excuses are allowed. Don't come late again. Lazy, unprepared, and dumb people come late, and they don't get anywhere in life, but they become a burden on other people," he scolded me.

I apologized to him again, noticing the oversize glasses that were too large for his small head. "I am sorry, but I'm only ten minutes late."

"Ten plus ten plus ten plus ten plus ten plus ten equals sixty! That's a whole hour, and before you know it, it's a lifetime. Don't come late again, or don't bother coming to class." Mohamed pushed his glasses back with his pointer finger.

"We are not in an operating room performing the surgery of the year. Relax, would you?" I rolled my eyes and sat across from him.

"If you were to perform surgery, your patient would have been in the grave by the time you got there," Mohamed said defensively.

"Right, like yours would have survived. You would have killed the patient by yelling at your nurses for coming two seconds late. Take it easy, man. Life is not about the destination alone."

"You are twelve! What could you possibly know about life?" He chuckled.

"I know more about life than you will ever know. You are laughing like you know anything about life yourself. You were born with a silver spoon in your mouth. Do you even know what the real world looks like?" I said.

"Just because you were born in the middle of nowhere under a tree doesn't make you an expert on life." He laughed.

"Good comeback, genius. You are learning how to talk," I whispered.

"Are you showing me your nasty attitude again? I am your teacher, young lady."

"My teacher? You wish! What do you know to be my teacher? You are a student yourself, trying to make it out of high school."

"All right, then, I will not teach you. And for your information, I am graduating with the highest score in the whole country. I also got into the best university in Somalia and the best university in the United Kingdom. Let me see you top that!" He returned to his reading.

"Come on, I was just playing with you. This is only my second time coming late to class. Please teach me. I promise I will never come late to class again."

"The first time leads to the second time, which will lead to the third time, which will lead to—"

Oh my God, here goes the broken tape again. Doesn't he ever get tired of thinking of the future and what's next?

"Okay, I get it! I am sorry, my great teacher. I will never come late to class. Now will you please teach me some math? I don't want to waste all my time arguing with you." I cut him off before he could finish his sentence.

"Say, 'Mohamed is the greatest teacher in the world,'" he demanded.

I looked at him, rolled my eyes, and said, "You are a great and awesome teacher. Now would you please teach me some math?"

"Yes, stu-dent," he said like a robot. "You may sit on the chair properly like a lady."

I sat straight, relieved, and opened my math notebook.

"Have you done any algebra yet?" he asked.

"Yes, it's all over the seventh-grade math book. I know how to solve most of the problems."

"All right, smarty-pants. Do you know how to solve equations with two variables and equations with three variables?"

"Yes, equations with three or more variables take me a little longer, but with practice I should be able to do them well. Could you teach me something that's cool and not in my textbooks?" I asked him, hoping to learn interesting things.

"Did you ever learn about matrices?" he asked.

"No, but it sounds interesting."

"Let us start from there, then. You won't learn it until you get to high school, but it's really cool, and you can use it to solve algebraic equations."

"Thank you, my awesome brother!" I said as I saluted him like a soldier.

He laughed and started telling me about matrices. About an hour and a half into the lesson, Halima, Uncle Ali's second-oldest daughter, came into the study room saying, "Nerds, come out, it's time for some tea. Everyone is waiting for you."

"Let's stop our lesson here today," Mohamed said. "I will show you more ways to solve matrices tomorrow. And don't come late to class. I don't want you to make it your habit."

"All right, let's go have some tea."

It was four o'clock in the afternoon and time for tea. The tea was sweet and aromatic with all the spices that Suad, our maid, had added to it. I could taste the cardamom, cinnamon, cloves, ginger, and mint with every sip.

Everyone came back from school, from work, from the library, or just from their rooms. Every one of us—Uncle Ali and Aunt Zainaba, their nine kids, Grandma and me, our watchman, Dayib, and Suad—sat on two large mats that were spread on the grass near Grandma's bedroom. Even though we had ten white chairs and white round tables in the yard, we all preferred sitting on the mats at teatime. There was something about sitting close to the ground and smelling the freshly cut grass. The only people who sat at the white tables were people who were reading and guests.

Everyone got a cup of tea and some cookies. Grandma started telling us a story about two men who were the best of friends. One was called Dheeg, and the other was called Dhuley. They were very poor and used to beg people in their village for food. They shared the food they got with each other every day. One day, Dheeg got greedy and did not want to share the food with his friend Dhuley anymore. He thought that if Dhuley were no more, Dheeg would have all the food to himself.

Dheeg and Dhuley did not have a home, and they lived in an area filled with lions that ate people. The friends used to sleep under the trees and keep an eye out for the lions. Dhuley used to keep watch on the first half of the night while Dheeg slept. They would then switch, and Dhuley would sleep while Dheeg kept watch. One night, Dheeg waited for Dhuley to fall asleep, and instead of keeping watch out for the lions, he left his friend there to be eaten.

Dhuley woke to the growling sound of hungry lions. He got up and ran for his life. He knew that he couldn't outrun the lions, so he ran to a cave with small entrance. He crawled through the small entrance, and he was fortunate that someone had cut down a thorny bush near the cave entrance. He used it to block the entrance so the lions couldn't come into the cave, and he stayed there for the night. The lions did not find him.

The next morning, Dhuley was woken by the sun's rays. He got up and looked around the cave, and he found a box filled with treasures and beautiful jewels. Dhuley guarded the cave for weeks to see if anyone returned for the treasures, but no one came. He went to the mosque for eight weeks asking if anyone had lost treasure, but no one claimed the treasure that he'd found.

Dhuley took the box with him and left a note saying, "My name is Dhuley. If you have left your treasure here, please come find me in the village. I promise I will keep your treasure safe for you." In time, Dhuley sold enough jewels to start his own small business. When he had enough money, he bought the jewels of the same quality and weight as the ones that he had sold to start his business, and put them back into the box with the rest of the treasure. He wanted to make sure that he didn't take another person's wealth, because it was forbidden in Islam. He also put half of the share of his business profit into the box, treating the owner of the jewelry as a business partner.

Ten years later, Dhuley became the most trusted businessman in all of Somalia, and he became the richest man in all of Africa. One day, the king came to Dhuley and asked if he had seen his treasure. The king told

Dhuley that he had hidden a treasure for his family in a cave when his kingdom was conquered by another kingdom and that he found Dhuley's note. Dhuley asked the king to answer several questions about the box and the treasure inside. The king got all the questions right. Dhuley gave the king the box and ten other big boxes filled with money, from his share of the business that Dhuley had started.

The king was impressed by Dhuley's honesty and business sense. He asked Dhuley to meet his only child, his daughter. Dhuley and the king's daughter met and fell in love. Dhuley and the king's daughter, Dhamo, got married. Before the king passed away, he named Dhuley as his successor. After the king passed away, Dhuley became the king of the land and had many children with his love, Dhamo.

Years later, Dheeg found out that Dhuley was the richest man in all of Africa and was the king now. Dheeg decided to ask his friend Dhuley how he had become king and how he had gotten all that wealth. Dhuley told him that he became rich from the place where Dheeg had left him. Dheeg wanted to find treasure, like his friend Dhuley, and so he went to the place where he had left his friend Dhuley. As Dheeg slept and dreamed of finding treasure, he was eaten by hungry lions.

"Don't ever dig a trap for anyone," Grandma said. "And if you do, don't dig it too deep. You never know—you might be the one who falls into your own trap."

About an hour before my bedtime, I got up and said, "Good night, everyone."

"It is not your bedtime yet," Aunt Zainaba said. "Do you have a test tomorrow?"

"No, I am just tired," I responded.

"You are not sick, are you?" Aunt Zainaba asked.

"No, I am fine. Sweet dreams."

"Are you sure? You are usually the last person to go to sleep, and you are going to sleep in the middle of teatime. You must be really tired."

"Yes, Aunt Zainaba. See you in the morning. Have a good night, everyone!"

In my room, I grabbed my favorite book, *Human Anatomy*. I had taken it from Uncle Ali's library; he had all kinds of books there. He said I might not be old enough for it, but I could read it, and I understood it very well. Every other night, I memorized at least two body parts, read what they did, studied their pictures, and tried to find where they were located on my body.

That night, I read about the muscles on my neck and shoulder: the trapezius and the levator scapulae. I repeated, "Trapezius, levator scapulae, trapezius, levator scapulae, trapezius, levator scapulae, trapezius, levator scapulae . . . ," until I fell asleep.

The next night was my night to write. I would alternate between writing and reading before I went to bed. I decided the next night to write a letter to my two younger sisters, Asli and Ramla.

Dear sisters Asli and Ramla,

I miss you so much and wish you were here to experience all the amazing things in Mogadishu with me. I have so much to tell you. It took us about a week to get here. Everything is different—in a good way, of course. It feels like Ruuraan is stuck in the past and Mogadishu is living in the future.

Remember when we were leaving Ruuraan and Dad put me on the camel with Grandma? Well, I was tired of just sitting there, so I decided to walk, but I got tired again and went back on top of our camel. I was bored, so I decided to take a nap, but Grandma woke me up.

"We are here! Look up ahead. Do you see the city?"

"Yes! I see it!" I said as excitement filled my heart.

It wasn't exactly a city, it was the village Mom used to go to for groceries and water. From afar, all we could see were shiny boxes and a long road that stretched to the sky dividing the village into two sides. Uncle Ali told me that this is what their huts looked like. They called them houses.

You wouldn't believe what happened after that! Oh, how I wish you had been with me to see everything. When we got off the camel, we got in a white box. It's taller than a cow but shorter than a camel. It was about the length of four cows lined up. It had four black round things, two on each side. Uncle Ali told me it was called a bus, and a smaller one of these creatures is called a car. He owns a couple of cars. There are so many cars in Mogadishu. More than animals!

"Are we here?" I asked. "Is this Mogadishu?"

"No, not yet," Uncle Ali responded to me. "This is not Mogadishu. We will take a bus from here that will take us to Mogadishu."

I was a little disappointed, but it was all right. We were a lot closer to Mogadishu.

"Grandma, when we get there, I am going to learn a lot of things. What are you going to do?"

My grandmother laughed as she hugged me from the side with her right hand on my right shoulder.

"I am going to take a shower and then sleep," Grandma said.

"No, Grandma, I'm talking about awesome things that we couldn't do in Ruuraan. Like learning or becoming a doctor! Or doing other fun things."

"Oh, dear, I am too old for those things. You will learn for me and become a doctor for both of us," Grandma said.

"But, Grandma, didn't you say that it was never too late to learn and turn your life around? You said that no matter what kind of life you were born into, you can always change it and make it better. Why can't you become a doctor?"

"It's too hard for old people to do those things. I was born in a time when girls in the city and girls in the nomadic area had pretty much the same roles in life. And I wasn't crazy like you to run away from home." Grandma smiled at me.

"Don't worry, Grandma, I will become a doctor for both of us."

When we got to the bus station, we said goodbye to Nuur. He took the two camels with him. I wished him safe travels back to Ruuraan. I miss our brothers too.

The bus was nothing like I had imagined. There were a lot of chairs on each side of the bus, and there was a little space about the length of my arm between the two sides. The inside was a dull brown color and looked like a long, rectangular house. I sat by the window, Grandma sat in the middle, and Uncle Ali sat right next to Grandma. Soon, people started filling the bus.

Then the bus driver came in and started the bus. It made a weird sound, kind of like lions make but stronger. It kept making that noise until we got to our destination and everyone got off. It was moving very fast—a lot faster than our father's horse.

We passed a lot of things so fast that they became blurry. I kept looking outside, but I got dizzy and threw up on Grandma's lap. From then on, I closed my eyes and didn't open them until we got to Mogadishu's bus stop.

"Ayan, wake up! We are here!" Grandma woke me.

We got off the bus and started walking through the city to get to another bus station where a bus would take us to Uncle Ali's house.

The sky was clear, with nothing but unending blue and scattered little white clouds. It looked like our flag. There were tall palm trees everywhere, and the roads were black. Unlike the roads in Ruuraan, red sand didn't fill our shoes. The roads looked as if all the sand were collected, turned black, wedged together, and then flattened on the ground like dough.

"Uncle Ali, why do the roads look like this?"

"They are paved roads. It makes it easier for cars and anything with wheels to move around."

I stomped my feet to see if the sand underneath my feet would scatter, but it didn't. It didn't even move a little. It looked smooth but had a texture so it wasn't slippery. The black roads looked as if they ascended into the heavens.

"Where do they take people? If I kept following it, would it take me to heaven? Would it take me to the sky? Would it take me to the edge of the world or maybe another world?" I asked.

Uncle Ali smiled and said, "No, dear, the world is round, so it doesn't have an edge. And no, these roads would just take you to other cities and other parts of the world. You have to work hard in this world and then die to get to heaven."

"The world doesn't have an edge? Then where does it end?"

"It doesn't end. If you keep traveling, you will end up where you started, like going around a circle," Uncle explained to me.

Can you believe that the earth doesn't have an end? I learned that it's like a big round ball. The earth is bigger than we thought it was, and there are all kinds of people.

I saw a lot of different people, people that don't look like us. Fathiya, Uncle Ali's daughter, told me that they came from other parts of the world. There are so many different things in this city. Everything is different. If only you were here with me! While we were walking to the bus station, I kept looking around, and people started to stare at us. I think they could tell that we were new to the city.

There were cars on the paved roads. Fathiya told me that they don't feel anything, and they don't have to eat vegetation like cows or camels. She told me that they only drink a special kind of water that is just for them. I later learned that it was called gasoline. They make different noises, and some even sound like they are whistling. People usually make them whistle when they are angry with other people and when someone doesn't follow the rules of the road. Everything here has a rule to be followed.

They have traffic lights that tell the cars when to move and when to stop. These traffic lights have three different colors: a green light that tells cars to go, a yellow light that tells the cars to get ready to stop or move faster, and a red light that tells the cars to stop. Uncle Ali and Aunt Zainaba have three cars. I like the white one best because it's bigger than the other two, it's comfy, and it smells nice. Once I become a doctor, I will come get you and bring you to the city. Some of the women and men wear weird clothes like the people in movies do. Oh yeah, movies!

There is this glass thing called TV, and when you put a VCR cassettes in something called VCR right below it, it plays a movie. Movies are people pretending to tell a story. Remember how Grandma used to tell us stories? It's kind of like that except you get to watch the story happening. We watch movies on Thursdays and Fridays since we don't have school on those days. We watch horror movies, where people get eaten or killed, action movies, romantic movies where people love each other, and, my favorite, comedies, which are funny.

Some women wear shoes that kind of look like our donkey Kalwa's hoofs. I miss Kalwa and my goats. I cannot come back now; Mommy and Daddy won't let me go if I do. I don't know why the women wear such things. I tried to walk while wearing them, but I kept falling. They are hard to walk in. This city is very beautiful. You should run away and come here too.

When we got to the bus station, we took another bus that was a lot smaller. And after a little bit, we got off. Uncle Ali said that we were in his neighborhood and we would walk to his house. On the way to Uncle Ali's house, I saw our flag almost everywhere; people here love our home, Somalia. There are no huts here, just houses and big buildings. Some of them go up to the clouds and feel like they are falling toward you when you look up at them. Sometimes I get scared looking up at the very tall ones, so I turn away from them.

We stood in front of huge gates that connected the wall from the right and the wall from the left around Uncle Ali's house. The gates were black and had golden flowers and leaves. I touched the gates, and they were hard. Uncle Ali pressed a button and it rang like a bell, and then Ramla, Uncle Ali's daughter, opened the gate. She was named after you, Ramla. She is so nice just like you; you should meet her one day.

"Daddy, you are here!" she screamed and hugged Uncle Ali.

"Yes, my daughter, I am here." he said, picking her up. "This is Grandma Asli, my mother, and this is your sister Ayan. Say hi to them."

"Grandma, you are here!" She hugged Grandma, and then she hugged me.

We entered and closed the gates behind us.

I became a city girl. I go to school, and I learn a lot of new things every day. You would love Uncle Ali's family. They are very nice.

Oh, I almost forgot—remember how Mommy used to tell us about the ocean, the big water she used to swim in when she was a little girl? Well, I have seen it. I wish you were here to see all these amazing things.

The ocean is blue. Sometimes it looks darker than blue, and it's very big. We go there every other Friday to swim. The water is strong, but it feels nice. Oh yeah, and they don't need to get water from other places, and they don't even have to store water like we did. It comes out of this thing that looks like a bent stick with a red wheel on top of it. Water gushes out of it like it's peeing, but fast when you turn the red thing around.

I have so much to tell you, sisters, but I have to go. I have class. Mohamed, Uncle Ali's son, teaches me math and science. He knows so much!

I miss you, and I will write to you again soon. Please take good care of yourselves, our family, and my goats. I promise I will bring you to the city as soon as I can. I love you.

Your sister,

Ayan

"Ayan, it's late, and we have school tomorrow," Fathiya said sleepily. "Please turn off the light and go to sleep."

"Perfect timing! I just finished writing. I will turn it off in a minute."

"What were you writing about?" Fathiya asked.

"Nothing much. Just a letter to my sisters Ramla and Asli," I whispered.

"We are blessed and happy that you are here with us. Don't worry, Ayan—one of these days, we will go together and visit them. I know you miss them," Fathiya said.

"That would be great. Thank you, Fathiya. Sweet dreams, and see you in the morning." I turned off the light and quickly jumped on my bed and put my blanket over me as if something were going to snatch me in the darkness.

"Sweet dreams," she said.

The next morning, everyone left early to go shopping, but Fathiya and I stayed back to watch the house. Well, that was more of an excuse. We didn't really want the headache of shopping for everyone. We didn't have school that week because it was the last few days of the monthlong fast that we observe each year—Ramadan.

The gate bell rang, and outside stood a woman with four young children. I could see a deep pain in her eyes. She had flawless skin and looked as if she were born into wealth but had been hit by adversity.

I didn't recognize her, and she was wearing what seemed like a hundred pieces of clothes patched together to make a dress and scarf. Her lips were dark, rough, and dry. Her eyelashes were long, curling up, but filled with dust. Her kids were very thin, as if they had been starving for a while. Their upper lips were covered with dried mucus, and they looked as if they hadn't washed their faces for days.

"May I help you?" I asked.

"Are your parents at home?" she responded in a weak voice.

"No, they went shopping. Do you want to come in and wait for them?" I asked her.

"Are there any elders at home?"

"That depends on who you consider elders. Fathiya is here. She is eighteen. Come in; I will call her." I held the door open to let her in. "Are you related to us?" I asked her.

"Could you please call one of the adults for me?" she requested.

I could tell she was holding her tears back. "Wait here. I will get her for you."

She waited by the gate while I went to get Fathiya, who was in the bedroom reading a novel. She enjoyed reading novels. Actually, she enjoyed reading in general.

"Fathiya, there is a woman with four kids asking for the adults," I told Fathiya.

"Who is she, and what does she want?" she asked, still reading.

"I don't know," I responded.

Fathiya put on a scarf that barely covered the end of her long hair, which extended past her hips. She was a little irritated that she had to stop reading. She put her index finger between the pages and closed the book, holding her thumb on one side and the rest of her fingers on the other.

I was surprised that she didn't read while she walked. I guess Grandma had taught her a good lesson.

A couple of weeks ago, Fathiya was lost in story that she was reading. She read it while she was walking to our room. Grandma called her name, but Fathiya didn't hear her, so Grandma walked close to her, but Fathiya didn't notice. Grandma then tripped her, and Fathiya fell to her face.

"Grandma!" Fathiya cried.

"Well deserved!" Grandma extended her hand to Fathiya to help her up.

"Grandma, seriously, grow up!" Fathiya held Grandma's extended hand lightly and got up.

"How many times did I tell you not to read while you are walking? Anything could happen to you." Grandma walked with Fathiya to our room.

Halima and I were watching. We burst into laughter.

Back at the gate, Fathiya asked the woman, "Hi! How may I help you?"

"Is anyone older than you at home?" she asked Fathiya.

"No, but I can help you. Who are you, and how may I help?" Fathiya asked.

"Thank you, dear, but I am not sure I can tell you my problems. You are too young."

"Fathiya? Too young?" I chuckled. "The only thing young about her is her face. She is an old woman inside."

"My kids haven't eaten for a while. I tried to get food for them, but I couldn't find any work. I don't really know how to do anything, and no one wanted to give us food." She stuttered on her words as tears filled her eyes.

"Don't cry, it's all right. You will get through this," Fathiya comforted her.

"I am sorry. I shouldn't be telling you these things." She wiped the tears from her face.

"No, don't be sorry. It's just a test from God, and you have the strength to get through it. God never burdens anyone with something that they cannot handle. You can handle it, and you will be all right. I am sure you will get through it," Fathiya tried to console her.

"Three months ago, I could have never imagined being in this situation—not in a million years." She lifted her head up, and I could see that her eyes were striking. She had amber eyes, beautiful but painful to look at.

"Please, come in." Fathiya brought her into the courtyard.

We took them over to the white chairs under the big tree whose green branches sprawled like an umbrella, creating the perfect shade. The branches were so close to the chairs that you could smell their sweet aroma as you sat at the table. Sitting on those chairs under the tree felt like being in a green hut, and it reminded me of our huts in Ruuraan.

She hesitated. "I don't want to make your white chairs dirty. May I sit on the grass?" she asked.

"No, no, you are not dirty. I would take you to the living room, but our parents aren't here. We will sit here with you. Please, go ahead and take a seat." Fathiya smiled at her.

She sat down, making herself small. She held her smallest child on her lap, and the other three sat on the chairs by her.

"We will get you some food. In the meantime, do you want to wash up?"

"Would that be all right with your parents?" she asked.

"Our parents are very nice people. I am sure they will not have any problem with it," I said.

Fathiya went to our room and brought a dress, undergarment, and scarf for the woman and clothes for her kids. "The bathroom is there. It has a shower and everything else you will need to take a shower. Towels are in the right bottom drawer."

The woman took her kids one by one and helped them shower, except the oldest one. She then took a shower and changed to the clothes Fathiya gave her.

We got a jug of fruit punch, a jug of milk, and spaghetti with sauce for them. We also got some for ourselves and ate with them at the table.

"May God bless you and your family. May he make a path for you in times of difficulty, and may he make everyone you come across like kin to you. Thank you. I will never forget your faces and the kindness that you have shown me today," she said with tears in her eyes.

"Please don't cry. It is all right. Life is not always easy," Fathiya said, trying to calm her down. "May God make everything easy for you."

"My mother told me that life is four seasons in a circle until death makes it a line segment," I said. "There is a relief after every hardship." Oddly enough, I somewhat felt her pain and gave her my hope.

I ran to my room and grabbed my mother's quote from the wall. I handed it to her, and she read it out loud:

Life is four seasons on a circular thread, until death cuts the thread and makes it a line:

The first season is the downpour season, the season of happiness. It puts a smile on our face as everything comes to life. It plants the seeds of inner peace deep in our heart.

The second season is the chilly season, the season of fear. It kills most of the grass and doesn't give a drop of rain, but it leaves just enough brown grass to feed the animals.

The third season is the season of scattered rain, the neutral season. It neither makes everything perfect nor destroys anything. It's the season of hope.

The fourth season is the season of famine, the season of destruction. Everything dries, deforms, or dies, except for that which endures.

In whichever season you find yourself, prepare for the next one and you will be of the few that endure.

"Thank you," she said, wiping away her tears. "Your mother is a wise woman."

"Thank you. She is! You are in the fourth season, and you should stay strong. The happy season is on its way," I said, realizing how much I missed my mother.

She smiled. "Thank you. I am sorry I forgot to ask, but what are your names?"

"My name is Ayan. It means luck. I am very lucky." My name was one of my favorite things about me. I often explained what it meant even though everyone who spoke Somali knew what it meant. For whatever reason, reminding people that my name meant luck had some profound pleasure to it, and I found hope in it.

"My name is Fathiya, which means victory. Not quite sure what my parents won, but, oh well," she said with a laugh.

"My name is Nura, and it means light. This is my oldest son, Awale. His name also means lucky. It is one of the male versions of your name, Ayan. This is my daughter Hibo; her name means a gift. This is Haboon, which means perfect. And this is Hodan; her name means fortune."

"Nice to meet you all," I said.

Awale was taller than I was and maybe a few years older. He had his mom's eyes. I couldn't help but look at his amber eyes that shone under the light.

"Our parents will be here shortly," Fathiya said.

"I will wait for them here. You can go inside if you would like," Nura said.

"Let me get my book. I will just read here." Fathiya grabbed her book and started reading.

A little later, Uncle Ali's second daughter, Halima, came in with Mohamed.

One after another, everyone came back from shopping and gathered in the yard. Uncle Ali, Aunt Zainaba, Grandma, and the younger children were the last ones to come home.

"Mom, Dad, Grandma, this is Nura. Nura, our parents," Fathiya said.

"Hi, Nura, I am Dr. Zainaba."

"And I am Dr. Ali."

"And I am Grandma."

"Grandma, don't you have a name?" Fathiya teased.

"Unlike you, I happen to have a genuine name. Actually, my name, which is Asli, means original."

"I have seen you somewhere." Aunt Zainaba tried to recall where she had seen Nura.

"Me too. Both of your faces look familiar," Nura said.

"Oh, now I remember," Uncle Ali said. "I saw you with your husband at the fund-raising dinner for the anti–female genital mutilation advocacy group. I am sorry for your loss. I heard about your husband on the news. He was a great man."

Grandma and Aunt Zainaba also gave their condolences.

After chatting for a little bit, Aunt Zainaba asked Nura, "To what do we owe this pleasant surprise from you?"

"I don't even know where to start. When my husband died, I lost everything! My children, my husband, my wealth, and my life. My husband's family decided that one of their sons was going to take over my husband's business and the family. And when I refused to marry him, he took everything away from me and tossed me out," she said.

"I am sorry to hear that," Grandma said. "Why didn't you get your family and clan elders involved?"

"Why didn't you go to court?" Uncle Ali asked.

"I don't know anyone here. I met my husband when he was on a business trip, we got married, and I moved here with him. I haven't seen my family for years. I couldn't go to court because I don't have money for lawyers." She choked on her words.

"I am sorry to hear that," Aunt Zainaba said, hugging her.

"It's all right; it's life. I just wish I had thought of those things beforehand. I was homeless for a few months. I was able to sneak into my house and steal my children, account information, and bank information that my husband had put away for our children," she said.

"Did you run out of money? Then what happened? Why didn't you go to where your family is?" Grandma asked.

"I went to the bank, but his men were monitoring it, and I almost got caught. I couldn't sell the small amount of jewelry that I have. I was scared of getting caught. I cannot go to my village; they know where I came from. I am sure they have people watching my family every day. I don't care about the business or about the money, but I cannot risk losing my children."

"I am very sorry to hear that. You can stay here for as long as you want, and no one will bother you here. Think of this as your house," Aunt Zainaba told her.

"Yes, please stay here," Uncle Ali added. "Your husband was a great businessman who did a lot for our people. He helped so many people and donated to so many great causes."

"Thank you. You are a wonderful family. I wish my husband's family were more like you. I will always remember your kindness," Nura said.

I couldn't help but look at her teary eyes with amazement. They were just so beautiful and yet so full of pain.

"It is an honor to have you in our house as our guest," Uncle Ali said.

"Ayan, Fathiya, go clean your room for your aunt Nura," Aunt Zainaba said. It was normal for us to be kicked out of our rooms every time guests came over.

"Eid is coming," Grandma said, patting her shoulder. "Cheer up, sister. You will get through this; you are very strong woman. I can see it in your eyes."

Eid was coming, which was why our family had been out shopping all day.

"Tomorrow, Ayan, Halima, Mohamed, and I are going shopping, and we will shop for you and your kids," Fathiya told Aunt Nura.

"Thank you," Nura said.

The next day, we went shopping, as Eid was only two days away.

On Eid day, we woke up before sunset to pray the morning prayer. Afterward, we got ready and went to the biggest mosque in Mogadishu. We parked our cars about a mile from the prayer site and walked the rest of the way. It was beautiful to hear the Eid chant from every mosque and every corner of the city. I have never seen so many people dressed up so beautifully, smiling, and greeting each other.

Hundreds and hundreds of people were walking from every corner toward the prayer area; most men were wearing white clothes, and women were wearing bright colors that lit up the whole city. The whole city was decorated, cleaned, and made beautiful for the Eid celebration.

As he did for other prayers, the imam stood in the front, men lined up behind him shoulder to shoulder, and women lined up behind the men. We prayed and then returned home to eat breakfast and sweets and to receive our gifts.

My favorite part of Eid was that we were free to go anywhere we wanted to go, and all the adults gave us money. I collected close to five hundred thousand shillings, which was a lot of money.

After we ate breakfast, Fathiya, Halima, and Mohamed decided that they were going to spend their Eid with us. They took us to the movie theater, and on the way, we bought some candy. We went to the city center to play, and then we went to visit our relatives, getting money from each one of them. We headed back home late that evening.

Grandma said, "Eid is the day of love and freedom."

"Grandma, February 14 is the day of love, not Eid," Fathiya said.

"Look around you on Eid day."

This year, we were especially happy, because Grandma had been healed of her illnesses and restored to good health. Even though she was better now, Uncle Ali and Aunt Zainaba said Grandma should stay in Mogadishu for a little while to recuperate fully where they could monitor her health. Personally, I think they were reluctant to see her leave. Everyone loved Grandma. Grandma told the best stories.

Eid was a day of happiness and love for everyone, and it was a day of freedom for kids as we freely roamed around the city. We bragged about all the money we had collected that day and told each other how much money we had.

It was sad that Aunt Nura and her kids couldn't go outside that day. They stayed at home, but we shared our money with them and brought them a bag of candy. Eid lasted for three days. Three days of celebration, love, and happiness.

On the last night of Eid, I was smiling from my heart. I was glad that I had decided to come to the city to live with Uncle Ali and his family. Though I missed my parents, I felt at home. I grabbed my journal and started writing about the day I'd told my family in Ruuraan that I wanted to go to the city.

Like the Cheetah Sprints Away

The sun was below the horizon, letting out beautiful rays of gold and maroon when we returned to our huts. I had left early that morning with my older sisters Shukri and Khadra to herd our goats and sheep with them. Shukri and Khadra were older than I was but younger than my sisters Ahado and Sulekha. I was nine years old, and my preparation for becoming a woman, a wife, and a mother had started with my circumcision.

I could no longer run around like a little girl. I had to be extra careful. Now that I was becoming a woman, I would learn to herd the goats with my older sisters.

"You are a woman now," my mother would remind me often. "From now on, you will be herding with your older sisters. Learn well from them. And remember, you are a woman. Don't run around a lot, keep your legs together, and don't even think of climbing trees."

"I know, Mother. I will behave like a woman," I reassured her.

We walked for most of the day, watching out for predators. We were herding over two hundred goats and sheep, so we had to constantly be on the lookout for lions, hyenas, cheetahs, and foxes.

The sun was beating down on us, its heat and rays getting stronger by the hour. In the afternoon, it got too hot. My sisters decided to sit under the shade for a little bit and to let the goats and sheep graze.

"So what do you guys do when you are taking a rest? Do you play games and tell stories?" I asked them, trying to break the ice into womanhood.

"Nothing, really. We just drink some water and talk," Shukri said.

"Talk? Talk about what?"

"Things you wouldn't understand," Khadra shut my question down.

"I am not a little girl anymore. I want to talk with you," I said.

"Shukri, did you find anything to wear for tonight?" Khadra asked, ignoring me.

"Not yet, but Mom bought a new dress last month! I am going to steal that. What about you?" Shukri said.

"I am going to wear that dress I got last Eid."

"Where are you going tonight?" I tried to join their conversation.

"You don't need to know, and you'd better not tell anyone," Shukri warned me.

"If you don't tell me where you are going and what you are going to do, I will tell everyone that you are planning to sneak out tonight," I said.

"Okay. But you will be in big trouble if you tell anyone. We are going to the dance tonight," Shukri said.

"Won't lions eat you?" I asked.

"Don't worry, sweetie. We are going in a large group with strong people," Khadra said.

"I promise I won't tell anyone. May I come with you?" I asked.

"You are too young. When you are old enough, you won't even have to ask us," Shukri said.

The heat was dissipating, and the mirage was disappearing little by little. I looked all around us and saw no sign of humans or human civilization. In the distance, the red sand blended in with the cloudless blue sky. Not too far from us, I saw two gazelles attentively grazing.

They stopped and lifted their heads as if they were listening to something, and then they started sprinting. Then I saw the cheetah stretching its body like rubber, hitting its tail on the ground, and raising the red sand like a dust devil as it ran after one of the gazelles. The gazelle ran in a zigzag and jumped up every few seconds. They soon disappeared into the distance.

Our sheep and goats stopped grazing and started bleating as they ran. My sisters jumped from the ground and tried to stop them from running far away. We reassured them that we were there to protect them, and they stopped running in all directions.

"It's going to get dark soon. We should start heading home," Shukri said.

We grabbed our sticks and turned our sheep and goats in the direction of our huts. By the time we got near home, the sun was setting beautifully. We put the goats in their pens, which were made from thorny bushes. Shukri and I counted the goats and the sheep—a total of 243.

Khadra then grabbed the bush that was cut right above its roots to close the opening of the pen. We sat by our hut, resting while our other older sisters got ready to milk the goats and the sheep.

My mother was making tea and traditional Somali bread, called *anjeelo* or *lahooh,* in front of a hut about two huts to the left of where we were resting. She was wearing her black-and-red shawl with its dress that complemented her caramel skin color. Her long, thin fingers were decorated with red henna. She chatted with Grandma and Aunt Ruun while they sat nearby on a mat. I greeted them and joined Grandma and Aunt Ruun. Soon, a total of eighteen women and children, including me, were sitting by the fire near my mother.

About four huts to the right of where we were sitting, my father, Arale, my four uncles, our grandfather, my six brothers, and number of my male cousins were sitting on mats and chatting about things I couldn't really hear—probably politics. There was a big plate of meat, five *dhiilood* and *haruubo* for them to use as cups, and three large teapots in front of them. They hadn't started eating yet. They were waiting for my sister to bring the lahooh.

As my sister was taking the bread to them, I decided to help her and take some plates to them.

"Where you going, Ayan? Come sit here by me," Grandma said when she saw me getting up. "I will tell you a great story tonight."

"Thanks, Grandma, but I want to help serve the meal." I felt too old to be listening to Grandma's stories. Ahado, Sulekha, Shukri, and Khadra didn't have to sit and listen to the stories.

"Ayan, listen to your grandma. Go sit by your grandma, or go join your older sisters. Besides, you didn't eat yet," my mother said.

They were my elders, so I couldn't say no to them.

"Okay, I will sit by my older sisters," I said as I walked to where my sisters and my youngest aunt were sitting.

"I wonder if his leaf is right next to mine," Aunt Siman said.

"What leaf?" I asked.

"No leaf," she replied hastily. "What leaf are you talking about?"

"I just heard you say, 'I wonder if his leaf is next to mine.'"

"What leaf are you talking about?"

"You heard wrong. We were just talking about my life leaf on the moon. And lower your voice—you don't have to shout." She said this so fast that I could barely understand her.

From the other circle, my younger sister Ramla asked, "Grandma, what leaf are they talking about?"

"There is a tree on the moon. Each human being that's alive has a leaf on it," Grandma told Ramla.

My sisters and aunt stopped talking when I joined them. I guess they were talking about boys. I got up to go sit by Grandma. I didn't feel like I fit anywhere.

"There is a tree on the moon?" I asked Grandma.

"Yes, dear. Look at the moon. Do you see the darker parts? That's the tree of life. Each one of us has a leaf on it, and when we die, our leaf dries and falls on our grave," Grandma said.

"I want to go to the city!" I said.

"Why are you screaming? You are a girl. Don't raise your voice," my mother said.

"I don't want to be here anymore. I want to go to the city. I want to go and stay with Uncle Ali and become a doctor like him," I said, using my newfound voice.

"You want to go to the city? Don't worry. You will go with us the day after tomorrow to get groceries," Khadra said.

"No, Khadra, I don't want to go to the village with you to get groceries. I want to go where Uncle Ali lives and stay there forever. I don't want to live here anymore." I tried to explain it to them, but they laughed at me.

"You are not going anywhere at your age. But in about five years, you can marry a man from the city and move there. I am afraid that's the only way to get out of this place. Now sit down," my mother said to me.

"I don't want to get married. I want to go to school and become a doctor like Uncle Ali. I want to move to the city. Please, Mother, please let me go there," I begged.

"You have shamed me enough, talking back to me and your elders. Don't bring more shame to yourself. Where have you seen a girl that leaves her family before she gets married? It's time for you to start acting your age," my mother scolded me.

"What's the point of a girl going to school?" Shukri said. "You will get married and will have to raise your children. You are a woman now. Start behaving like one."

As soon as I finished my dinner, I got up. I went to the hut and tried to sleep, but I couldn't. I just stared at the vast darkness and thought of my options.

Outside, my family was chatting, laughing, joking, and sharing stories as if what I had said meant nothing. I could only think of three options: to run away, to live here until I got married to a man from the city, or to just live here forever as a nomad chasing the rain—none of which seemed plausible to me at the time, but I had to do something. My sisters came into the hut, and I pretended to be asleep.

"I am too tired to dance tonight. Let's go to the dance tomorrow night," Shukri said.

"Oh, come on, we have been planning this for days," Aunt Siman said.

"Awwww, are you dying to see him?" Khadra teased her.

"Shut up. I am not dying to see anyone," Shukri said.

"But we haven't done anything fun for a while," Khadra said. "People our age are enjoying their lives and going to dances."

"It's a little late, and our fathers, brothers, and cousins are all home. Imagine if they find out that we snuck out; we would have to dig our own graves," Shukri said.

They decided not to go to the dance that night, and instead, they went to sleep. There was something off about that night. Soon enough, everyone was asleep but me.

The cool and calm night seemed to go on forever. I could hear my sisters and aunt breathing deeply. I could hear the roars of wild animals in the distance. I loved listening to the sounds of animals, wild and domestic, mixing with the sound of the wind. There was something so calming about it. For a moment, the sounds distracted me from my burning desire to go to the city.

Everyone was in a deep sleep when I heard a lion roar so close that it felt like the lion was in the hut with us. Our goats, sheep, cows, and camels started bleating. We were under attack by a hungry lion.

My father and uncles rushed outside with their guns.

"Keep the children inside! Keep the children inside!" my father screamed.

My sisters jumped up and hastily lit the torch with a match. Our father and uncles walked our mother and Grandma to our hut to stay with us. Aunt Siman handed each of the men a torch that burned brightly.

"Make more fire! And keep all the children inside," Uncle Gutaale said as he walked out of the hut carefully so he wouldn't set it on fire.

The men in our family stood in front of our hut and carefully listened for the roar.

"The roar is coming from the goats' pen. Let's head there," Uncle Gutaale said. Cautiously, they followed each other toward the goats' pen. They were ready for the lion. No one was watching me, so I followed silently behind my uncles as they tracked the lion.

When they got near the goats' pen, my brother beamed a big flashlight in the direction the noises were coming from. He beamed it right at the lion's face, and we could see its huge fangs dripping fresh blood. One of our goats was lying below the lion and fighting for its last breath.

The lion's eyes reflected the light more like a jewel than eyes. The lion started growling at them and bluffing to scare them. My father shot the lion once, and it fell to the ground. But then it got up and started running toward them.

My heart started racing. I had gotten more excitement than I had bargained for. They shot the lion again and again and again, until it fell to the ground, less than a meter away. Uncle Guleed shot the lion in the head a few more times, just to make sure it was dead.

"Never trust a wild beast!" he said.

I was covering my ears in terror, but I could still hear the shots.

I felt like crying, but I was holding it back so I wouldn't get in trouble. My brother Mu'allim looked back and saw me covering my ears and crying silently.

He was furious; he slapped me and told me to run to the hut. I couldn't run or move. I just stood there sobbing like a baby until my mother ran out and dragged me back to the hut. She hugged me and tried to calm me down while also yelling at me and scolding me at the same time.

My brother yelled after me, "Didn't I tell you to stay in the hut? Why did you come out? You could have been a lion's dinner tonight!"

I heard so many stories about lions and how strong they were. Lions were always strong, brave, and the leaders of all animals. I just wanted to see what that amazing animal looked like.

My father took out his pocketknife and said, "In the name of God!" He cut the goat's throat, and its legs stopped moving. We were not allowed to eat meat unless it was slaughtered properly.

They then dragged the goat and covered it with thorny bushes so other wild animals wouldn't eat it before the sun rose.

My father came back and told everyone to calm down and go back to sleep. He told us to scream if we saw or heard anything.

Everyone went back to sleep, but I kept thinking, *What if all the lions see their dead lion and decide that they want to go to war and kill the people that killed him? What if all the lions gang up to attack our family? What will we do? There is God and Allah will protect us. Also, my father, uncles, brothers, and cousins are all here. They will fight with the lions and protect us.* I calmed myself down and tried to go to sleep.

The next morning, we did our ablutions right in front of the hut and prayed inside our huts. No one went to pee, and no one went to the other huts to wake up the rest of the family for the morning prayer. For a while, I couldn't even think of going to the city, I was so scared that a lion would eat me on the way there.

I went with my cousins Ulumo and Fozia and Aunt Siman to herd the goats and the sheep. It was their turn that day. While we were resting, I saw a cheetah sprinting after a gazelle. This time, it caught the gazelle. The cheetah held the gazelle's neck with its fangs. After a while, it dragged the gazelle under a tree.

Out of nowhere, a lion appeared and threatened the cheetah. The cheetah tried to defend its prey, but the lion was too strong. The lion chased the cheetah away.

Following the same routine as before, we headed home before the sun set. It was like any other night for everyone else.

"Grandma, what would you do if you were alone and you saw a lion? Or if a lion tried to attack you?" I asked while we were eating dinner.

"Only lucky people see lions before the lion sees them. I would climb the closest, strongest, and tallest tree I could find," she told me.

"Why would you climb a tree?" I asked.

"Lions can't climb trees, but they are very smart animals. They will pretend to leave and hide close by to trick you. If you climb down, they will jump at you and eat you!"

"Grandma, can a human outrun a lion?"

"No, dear, they are faster than we are. Just climb to the top of the tree. That's the safest place to be," she replied.

The following week, I started practicing climbing trees fast. About three weeks later, I decided that I was ready—ready to run away to the city.

While my sisters were milking the goats and the sheep, I hid a flashlight, water bottle filled with water, and my shawl behind the bush that I had used to wash up on the day that I was circumcised. I ran back to the huts before anyone noticed.

That morning, I was herding with Fozia and Shukri.

"Fozia, Shukri, keep going and I will catch up to you. I forgot something at home. I will follow your footsteps," I told them as I ran back to the huts.

I hid behind our hut and waited for them to disappear into the distance. I then sprinted to the bush where I had hidden the flashlight, shawl, and water bottle. They were still there. I put on my shawl and slung the water bottle's strap over my shoulder. I then started running as fast as I could on a narrow white path that took people to the city. I had nothing to eat or drink, except the water bottle filled with dirty brown water.

The sun was getting hotter and my feet were getting tired, so I decided to take a quick rest under a tree. There was nothing around me but shrubs, trees, grass, and a wind that kept blinding me with hot red sand. I started to doubt myself. For the first time, it felt like I was doing the wrong thing. I couldn't decide whether to keep running or to head back home. I wanted to rest longer, but I smelled danger at every corner around me, so I decided to keep moving and reach my dream of living in the city.

As it grew darker, I could hear lions roar and hyenas laugh near me. I was petrified, but I knew going back was not an option. I walked as fast as I could and climbed the tallest tree I could find. I then took off my scarf and tied myself to the highest stable branch so that I wouldn't fall down when the lions shook the tree or when I fell asleep.

The moon was full, and I sat there in the tree watching the beautiful stars, the Milky Way, and the full moon. I was mesmerized by the beauty of the night sky but felt lonely for the first time in my life. Little did I know that this would be a feeling that would become part of my everyday life. At some point in the night, I fell asleep.

The next morning, I woke up to the sun's golden rays. I looked around for any sign of lions, cheetahs, or hyenas. I saw no lions, but I could see their paw prints all around the base of the tree. At that point, I was scared, because I remembered what Grandma had said about lions hiding nearby, so I decided to stay in my tree for a little longer in case the lions were still around. In the distance, I heard a camel bell, which we called a *koor*.

Our camels had koors around their necks to make it easy for us to find them and to hear when people were coming. I could see the camels and their riders in the distance, but I couldn't make out the people's faces. I was scared that they were my family.

What do you have to lose, Ayan? If they are your family, they will take you back and you will run away again. If they are not, you will meet people you can travel with, and you will go to the city with them. I gave myself a little pep talk and waited for them.

5

It was late, and I had school the next day, so I stopped writing and went to bed. I woke up to the call to morning prayer. There were six mosques in our neighborhood alone, and they all called to prayer at the same time with the rest of the mosques in Mogadishu. It was impossible to sleep through that.

I got up to use the bathroom, but Halima was in it, and Siham, Yahye, and Ridwan—Uncle Ali's kids—were in a line waiting for it. I sat on the floor at the end of the line, and it wasn't long before I dozed off.

Later, Ridwan said, "It's your turn, Ayan."

"Oh, thanks, Ridwan." I rushed to the bathroom. When we were all ready, we went to our mosque and prayed there.

After prayer, Aunt Zainaba told us a story of a man who was the size of a thumb and who married a giant. He was a brave man, and everyone admired him and his wife for marrying each other despite their big differences.

His wife, the giant, had to use gigantic silverware, and he had to use tiny silverware. He had a hard time navigating through their gigantic house and kept falling into her silverware and other items. His wife also had a difficult time navigating through the house, as she kept stepping on his tiny things. She constantly worried about stepping on him, especially since she had impaired sight and hearing.

Although they both knew how hard life was for them, because they were living together, they never talked about it and did not try to find any solutions to their difficulties. They both ignored their feelings, their needs, and the struggles that they were facing.

They assumed that if they talked about the difficulties they were having and the problems they were dealing with by living together, they would have to break up. They loved each other very much and did not want their relationship to end. One day, he accidently fell into her milk bowl and drowned.

The giant, now a widow, cried, "Oh, how I wish we had talked about our problems and what we each needed! Oh, how I wish we had found a plan to deal with our differences! Oh, if we had only talked about how to prevent him falling into my milk!" The widow cried in regret as she put her husband to rest in his tiny grave.

"The moral of the story is, don't bite more than you can chew. Don't take up more than you can handle. And if you do, make sure you have a plan in place to handle it. If you take on more than you can handle and have no plans, you will drown like Mr. Thumb. From time to time, people face difficulties—that is just part of life—but they have to talk about it and find the right ways to deal with them," Aunt Zainaba said.

"Or you lose your teeth?" Grandma said jokingly, and we giggled. "Time to get ready for school and work. Go get ready, everyone," she said, smiling.

Once I was done with my breakfast, I went into my room to put on my blue-and-white uniform like our flag. As I was getting ready, I felt uneasy, like something bad was going to happen.

"I hope nothing bad happens today," I said.

"Ayan, let's go. We are late!" Aunt Zainaba called.

I walked out of the room and got into the car that Uncle Ali was driving.

Uncle Ali dropped us off in front of the school and left for work. I walked at a normal pace while the kids chased each other into their classrooms. I felt a black shadow hovering over me, its weight pulling my shoulders down for the whole day. I knew a dark feeling had fallen on me, but I couldn't put my finger on what it was.

At school, my friend Layla asked, "Ayan, are you all right? You seem distracted today."

"My shoulder keeps twitching. I feel like something bad is going to happen today. I've felt this dark weight over me since this morning," I said.

"Doesn't your shoulder twitch when it's going to rain? Don't worry; nothing bad is going to happen. It will rain today," Layla said.

"No, that's when your eye twitches. It's bad when your shoulder twitches. It means something bad is going to happen," I said.

"It's all a superstition. Only God knows what will happen. Don't worry, nothing bad is going to happen, and if it does, it has nothing to do with your shoulder twitching."

"Shhhhh, the teacher will hear us," I said.

My feelings of a bad thing happening that day intensified, and my fear grew. School was dismissed in the afternoon, and Uncle Ali came to pick us up from school.

"Are you all right, Ayan?" Uncle Ali asked.

"Yes, Uncle, I am fine. Why?" I asked.

"You seem uncharacteristically quiet today. Is there something bothering you?"

"No, Uncle, I am just tired," I said.

I didn't want to worry him, so I quietly thought of all the bad things that could happen. It seemed like it took forever to get home, even though it took us a little less than thirty minutes.

As we drove home, I looked at the white buildings on the sides of the road. A lot of the buildings were big and beautiful. Their color and the palm trees around them fit in perfectly with the beautiful Somali sky and ocean.

At the traffic light, I watched the cars being released in groups like camels being released to drink from a water well. I watched them and tried to figure out the pattern, but we never stayed still long enough for me to figure out the pattern that the cars were being released in.

I loved lowering the window to feel the wind on my face and my hair. It reminded me of Ruuraan. Palm trees lined the sides of the road, and most of the buildings we drove by were white or tan with beautiful carvings on their walls.

When we got home, Grandma was crying frantically, and there were three men I didn't recognize trying to console her.

"Asli," one of the men said, "I am very sorry. It's tragic, but crying won't bring them back. Please calm down. We all belong to God, and we are all going to go back to him. Every one of us has a time, and when that time comes, we have no choice but to go. I am very sorry for your loss."

When I heard his words, it felt as if someone had soaked me with ice water. I struggled to move my legs toward them. When I saw the tears in Grandma's eyes, I knew something very bad had happened.

Uncle Ali ran toward her and started questioning her. While I walked slowly toward them, my heart beat so fast that it felt as if it wanted to escape through my ribs.

"What happened? Why are you crying? What happened, Mother?" Uncle Ali asked hastily.

Grandma Asli hugged Uncle Ali tightly and started sobbing. "They are gone! They are all gone! All of them! *Gone!*"

"Who is gone, Mother? Who? Who died?" Aunt Zainaba asked worriedly.

"They are gone! Oh, God! Oh, God! Why didn't you take me instead?" Grandma Asli kept sobbing.

One of the men who had been calming Grandma said, "I am very sorry to tell you this, but your family members in Ruuraan have all been killed in a tribal dispute. I am very sorry. May God bless their souls and give you the strength to deal with this."

Ruuraan?

My family! My parents, my siblings, my uncles, my aunts, my cousins, and my grandfather?

"Grandma, they are lying, right? That can't be true!" I said in denial. "How can they all die at the same time? One person dies at a time, right? They are lying, right, Grandma?"

Grandma looked at me, her eyes full of tears and pain. She hugged me tightly and kept sobbing.

I hugged her, thinking, *Who am I going to cure now?* A dark cloud had fallen over our family. It all seemed like a bad dream. I let go of Grandma and ran to my room. I sat on my bed, grabbed my blanket, and tried to sleep. I hoped that it was just a bad dream and that when I woke, it would all be gone. But I couldn't fall asleep. I could hear the crying and the weeping of my family members in the yard. I don't know what I was feeling; I had no words to express it. It was a feeling that I wouldn't wish on my worst enemy. It felt as if someone had thrown a boulder with sharp knives on my chest.

I covered my head and started chanting words, whatever came to my mind.

"Deep limbic system, prefrontal cortex, anterior cingulate gyrus, basal ganglia, temporal lobes . . . Deep limbic system, prefrontal cortex, anterior cingulate gyrus, basal ganglia, temporal lobes . . . Deep limbic system, prefrontal cortex, anterior cingulate gyrus, basal ganglia, temporal lobes . . . 2 times 2 is 4 . . . 4 plus 678,423 is 678,427, and 678,427 doubled is 678,427 plus 678,427, which is 1,356,854! Think of school! Think of school! God, God, God, the Creator of the Universe, the most Merciful, Almighty God! God! God . . ." I kept trying to think of other things, but I couldn't get it out of my head that they were all dead, all of them gone. My eyes were dry. No tears dropped from them. I removed the blanket from my face and stared at my mother's handwritten quote on the wall.

I kept seeing my mother's face, her gentle hands, the wise words she had told me, her unconditional love, and the care she had given to everyone.

"How can she be dead?" I kept staring at the quote, paralyzed by darkness and unfamiliar feelings. Little did I know that these feelings were going to become a familiar part of my life. I put the blanket back over my head as I closed my eyes and imagined walking back through Ruuraan. I could see the faces of my loved one, their smiles, their walk; I could hear their voices.

Aunt Zainaba lifted the blanket from my head and hugged me, "Cry! Cry, my honey. It will help you. It's all right to grieve." She held me tightly while she cried.

"How can they all be dead? What about Asli and Ramla? I was going to bring them to the city when I was old enough. How could they just be dead? How? I should have been there with them! I shouldn't have left them. Who am I going to cure now?" I cried on Aunt Zainaba's shoulder.

"It's not your fault, dear. There is nothing you could have done. Everyone has to die at some point in their life. Don't despair, dear; they are in a better place," Aunt Zainaba tried to console me.

6

Later that night, Uncle Ali called everyone to the living room.

"Let's not overreact," he said. "We are not even sure if it's true. If they died, everyone has to die, and we will hold a funeral for them and pray for them. They don't need our tears; they need our prayers. Death is an inevitable truth that human beings must experience at the end of their time on this world. I will send some people to confirm it. Until then, let's pretend we have not heard anything. Have faith and be strong," Uncle Ali said, fighting back tears.

"There is no need to pretend! It's true!" Grandma cried. "These men would never lie to me. Why would anyone lie about such a thing?"

"Mother, please, calm down. I don't want your blood pressure to rise. Don't risk your life for something we are not even sure of. Please, Mo—" Uncle Ali said and slumped to the floor as he fainted.

"Ali! Ali! Ali!" Aunt Zainaba yelled. And then to us, "Go! Get me some water."

Suad ran into the room with a cup of water.

"Open the windows and the door," Aunt Zainaba said as she sprinkled water on Uncle Ali's face. "Give him space to breathe. Move to the sides."

"Get me some sweets from the kitchen. Hurry!" Aunt Zainaba said.

Halima brought honey, Fathiya brought sugar and candy, and Suad brought cookies. Aunt Zainaba put honey in Uncle Ali's mouth, and he began to stir.

"Ali, are you all right?" Aunt Zainaba asked.

"I am fine, Zainaba. My blood sugar level was a little low, that is all. I forgot to eat," he said, holding on to Aunt Zainaba's hand.

"How could you be so careless and forget to monitor your glucose?" Aunt Zainaba asked as tears rolled down her cheeks. "I'm going to call my cousin Samatar to make sure you are okay."

"Don't worry, dear, I am all right," Uncle Ali said. "Nothing will happen to me."

"Mohamed, come help me take your dad to his bedroom. Halima and Fathiya, take Grandma to her room," Aunt Zainaba said.

Fathiya and Halima helped Grandma walk to her room. I sat in the living room for hours, until Uncle Samatar arrived to examine Uncle Ali. He was our family physician and Aunt Zainaba's first cousin.

"May peace be upon you. How are you, Zainaba? How is Ali?" Uncle Samatar greeted Aunt Zainaba.

"We are doing well, but Ali fainted a little while ago. That's why I called you here. He keeps insisting that he is fine, but I want you to check him," Aunt Zainaba said.

"Where is he? Did something happen to disturb him?" Uncle Samatar asked.

"We received terrible news today. We heard that our family in Ruuraan has been killed," Aunt Zainaba said as tears rolled down her cheeks.

"We belong to God, and to him we shall return," Uncle Samatar said, repeating it several times. After a moment of silence, he asked, "When did this happen? Are you sure?"

"That's what we have heard. We don't know for sure, and we don't know when," Aunt Zainaba said.

"We belong to God, and to him we shall return. May God bless them and forgive all their sins. May he bless us all with strength and faith to deal with this tragic loss. All of them? The whole family?" he asked in shock.

"Yes, the whole family, at least that's what we have heard. It was a tribal dispute. The tribe of Qansah took all our family's livestock and burned all their huts too," Aunt Zainaba said.

"We belong to God, and to him we shall return," Uncle Samatar said. "This is a dark day for your family. I will go check on Ali. What they say about women is true—they are who they marry. You are talking like you are not from the tribe of Qansah," he said as he walked to Uncle Ali and Aunt Zainaba's bedroom.

We decided not to inform anyone about what had happened until we were certain.

The next day, Uncle Ali sent some people to Ruuraan to confirm the sad news that we had received. I prayed that it was just a horrible lie or a bad dream, but in my heart, I knew it was true. That entire day, I had had a feeling that something terrible had happened.

We waited many days for the men to verify the news, and those days seemed longer than normal days. It felt like an eternity. Nothing was the same. There was very little talking and not much laughter. Grandma stopped telling us stories and spent most of her time in her room crying. I felt as stiff and voiceless as a mannequin.

Two weeks later, the men returned and told us that it was true. Everyone had died, all our livestock was looted, and the huts were set on fire.

"We belong to God, and to him we shall return. I was not expecting to hear anything else. I knew they were all gone," Grandma said as tears filled her eyes.

Uncle Ali thanked the men, and they left us in the darkness.

"Let's prepare the funeral. I hope they were buried properly!" Grandma cried.

Uncle Ali and Grandma continued talking, but I couldn't listen to all the details of what had happened to my family, so I went to my room and cried.

The next morning, Uncle Ali and Mohamed bought five goats that were to be slaughtered for the funeral. A lot of relatives, neighbors, and other people came to help and give their condolences. Hundreds of people showed up—some to help, some to give condolences, and some with a proposal to take revenge on the tribe of Qansah. Uncle Ali and Grandma Asli condemned any such proposals.

"Killing other people and making other families cry will not bring our family back. It will only make the matter worse. We don't want to start another endless tribal war between Qura'a and Qansah. The people who were killed were my family, and I don't want any one of you going after anyone from that tribe. We don't want blood money, and we don't want revenge," Uncle Ali told them all.

"I have always known how weak you are!" one of the men taunted Uncle Ali. "They killed your family, coward! Where is your blood? This is not your decision alone! This is for the Qura'a tribe. They might have been your family, but they are also part of our tribe, and we will get them justice whether you like it or not!"

"Please leave!" Uncle Ali said and showed him to the door.

When the funeral ended, we went back to our old way of life even though nothing felt the same. I started hiding from Grandma, because every time she saw me, she would remember my father, my mother, and everyone else we had lost, and she would then start crying.

"Uncle, Grandma hates me. Every time she sees me, she cries. Why does she hate me?" I cried to Uncle Ali.

Uncle Ali hugged me and said, "She doesn't hate you. She loves you a lot! It's just that you remind her of everyone that we have lost. She is having a hard time. Please try to understand her and give her a little bit more time. And know that no matter what happens, your grandma loves you more than anyone else."

"Thanks, Uncle."

About a month later, everyone was starting to get the hang of life again. Things were never normal, and I doubted they would ever become normal. But Grandma Asli stopped crying whenever she saw me. I could still see the pain in her eyes.

I stopped eating dinner with everyone and spent most of my time in my room. Aunt Zainaba came into my room with a plate of food. I was sitting on my bed with my back to the wall, an open book on my lap. I was reading, but before I knew it, I was just staring at the pages as if my mind were no longer registering letters. My mind was far away in Ruuraan.

Aunt Zainaba pushed my blanket aside and sat next to me on the bed. She took the book from my lap and placed it on my table. She gently put the food on my right side and started stroking my hair as tears filled her eyes. I felt that she could feel the pain that I was feeling. She put her hand on my face, her fingers under my ear, and her thumb on my cheekbone. She kissed my forehead as tears rolled down her cheeks.

"Here is your dinner, dear. Eat it, and I will come back to check on you," Aunt Zainaba said and joined the rest of the family for dinner.

When she returned an hour later, the untouched plate of food was sitting where she had left it.

"Ayan, why are you not eating your food?"

"I am not hungry," I replied.

"You haven't eaten today. You haven't eaten for the last couple of weeks. You have lost so much weight, dear, I am worried about you," Aunt Zainaba said. "You have to eat food. Look at you; you are becoming walking bones. Here, eat some." She picked up some of the food and tried to feed me with her hand.

"I am not hungry. I don't want to eat."

"I don't care whether you are hungry or not; you have to eat some food. Eat!" Aunt Zainaba said. "Do you want me to continue to feed you with my hand? I promise I will do it."

"I don't want to eat. Please, Aunt, I don't want to eat anything." I pushed her hand away from my face.

Grandma came into the room for the first time since our family had been killed.

"It has been more than a month since that tragedy happened. You have to continue with your life. I am sure that's what your parents would have wanted you to do. Please eat some food," Aunt Zainaba said.

"Zainaba is right," Grandma said. "You have to eat something. I lost my sons, my daughters, my daughters-in-law, my grandkids, my—"

I cut in before Grandma could finish her sentence. "Okay, I will eat it!" I grabbed the plate from Aunt Zainaba, and I put as much food as I could in my mouth and swallowed it without chewing. By the fifth bite, I threw up.

"I am sorry. My body doesn't want to eat!" I said, upset.

"You don't have to eat right now, dear," Grandma said and took the plate from my hands. "I just want you to not starve yourself to death. We have already lost enough family members. We can't afford losing you. Just try eating slowly, little by little. Take some rest, and get a good night's sleep."

Grandma brushed my hair back and kissed my forehead. "I lost a lot of my loved ones, dear. I don't want to lose you too. I love you more than anyone else on this planet, so please take care of yourself, for me and for your parents."

"I will take care of myself, Grandma. I promise." I kissed her hand and her forehead.

"That's my girl. Let's stay strong, okay? Get some sleep, sweetie."

Suad came into the room to help me clean up my vomit. Once we were done, I took a shower, and then I started writing again. I wanted to write about my family in Ruuraan and the last time that I had seen them.

As the Bird Is Released

As the figures came closer, I realized that they looked like my brother Mu'allim and my cousin Hassan, but I wasn't sure.

Mu'allim and Hassan each carried a water container, called *ubbo* or *wayso*, on their shoulders. Hassan was wearing a white T-shirt that had turned tan from the dust, with green macawis that had a diamond pattern. Mu'allim was wearing a blue T-shirt and blue macawis with white stripes. Each of them had a stick, called *hangool*, which was curved like a hook at the top and branched out to two branches at the bottom.

There were trees and shrubs as far as I could see. The shrubs and trees were so thick that in some areas I couldn't even see the sand beneath them. It looked like the perfect place for lions, cheetahs, and hyenas to hide. I was scared of being eaten if I came down from the tree.

There were several red termite mounds around me, some morphed around trees and some standing alone.

"Hey, you! Come down from the tree right now!" Mu'allim yelled, looking up at the tree where I had spent the night. He struck the tree with his hangool.

"I am not coming down! Grandma told me all about you. I am not coming down. Go away, cannibals!"

Mu'allim and Hassan started laughing at me hysterically.

"Laugh all you want. I know what you want," I said. "You want to eat me, don't you? I am a brave girl, and I am not scared of you. Go away before my family comes and kills you." I tried to scare them off, but they laughed at every word that came out of my mouth.

"Hold these for me." Mu'allim handed his hangool and ubbo to Hassan. "I will go up there and bring her down." Mu'allim turned to me and said, "I am coming up there, and I am going to take a big bite out of your hand, then your leg, then your fat cheeks, and then we will eat you. Here I come! You could tell me your last wish while I climb up the tree."

I started screaming and crying out loud. There was no place to run to.

He untied my shawl and carried my little body down to the ground. We sat under the shade of the tree.

"Here, eat this bread and drink some water. You look like you were tied to that tree for days. Oh, wait, you were," Mu'allim said, and they started laughing again.

"Is this your way of running away? Trees don't move. Did you not know that?" Hassan mocked me as they kept laughing.

"I am not eating it!" I said. "I know that you trick kids into eating so you can eat them when they become chubby. I won't eat anything."

"We don't care whether you are fat or skinny; we are going to eat you. You might as well eat some food so you have energy to fight us or pretend to run away," Hassan said.

I was starving, so it wasn't hard to convince me to eat. I grabbed the food from Mu'allim and started eating as fast as I could while they waited for me. Once I finished eating, I got up and sprinted. Laughing, Mu'allim caught me before I took five steps.

"You are a woman now. We cannot put you on the camel. You have to walk. Let's go." Hassan grabbed my hand, and we started walking.

"Where are you taking me?" I cried.

"To our house, where we cook and eat all the little kids that run away from their homes," Mu'allim said.

"I am never going to run away again! Please take me to my mother!" I cried.

"You should have thought of that before you ran away," Mu'allim said.

I was convinced that they were Qori Ismaris, the shapeshifting cannibals, who had taken my brother's and cousin's forms and that I was going to be their dinner that night.

The next day, we got to an area that looked familiar, and before the sun set, we arrived at our huts in Ruuraan. Everyone came out to look at me as if I were a circus animal.

"She is alive! She is alive! Thank you, God! Thank you, God, a million times," my mother cried and hugged me tightly. "Thank you, God almighty."

That night, we had dinner with everyone else, and Grandma told stories about kids who ran away from their homes who were eaten by cannibals—and lions, of course.

When it was time to go to sleep, my mother asked me to come with her. She told me to sleep by her for the night and that we were going to talk first thing in the morning.

"Sleep here, and don't even think about running away!"

I knew she was very angry with me. She was just waiting for the morning to come.

"It's not my fault! I want to go to the city and become a doctor like Uncle Ali. I don't want to live in this place, Mother. I told you, but you won't let me go to the city!" I cried to her.

"Shh, people can hear you. Stop crying like a little baby and give me your hand. Oh boy, if you only knew the day that's waiting for you tomorrow! If I were you, I would go to sleep now, quietly."

The next morning, I became the entertainment and scolding channel for everyone. From that day on, everyone in the family started watching me like a hawk. There was no chance of running away again.

You will have to give up on your dream, Ayan, I thought. *You will become like them—grow up, get married, have children, and then die without realizing any of your dreams.*

No, the fighter in me responded. *Somali people say one eye cannot watch another eye. They will forget about it soon. They cannot watch me forever. I will run away once they let their guards down, and this time, I will make sure that I don't get caught.*

I could no longer herd goats or do anything. I was not even allowed to play outside of the huts. My family knew me a little too well. Weeks went by, then months, until one day Grandma got sick. She was very sick, and none of the traditional doctors could heal her. Our grandfather then sent my brothers and cousins to the city to call Uncle Ali.

Four days later, they came back to Ruuraan and told us that Uncle Ali was on his way to Ruuraan.

Everyone was worried about Grandma and forgot about me, so I planned to run away that night. But before I could leave, my mother called me to her.

"Ayan, I am your mother, right?" she asked.

"You told me you are my mother. Are you?" I asked her.

"I am serious. Who am I?" she asked again.

"You are my mother, I think," I said, looking at her dark brown eyes.

"Ayan, stop playing around. What did God say about your mother and listening to her?" my mother asked me.

"He said to listen to your mother and that heaven is under her feet," I said.

"I am your mother. Please just listen to me this once. Don't run away. If you run away, I will curse you, and you will not go to heaven. I will complain to God about you, and you will not be my daughter anymore." I could tell she was serious.

"You will forgive me when I become successful doctor," I said. "Uncle Ali ran away too, but no one is mad at him now. Everyone is proud of him, and he helps people."

"The world was a different place when Uncle Ali was young. It was a lot safer, and he was helped by his brothers. He was much older than you are now, and he knew what he was doing. It was safe for him to go out into that world, but it is not safe for you!" my mom tried to reason.

"We still live in the same place. It is safe for me to go out into the world like Uncle Ali did!" I said.

"What if you run away and your grandma dies? What if I die before you become successful and before you come back? What if I die? Or you die before you become successful? You are my beautiful daughter. Please listen to me and promise me that you will not run away," my mother begged me.

"If you die or I die before I become successful and before I get a chance to ask for forgiveness, I will ask you to forgive me in the hereafter, then," I said, refusing to promise her.

"There is no way to convince you, is there? Here is the thing: I dare you to try running away. Mu'allim and Hassan will catch you again, and I will break both of your legs when they do. I was too nice to you this time and let you off the hook. Try running away again. I promise you that you will spend the rest of your life in this little hut with broken legs, and no one will marry you. Just try running away!"

"You? You will break my legs? Come on, Mom, you couldn't watch me get circumcised, and you cried that time I broke my finger. How will you break my legs?" I asked, laughing.

"Go ahead and try running away! I should have just slept that night I stayed up in pain trying to give birth to you. You wouldn't have been talking to me like this today."

"I am sorry, Mom. I love you. I know the pain you went through for my siblings and me, and I know the pain all women go through here, with no hospital, doctors, or anything to lessen their pain. That is why I have to go to the city to become a doctor," I said and hugged her.

"You don't know half the pain I went through to have you and all the ridicule I get from your aunts for spoiling you. If you love me, you will not run away. If you do, I will have a funeral for you," Mom said.

"I know what it feels like to have your private parts cuts with a blade. I know it's nothing compared to what you went through, but I know. That is why I want to become a doctor. I want to help mothers give birth, and I want to fight against female genital mutilation. I don't want any other girl to go through what I went through, and I don't want any mother to go through the pain you go through every year to have children. Please, Mom, let me go to the city and become a doctor," I said.

"Life is not perfect, dear, and this is something that is part of our life. It's nothing that you can change. It has always been that way and will always be that way. I don't want to lose my daughter. If you decide to go, I will know that you don't care about your mother," my mom said.

She left the hut, and I went to sleep. I had been planning to run away early that morning, but Mom woke me up and I realized it was too late.

I will run away tomorrow, I told myself and got up.

Grandma's situation was getting worse. Fortunately, Uncle Ali came two days later. He checked Grandma and said that she had malaria, anemia, and pneumonia.

"I have to take her with me to the city," Uncle Ali said.

The rest of the family agreed and started preparing for Uncle Ali to take

Grandma to the city. It seemed like God was working with me. My mother trusted my grandma more than anyone else and never said no to her. I knew what to do.

I went to Grandma, even though she could barely speak. I massaged her legs, which burned with fever, and I asked her if she could let me go with Uncle Ali to become a doctor like him.

"Grandma, can I please come with you to the city? I want to become a doctor like Uncle and help people," I asked her.

"No, dear, your mom will worry. Besides, you are a girl. What's the point of you becoming a doctor? Your duty is to your family. Be a good daughter and listen to your mother," Grandma said in a weak voice.

"I know I am a girl, Grandma, but I want to become a doctor. I promise you, I will be a good woman. I will take care of my family and become a good doctor. Please, Grandma, please let me come with you. I promise I will be good," I begged.

"You have to ask your mother, dear. I cannot make a big decision about your life without your mother," Grandma said.

"My mother wouldn't let me go to the city. She wants me to waste my life here. Grandma, please tell her to let me go. She will listen to you."

"Your mother loves you very much and wants what's best for you. You have to respect her and listen to her." Grandma refused to ask my mother to let me go to the city.

"Please, Grandma, I promise I will be a good girl. Please, please, please, Grandma, please talk to her. I really want to become a doctor like Uncle Ali and help others. I want to cure our family when they get sick and take care of them. Please, Grandma, please talk to her. Just once. You will be there, Uncle Ali will be there, Aunt Zainaba and their kids will be there too. Please, Grandma, I don't want to stay in this place. Please, let me go with you."

"I will see what I can do. Go call your mom," Grandma said.

"You are the greatest grandmother! I love you," I said and kissed her forehead.

"I love you too, dear," she whispered.

I ran out of the hut, calling my mother, "Mom! Mom! Mom! Grandma is calling you! Grandma is calling you."

"Shh! Stop running and yelling! You are not a little girl anymore. You are a woman now; start acting like one," my mother whispered.

"I am only eight, Mom," I replied.

"I used to take care of the whole family when I was your age, and here you are pretending to be a little girl. You are almost nine years old; start acting your age. You are five years away from marriageable age. And why is Grandma calling me? Did you say something to her?" Mom said.

"Grandma is calling you, Mom; please hurry up. She is sick, and she is waiting for you. Hurry up. What kind of daughter-in-law are you? Making your sick mother-in-law wait for you."

"You said you are a little girl, and you shouldn't be talking like that," Mom said, but she was smiling as she walked to Grandma's hut. "Mom, did you call for me?"

"Yes, dear," Grandma said. "Come, sit down."

Mom knew what Grandma wanted to talk to her about.

"I want Ayan to come with me to the city. She will stay with me and Ali's family in Mogadishu and go to school there. I know, as a mother, you will be concerned, but I promise you I will take a good care of her," Grandma said.

"I don't want my daughter to grow up without me in the city. Nevertheless, I respect your wishes; you can take her wherever you like, but I would prefer it if you could leave her here with all of us."

"Please let her go from your heart and pray for her so that God may put blessings in her life," Grandma whispered.

"Okay, Mom, she can go with you," my mom said, holding her tears back.

I knew Mom would agree, so I went to the hut and started preparing for my journey to the city. I spread my other scarf and my other dress on the floor of the hut and gathered my hair comb, my mirror, and my small bag that I had sewn from grass and a dyed rope.

"So you already know?" Mom said as she entered the hut.

"Yes, I know that you can never say no to Grandma," I said, smiling.

Mom sat in front of me and held my hands. "Are you that happy to leave us?"

"No, Mom, I am not happy at all, but I really want to become a doctor. I want to cure you when you are old like Grandma, and I want to help everyone feel good and not go through unnecessary pain. Please, Mom, forgive me and let me go," I said to her.

"I want you to know that I love you so much, and I will pray for you every day for as long as I am alive. Be a good daughter and listen to your uncle and aunt and Grandma. Study very hard and become the best doctor in the world, like the best daughter you are." Tears filled Mom's eyes.

I hugged her and wiped her tears. "I will, Mom. I will become the best doctor in the world, and I will become a good daughter. I will never lose my culture and religion in the big city and will never do anything to make you sad," I said as tears rolled down my cheeks.

"Don't cry, dear. I don't want people to say Dahabo's daughter is weak. Don't ever let anyone see you weak. You are very strong." She wiped away my tears.

"I will never cry again, Mom. You should stop crying too. I don't want people to say Ayan's mom is weak."

Mom laughed as she hugged me tightly.

"I will miss you so much," I said and kissed her forehead.

"I will miss you too, dear. I don't know what I will do without you," Mom said with her hand on my cheek.

"You have ten other kids. I am sure they will keep annoying you until I come back. When I come back, I will yell at them if they haven't been taking care of you."

"Remember my words, dear—life in the city is hard. Life everywhere is hard; you have to be very strong and never forget your aim no matter what happens. Nothing bad lasts forever, and nothing good lasts forever. Everything comes to an end at some point, so cherish the good while you have it and look forward to the end of the bad while you are going through it. Always remember to pray to Allah. God is always there with you," Mom said and wiped the tear from my face.

"I know, Mom. I will be all right. I promise."

Part of me wanted to stay, and another part wanted to become a doctor. I have never forgotten how my mother's face looked that day.

"It's time to go," my dad said from outside the hut. "If you two are done, please come out."

I bid farewell to everyone in the family and left home. I remember Mom standing there, looking at us disappear into the distance as she hid her tears from everyone else.

7

During the last quarter of eighth grade, the rumors of violence in the countryside grew into a reality. The civil war had started in some parts of Somalia. We went on with our daily routines, our hearts filled with fear of whether or not Mogadishu was going to be hit by the disease and the destruction sweeping through our nation.

About four months earlier, we had gotten the good news that Aunt Zainaba was pregnant with her tenth child. I remember that evening when she made the announcement that she was pregnant. We were sitting in the yard, waiting for dinner. A cool wind was blowing my hair to the left, a feeling I have always loved.

Aunt Zainaba collected my hair together and tied it back in a messy bun like my mother used to do in Ruuraan. I noticed an empty spot in my heart, but Aunt Zainaba stroked over it so gently like a careful painter that she concealed the empty space in my heart.

"I have good news tonight!" Aunt Zainaba said. "You are going to have another sibling!"

"You are so shameless," Grandma chuckled. "You are not supposed to tell that you are pregnant; it's a bad omen for you and the baby. You should know this by now. It's not like this is your first child."

"Oh, come on, Mother. What's there to be ashamed of? You know what they say—I won't tell, but don't let nine months tell you." Trying to hide her disbelief in my grandmother's superstitions, Aunt Zainaba calmly laughed.

"Pregnant! Are you serious, Mom?" Halima said. "When will you stop having kids? There are, like, hundreds of us. What do you need more kids for?"

"Not until I have my own teams. I want to give birth to an entire soccer team so we can win the World Cup for Somalia! You can be our manager if you would like, since you have no athletic abilities," Aunt Zainaba said, teasing Halima.

"I am not kidding, Mom. Please stop having kids; you don't need any more kids. You are a doctor, and you always talk about family planning, yet you don't practice it yourself." Halima marched to her room.

"I will keep having babies for as long as I can have them. Kids are a blessing from God, and I will have twenty-four of them if possible," Aunt Zainaba said, smiling.

"What wonderful news. Thank you, Mom! I hope it's a boy. If it is, I will name him," Fathi said.

"Halima is seriously brainwashed!" Grandma said. "You should tell her to stop watching those movies or soon enough she will tell you it's wrong to have more than one child."

"I wonder who spoiled her rotten. Why don't you talk some sense into her, since you are the only one who knows the right way to raise kids?" Aunt Zainaba teased Grandma.

"You are her mother; it's your job to teach her. But since you don't know how to do your job, I will talk to her," Grandmother said jokingly.

"Don't you ever get tired of bickering?" Mohamed asked.

"What fun is life without teasing and having fun with your loved ones? This is how we show our love, dear. Men are too slow to understand this," Grandma said.

Halima came back and sat by Grandma to eat her food. We had dinner and went to bed after about an hour of sharing stories and laughing.

Aunt Zainaba's belly grew bigger, and so did our fear of civil war destroying our home. Grandma, Uncle Ali, and Aunt Zainaba's conversations were often consumed with discussions of the war, trying to make sense of what was happening to our country. Although they did not always agree as to what was the cause for our country's downward spiral to destruction, they agreed that it was speeding toward a cliff.

I remember one night when Grandma, Uncle Ali, Uncle Samatar, and Aunt Zainaba discussed the war over dinner. The adults were sitting on the white chairs, and the rest of us were sitting on a mat on the grass near them. When we had guests, Uncle Ali and Aunt Zainaba would sit with them at the white table in the yard. The children would spread our mat near them so we could have dinner together.

"It looks like we are headed for destruction," Grandma said, shaking her head.

"Tribes have been fighting for centuries in Somalia," Uncle Samatar said. "It's nothing new. I don't think this one is any different. Just like the other wars, this one will pass, and we will be all right."

"I have lived long enough to know that this is not like any of the other wars we have had," Grandma said. "I always knew that one day our country's lack of fear of God was going to destroy it. Sins tend to catch up to people. Our country is going to be destroyed because we have forgotten our maker, the one who blessed us with so much. What is worse is we remained silent when the government killed the scholars of God because they refused to change the words of God. This is a punishment for our sins. And it breaks my heart to see this disease spreading so fast. It is taking over our country. Brother against brother for no apparent reason."

"We are in this situation because of the colonizers and communists," Aunt Zainaba said. "They have divided us and made us materialistic people. They made the land part of our identity and turned us against one another and left us in a downward spiral to destruction. Not just us. They have set up Africa for conflict for centuries to come. I hope the colonized world wakes up before the whole world is in flames again."

"Aren't you giving them too much credit, dear?" Uncle Ali said. "We are in this situation because of the ignorance of our people. Although colonial systems had something to do with it, lack of adequate education and resources are the primary causes driving this conflict."

"Zainaba has a point," Grandma said. "Tribes married from one another and lived together in harmony for centuries. We were nomads following the rain. There was no sense of geographical identity until the colonizers came to Somalia. Somali people were noble people who lived peacefully with each other, with no lust for materialistic things and power. We were a beautiful nation of poets."

"I agree with both of you that colonizers used the divide-and-conquer method to gain power and colonize us, but they are not the ultimate cause of our problems," Uncle Ali said. "If you look at almost every tribe-related conflict, it started because of water, water wells, land, or other resources. Yes, the colonials might have intensified the tribal feuds and differences, but they are not the primary cause of our problems. They left our country almost thirty years ago—the problem is our people."

Grandma chuckled in disagreement, and Aunt Zainaba said, "Lack of resources has fueled many conflicts around the world, but it's not the cause of it. We have farmlands that can feed all of Africa, we have one of the longest coasts in Africa, we are in a strategic trade route, businesses are booming, we have oil and natural gas, mountains rich in minerals, and livestock in the millions. Do you really think we don't have enough resources? Colonizers and communist ideologies are the cause, dear. They tricked us into organizing us into geographical areas and tricked us into making those geographical areas part of our identity. They also introduced the idea of one tribe being better than the other tribe. They brought this disease to our land. They are the cause of it."

Uncle Ali responded, "You can't give them that much credit. There is no way anyone can have that much power over a whole nation unless that nation is the problem. Our people are the problem—we are the ones killing each other, we are the ones who let outside forces influence our country. We are the ones not realizing the kind of world we live in and what is important and what is better for all of us. Even if everything is due to the colonists and the meddling of the neighboring countries, none of their plans would have worked if it was not for our people implementing their plans. Therefore, the problem is our people, and no one else is to be blamed."

"It is Ethiopia and Kenya!" Uncle Samatar broke in. "Both Ethiopia and Kenya received large areas from Somalia, wrongly given to them by the colonizers. Both areas are rich in oil, minerals, and other natural resources. If Somalia were a strong country, we would have taken both areas back by now like we kicked Ethiopia's ass in 1977."

"Samatar, while you have a point that Ethiopia and Kenya both contributed to the downfall of Somalia, you are giving them too much credit and a power they simply don't have. The issues are internal. We enabled colonizers and foreign powers to impact the downfall of our country. The issue is our people. The credit of destroying our country belongs to us," Uncle Ali said.

"Ali, suppose you invent a new disease, you purposefully make someone sick, and the disease keeps spreading. Suppose there is an epidemic of that disease, let's say a hundred years later. Are you the cause of that epidemic, or should you blame the patients?" Aunt Zainaba said.

"This is not the same, dear. You cannot use that analogy," Uncle Ali said.

"Yes, you can, dear. You know I lived with a historian for over fifty years," Grandma said.

"You should have been a judge, Mom." Aunt Zainaba laughed.

"When a nation forgets to fear their creator, they are bound to fail. This is the result of our sins. God told us to be humble and told us that all humans are equal. No one is better than another person, but our people forgot that. They take pride in the family they are born into as if they have earned it and think that they are better than other tribes. What is worse is that human life has become less valuable than dirt," Grandma continued.

"How about this," Aunt Zainaba said. "Let's just say Somali people, Somali tribal system, neglecting Islamic teachings, neighboring countries with their own interests like Ethiopia and Kenya, colonizers and other foreign ideologies, and a lack of resource utilization have all contributed to the downfall of Somalia."

A summary of the complex reasons for the downfall of Somalia [handwritten margin note]

"The food looks good; let's eat," Uncle Ali said.

"Yes, please, let's eat before someone gets high blood pressure," Fathiya said, laughing.

"Do you ever think of anything else but food?" Grandma asked, laughing. "Stop being obsessed with food. I don't want a divorced granddaughter because she ate too much food. Learn how to control your appetite."

"Obsessed? Me? Come on, Grandma, we both know who the doctor told to cut down on eating," Fathiya teased Grandma.

"For your information, he said to cut down on fatty foods. And I am not the one who makes three hundred crepes every morning to take with her," Grandma said.

"The crepes I make for the homeless people in our community? That's a new low, Grandma." Fathiya smiled.

"That's what you tell us. I am no fool, dear. I know all your secrets," Grandma said, laughing.

"Oh, come on, Grandma, you have helped me give out breakfast so many mornings."

"Really? Did I? I am having a hard time remembering that," Grandma said and started eating.

We laughed, shared stories, and joked with each other until it was time to go to sleep.

As the reports of fighting near Mogadishu intensified, Grandma called for a family meeting. Family meetings were always held in the living room because it was the only room that could hold all of us at once. Aunt Zainaba, Grandma, Uncle Ali, Fathiya, and Mohamed were sitting on the leather couches. The rest of us sat on the carpet. I sat right under the chandelier. I admired that chandelier and was amazed by how people could put such a beautiful thing so high and how the roof could support it. It looked heavy to me.

The person who called for the family meeting was always the one who started it. Grandma sat on the single-seat couch and started the meeting.

She wanted Uncle Ali to leave the city with Mohamed. They were the only men left in our family, and many people knew them.

"I am concerned about your safety, Ali. I want you to take Mohamed with you and leave the city. Aside from the children, you are the only men left in our family. God forbid if anything happens to you two. It would be the end of this family," Grandma said.

"Where would we go, Mom? The whole nation is burning. I cannot leave you. I am responsible for all of you," Uncle Ali said.

"I don't care where you go as long as you leave this place. I cannot bear to lose another person in my family. I will die if something happens to either one of you," Grandma said as tears rolled down her cheeks.

"Mom, I understand and know how you feel. Nothing will happen to us. We will be all right. Mohamed will grow up and have twenty boys for you," Uncle Ali said as he hugged Grandma.

"I am your mom! If I tell you to jump, you ask how high! I am not going to lose another one of my family members. You and Mohamed are leaving this city. I took out all my money from the banks and put them in these shoes," Grandma said in a stern voice. She took out a bag filled with shoes for each member of our family.

"I've hidden money in the middle of each shoe for every one of you. Make sure you wear these shoes everywhere you go, and only use that money in case of emergency."

"Ewww, they are so ugly," Halima said. "There is no way I am going to wear these shoes!"

"Halima, I am not joking! Everyone, try them on right now!" Grandma said, handing the shoes out.

"Mom, if something is meant to happen to us, no one can stop it from happening, and if something was not meant for us, it will never happen to us. Why are you so worried?" Uncle Ali said. "Have faith, please. Nothing will happen to us."

"Victory is for those who prepare for it. I am not going to just sit by and wait for something bad to happen to my family. I have to do something, and you have to work with me to save our family!" Grandma said.

"Mom, nothing is going to happen to us. This is just a small tribal war, and it will end before you know it," Uncle Ali said.

"You know very well that if any tribe had an issue with our tribe, you would be the first one to get killed. Do you not remember what happened to our family?" Grandma asked.

"Mom, please don't worry. I do remember what happened in Ruuraan; I can never forget that. I understand where you are coming from, but leaving our home is not going to solve anything. Even if all the tribes fight, I am mixed with all of them in one way or another. Why would anyone want to kill me?" Uncle Ali said, refusing to leave the city.

Grandma agreed to wait for a little bit more to see if the situation grew worse. She made Uncle Ali and Mohamed promise that they would leave the city if things took a turn for the worse.

The military and the armed civilians started coming to Mogadishu but remained on opposite sides of the city. From that time on, everyone was sure that the war was going start at any moment. I could not understand the reason for the fighting, but I was aware that war meant the end of our world as we had known it.

One afternoon, Grandma was sitting in her room and holding her forehead with her hands. She did not notice that I was there until I talked to her.

"Grandma?" I said. She jumped as if she were woken up from a nightmare.

"Yes, dear?" Grandma whispered, lifting her head up to look at me.

"Grandma, why are our people fighting with each other?" I asked curiously.

Grandma shook her head as tears rolled down her cheeks. "Sweetie, there is no reason to justify what is happening. It is a disease! I wish there were a reason, but there is no reason good enough to justify the lives of the innocent people who are being killed!" she cried loudly.

"Grandma, I will become a doctor and find a cure for everyone infected with this disease!" I exclaimed with words full of dreams and hope.

Grandma started laughing. "That's my granddaughter! Never treat anyone differently because of their tribe, race, religion, nationality, or any superficial label attached to them. We are all human beings, dear, and God created all of us." Grandma kissed my forehead.

A couple of weeks later, I was reading a book in the living room when Uncle Ali, Aunt Zainaba, and Uncle Samatar came into the room.

"Ayan, we need to talk privately with Uncle Samatar. Please go read your book in the yard or one of the other rooms. You can come back to the living room once we are done," Aunt Zainaba said.

I walked out of the room, and Aunt Zainaba closed the door behind me. I sat on the stairs of the living room and continued to read my book, and in the background, I could hear their conversation.

"Dr. Ali, as you now, we have been friends for many years," Uncle Samatar said. "We are also in-laws, as you are married to my first cousin Dr. Zainaba. I like to think that the two of you wouldn't have been married today if it weren't for me. I am also your family physician and have done many things for you and your family. What I am about to say is contrary to the Somali culture, but I think it is all right given our relationship."

"Dr. Samatar, you are right we have been friends for many years, and you are Zainaba's cousin," Uncle Ali said. "We have a long history together as friends and as family. What is it you want to ask for?"

"I would like your son Mohamed to marry one of my daughters. I know this is contrary to the Somali culture, as the man's family is supposed to ask for the woman's hand. But given our history, I hope this is all right," Uncle Samatar said.

"I appreciate that you want my son to marry one of your daughters, because that must mean that you see some good in him. However, I don't think my son is compatible with your family," Uncle Ali said.

"Samatar, I know we are family, and I love your daughters," Aunt Zainaba said, "but I agree with Ali. My son and your daughters are not compatible."

"What do you mean my daughters are not compatible with Mohamed? Your nerdy son is not exactly a catch!" Uncle Samatar said.

"Samatar, we didn't mean to upset you, but your daughters' lifestyles are very different from Mohamed's. Your daughters love nightlife—they club, they drink, they don't cover up, and they don't respect anyone. Like you said, Mohamed is a nerd. He doesn't drink, he doesn't club, he doesn't like nightlife, he is a practicing Muslim, and he cares deeply about Somali culture. I just don't think your daughters and Mohamed would get along. They don't even get along when they meet at family events. What would a marriage be like?" Aunt Zainaba asked.

"What are you trying to say, Zainaba? That my daughters are not good enough for your family?" Uncle Samatar yelled.

"Please don't raise your voice at my wife. We are not saying your daughters are not good enough for us. We are saying that none of them are compatible with Mohamed," Uncle Ali said.

"What about my two oldest sons? Would you agree to letting them marry your two daughters Fathiya and Halima?" Uncle Samatar asked.

"No! I don't think they are compatible either," Uncle Ali said.

"Stop trying to use compatibility as your get-out card. Why don't just say that my family is not good enough for yours. I have done so much for you and your family! This is how you repay me?" Uncle Samatar continued to raise his voice.

"Your sons have asked my daughters out, and they both rejected them. I am sorry, but we are just not compatible with each other when it comes to marriage. We know all what you have done for us and for our family, and we thank you for that, but our kids are not going to marry into your family," Aunt Zainaba said.

"You finally showed your true colors! That's women for you! Isn't my family your family? You think just because you are married to him you are part of his tribe now?" Uncle Samatar said.

"Samatar, do not raise your voice at my wife again! We worked very hard to instill moral values into our children and raise them with religion and culture. Your family is the total opposite of that, and we will never allow your kids to marry into our family or allow our kids to marry into your family. I am sorry, but that's just how it is," Uncle Ali said.

"You ungrateful, backward, uncivilized garbage will regret this! Mark my words! You will regret this! I have done so much for you and your family. And you repaid me by insulting me! You will see!" Uncle Samatar said, banging the table.

"Please leave!" Uncle Ali said. "We thank you for all that you have done for us, but that doesn't mean we owe you anything! We have also done so much for you and your family, but we don't act as if you owe us anything!"

Uncle Samatar stormed out of the room and went to his car. He beeped his car horn to signal to Dayib, our watchman, to open the gate, and he almost ran over Dayib in his haste to leave.

The bad day started like any other day. In the morning, we all went to school, and our parents went to work. But right after the second class ended, we started hearing loud noises outside the classroom.

We heard *bang, bang, boom, boom, wisheeew.* The noises were very loud like something I had heard only in action movies. I wished that they were shooting a movie outside. I wished it were all a bad dream that would end when I woke up. And I wished it were just my imagination. I prayed to God.

Our teacher told us to get down on the floor and under the tables. We started panicking, with some of the kids crying and screaming instead of getting on the floor. Our teacher grabbed them one by one and made sure everyone was on the floor and under the tables.

She yelled to us, "Stop screaming and crying! If you cry, they will come get you! If you don't want to get killed, stop crying!" She was as terrified as we were, but she cried silently. She was the teacher and had to be strong for us, but we could all see it on her face. She was shaking and biting her nails while she tried to figure out what to do. Everyone was terrified and wondered what was going on.

Nothing could have ever prepared us for what happened next, not even our worst nightmares.

Our classmate Layla wouldn't stop crying; our teacher walked toward her and told her to be quiet or she would get us all in trouble.

"I am scared!" Layla said. "Are we going to die? What if we get shot? What if . . ."

Our teacher hugged Layla and tried to calm her and the rest of us. She told us that nothing was going to happen to us and that this was going to end soon. We huddled around her, and she told us that we would be fine as long as we got on the floor and calmed down. She told us to pray so that Allah would protect us. "Pray, pray, pray Allah will protect us all! You should always call for Allah's help when in need of help! Allah is great; Allah is grea—" She fell to the ground before she could finish her sentence.

We did not know what happened to her. We all got up and ran to where she was lying lifeless. A thick pool of dark red blood slowly flowed from her body. We called her name, but she did not respond. She lay there like a log. I looked where she had been standing moments ago. The wall had a hole on it.

Was it there before, or did a bullet come through and kill our teacher? I wondered as tears flowed. I tried to make sense of all of this in my little terrified head.

All the kids stood there like stones, not knowing what to do. Their eyes filled with fear and with tears. We all started crying, but no one came to stop us from crying, no one calmed us down, and none of us knew what to do. We stopped crying when we could not cry anymore.

Eventually, parents dashed in one by one and rushed their children out of the classroom. Soon the only children left in the classroom were me and couple of other students. Our dead teacher's body was covered by a small shawl that one of the parents had placed over her. We could still see the pool of blood around her.

I waited and waited; the loud noises, the screaming, and the fear increased as time passed ever so slowly. It was like those moments were things happening so fast that the brain couldn't process them and make sense of them yet. Time moved so slowly because I wanted it all to end. I sat there, staring at our dead teacher.

Layla and I held hands tightly as we sat on the floor crying until we heard footsteps. Each time we heard someone coming, we didn't know whether to be happy or scared. We heard footsteps of two people coming, and our hearts started racing. *Thud-thud . . . thud . . . thud.* Sweat ran from our skin. *Oh, Allah, please let these people be our family.*

Halima entered with a strange-looking person. I looked at the other person curiously; I had seen his eyes somewhere, but I wasn't sure where. I hugged Halima tightly and started weeping. She calmed me down.

The loud noises and the gunshots started to move farther away.

I asked Halima who the other person was. The strange-looking person startled me before Halima could answer me. He said, "Ayan, it's me, Mohamed!"

"Mohamed? Why are you dressed like a woman?" I whispered to him.

"Grandma made me wear this; she said it was for my safety. The family is waiting for us. We are going to leave the city. The situation is getting worse by the minute! Let's go!" Mohamed said fearfully.

"Ha ha, you are scared!" I cracked a little laugh.

"Your tears are still wet! We don't have time for jokes. Let's go!" Mohamed said, grabbing my hand.

We had to leave the school, but I didn't want to leave my friend Layla there alone. We cried and begged Halima and Mohamed to take Layla with us or to stay with her until her parents come. But Halima and Mohamed told us that we couldn't take her because her parents would be worried if they didn't find their daughter, and we had to leave because our family was waiting for us.

Halima said, "It's too dangerous; we have to leave now!" Layla and I clung to each other, but Halima and Mohamed dragged us apart and pulled me outside the classroom. I struggled with Mohamed's hand, trying to free myself, but he was too strong for me.

Halima scolded me, "Ayan! Stop acting like a baby. We have to be very strong, and you need to act like a strong person if you want to make it home safely. Stop this childish behavior. Layla will be all right. Her family will come and take her. You can come back and see her when things get better. We will come back in couple of days when the fighting subsides. Let's go!"

If there was anything I had learned from the stories that Grandma told us, it was to help those in need. I couldn't leave my friend there, alone with our dead teacher. I knew that was wrong. I begged them, cried, and even threatened them that I wasn't going to go with them. They knew that they would get in trouble with the Uncle Ali if I wasn't with them.

They finally agreed to wait with me for Layla's parents to come, but only for thirty minutes. The clock ticked slowly. As time went on, Layla and I started worrying that maybe her family was not going to come and that we would have to leave her alone.

Twenty-eight minutes in, Layla's family finally came. Layla burst into tears and ran to her mom, hugging her tightly. Her mother calmed her down, and it was time to say goodbye to each other. We hugged and promised to look for each other when we came back.

We left the school like thieves, moving from one side of the road to the other, hiding in corners, and scanning the area before making a move.

The fighting had returned to our part of the city, and the sounds of the gunshots, missiles, screams, and chaos all around us deafened us. The calm, cool weather of our city was nowhere to be found; it felt like we were in foreign land. I could barely recognize the roads that we had been walking on almost every day since I had started going to elementary school in Mogadishu. They were nothing like the roads they used to be.

We could hear bullets hitting the walls, sometimes explosions nearby and bullets passing so close to us that we could feel the change in the air pressure.

There was blood, dead people, and men with guns everywhere. People were running and walking around as if some sort of alien force had taken over our home. People were looting stores, houses, and anything of value. The white marble buildings were smeared with blood. The beautiful sculptures were destroyed. The palm trees were on fire. The cars were not stopping at lights, and traffic was not flowing smoothly as it used to. It was chaos all around.

"Ayan! Stop watching and get going! We don't want to get killed! You will be more scared if you look around you. Just follow us quickly. We need to get home before anything happens to us!" Halima exclaimed as if the words would be stolen from her.

We kept walking until we got to our neighborhood. We felt relieved thinking that we had finally made it without being killed, but what we saw when we got home was something that we could have never imagined.

As we got closer to our house, the hair on my arms and neck started standing. I had an eerie feeling. My fear grew bigger. Our neighborhood didn't seem so safe anymore. There were dead bodies in front of our house. Someone felt sorry for them and had covered them with bedsheets. We looked at the bodies with terror, as if looking at them would make us among them or they would come to life and get us.

"Oh my Allah, some people were killed in front of our house! May Allah bless their souls and forgive them," Mohamed said, shivering with fear.

My heart was racing and pounding hard; it felt as if my heart were in my throat. The whole world suddenly became frightening.

Stunned with fear, we stopped moving; the gate to our house was wide open. Our gate was always closed, even before this strife had swept through our city. A dark cloud of fear came over us.

"Don't go in. Don't go in there," a voice said quietly.

We looked around, but we could not see anyone.

"Don't go in there," the voice repeated.

"I am so scared that I started imagining that people are telling us not to go in our house," Halima joked, and we laughed nervously with her.

"I hear it too," I said, stuttering.

"Me too!" Mohamed whispered.

We stood there petrified, unsure what to do.

"Maybe the gates are open because the house was looted, maybe the bad guys are in there, maybe our family already left us because we were late, or maybe our family opened the gate for us in case we come running . . ." We thought of all the reasons why our gates were open.

We heard gunshots nearby and decided to go through the gates to safety, but we heard the words again: "Don't go in there!" The voice seemed familiar, and we knew that we were not imagining things this time.

I saw a hand covered in blood moving out from under the corner of the bedsheet.

We jumped with fear.

"Allah! Talking dead body!" I screamed.

"Shush! I am not a dead body. It's me, Grandma. Go and hide before they come." It was Grandma's voice, but we couldn't believe it was our grandmother.

She should be in the house waiting for us. Why would she be one of the dead bodies covered in blood? We ran to the pile of bodies where our grandma claimed to be.

Mohamed lifted the bedsheet with the tips of his two fingers. It was Grandma! We held her hand, questioning her as we shook with fear.

"Grandma, what happened?" Halima cried.

"Nothing. I am just hiding here. Go and hide quickly before they come out," Grandma said weakly.

We looked around, but there was nowhere to hide and nowhere to go.

"Come in here quickly, under the bedsheet, and pretend you are dead! Do not move or make any noise, no matter what happens!" Grandma cried.

We lay down among the dead bodies and Grandma. Seeing Grandma alive calmed us down, even though we were scared.

As I lay beneath the sheet, I turned to my left and saw Uncle Ali lying there. He looked pale and lifeless. A terror pierced through my heart like a million knives hitting at once. It felt like a scene from a horror movie.

I moved my hand slowly and touched his hand. It was the same hand that had brushed my hair, the hand that had wiped my tears when I cried, that same hand that had taught me how to read and write. But it wasn't the same. It was lifeless, missing its warmth, and heavy. I wondered if he was dead or just really good at pretending to be dead.

No, he cannot be dead! I tried to brush the bad thought from my head.

I nudged him and whispered, "Uncle Ali, Uncle Ali, Uncle Ali . . ." But he didn't respond to me.

I thought, *Maybe he fell asleep. No, he probably doesn't want to talk to me because we are pretending to be dead.*

I lifted the bedsheet up a little to look past Uncle Ali and saw the rest of the family under the sheet. Aunt Zainaba was there, the same color as Uncle Ali.

I was feeling uneasy, so I got up and removed the sheet from everyone. And for a moment, I wished my eyes were deceiving me.

"I must be dreaming. I must be dreaming. I have to wake up from this nightmare!" I cried as salty tears rolled down my cheeks.

I looked at Aunt Zainaba, hoping that she was pretending, just like Grandma, Halima, and Mohamed. She was covered in blood. Her mouth was open, and her eyes were not in this world. I touched her face; it was cold.

I tried to wake her, but she wouldn't. I knew she was gone. I looked at her belly, hoping that at least her belly was safe. Her belly was no longer round and big; it looked as if it had burst open and a pool of blood was on her left. Inside her dress, by her belly, the baby inside her womb and everything else in her belly was visible.

My whole world turned black, breathing got harder and harder, my brain felt overwhelmed. My veins swelled so that I could see all of them rise on my skin. My heart weakened, my head started pounding, and my world become so tiny that it could no longer hold me.

My heart shattered into a million tiny pieces like a broken glass. I couldn't do anything but stand there and feel numb. I couldn't bring them back to life; I was hopeless. I had never felt so weak before.

I started throwing up and crying hysterically. Halima and Mohamed were on Grandma's side. When they heard my cries, they sat up with terror, as I couldn't stop vomiting. Halima started vomiting with me.

Grandma urged us to put the bedsheet over us and go back to pretending to be dead, but we couldn't knowing that everyone in our family was dead and lying on the ground lifeless as their blood pooled. It was hard to believe what was around us, let alone go back to pretending to be dead. I felt my body shutting down as if someone had turned off the lights. I started shaking, and I kept throwing up even though there was nothing left in my stomach to come out.

"Put the bedsheet back and get back to your position! *Now!*" Grandma said. She was concerned about our safety. We didn't know what to do.

Mohamed held me, and Halima tried to calm us down. Halima fainted. He took her and put her by Grandma and covered everyone.

Everything around us was getting too real; too real yet too far from reality. I didn't know whether to believe it or whether this was just a bad dream or a scene from a horror movie.

I sat down and looked at the faces of all the bodies closely. They were all our family. I looked down to my right, and there was Fathi, dead, then there was Hassan, the youngest of the family, just two years old, lying on the ground, lifeless. It was unbelievable, unimaginable, and unthinkable to me that someone in their right mind would kill a whole family from a two-year-old child to the grandmother, who was already in the last days of her life.

I sat there praying, "God, why are you taking my family? Grandma was right. A disease has certainly infected our home. Please give my family back to me or take me with them."

I heard footsteps approaching from inside the courtyard.

"Get under the sheet right now!" Grandma hissed at us with all her strength. We covered everyone else and got under the bedsheet with our dead family.

The footsteps and the voices grew closer. After a little bit, something heavy fell on the ground. From the sound it made as it landed, we could tell it was a body, but I didn't know whose body it was and I couldn't find the strength to look it. At least not right away. My heart was filled with fear; I thought no one was going to survive. I could smell the horrible odor of my family's blood all around us.

"That bitch! Who does she think she is?" a familiar voice boomed nearby. "She thinks I am fool or what? Ha ha, she actually thought I would give her half of everything. See, Ali! Do you see what you have done to yourself and to your family? Everyone will think that you were killed because of the tribal conflict, I will get away with it, and there is nothing you can do to stop me! I told you not to reject my proposal for your son Mohamed to marry my daughter! I told you that you would regret it one day! After all, every dog has its day! I tried to get on your good side and even let you marry my stupid cousin, but what did you give me in return? You gave me nothing but humiliation and rejection. Everyone has been telling me, 'Look at Ali. You are the same age and you went to the same school, but he has everything and made a huge difference, while you accomplished little and have nothing compared to him!' Ali, this is what you get for rejecting me and making my life miserable for years! I told you that at the end of the day, I will have the upper hand, and I do now!" He went on and on venting his anger on the corpse, yelling at the lifeless body of Uncle Ali.

I wondered what terrible thing Uncle Ali had done that this man was still not satisfied even after killing our family. He was not satisfied with the sight of our family's blood and the people he massacred, whose wet blood was still running in the street.

I had no doubt whose voice it was, but part of me didn't want to believe it. But I had to make sure. I had to make sure who did this to my family. I had to look at their face even if I would be killed for it.

But I couldn't move my hand. It was as if my hands were glued to the ground. I was scared, but I had to look at that person—the person who had painted the street red with my family's blood. I had to see the face of the person who had shattered my dreams, the person who had killed my beloved family. How could I not see his face?

I have to look! I convinced myself. I used every bit of strength in my body and lifted the sheet from my face.

My eyes widened in disbelief. I closed my eyes and opened them again. He was still venting his anger on my uncle. Turning my eyes away from him was harder than gathering the courage to move the bedsheet from my face. I closed my eyes and silently prayed to God.

I kept closing and opening my eyes repeatedly, as if blinking was going to prove me wrong or at least replace him with someone else, but it was the same person every time. No matter how long I closed my eyes, no matter how many times I blinked, it was still Uncle Samatar, the uncle we all loved and respected so much. It was Samatar; he had killed his cousin Aunt Zainaba and murdered her unborn child. Uncle Samatar had killed her and her family.

He was covered in blood, the blood of his own cousin and her family. He looked very dirty, as if nothing in this world could ever make him clean again. It was the same face, the same body, and the same voice. For some reason, it did not feel like him. He looked as if he were possessed.

The strap of a long, ugly gun was on his shoulder. It was the gun he had killed my whole family with. The gun whose bullets went through my family's flesh, through their hearts and bones, through their veins and muscles. He was carrying the gun that had shed my family's blood. I was numb. I lay there as if frozen in time. The air stood still as I watched him vent over the corpses of our family.

Oh, how I wished that I could jump at him and slice his heart into tiny bits and feed it to the vultures. But for some reason, I couldn't find the strength in me. I had no power, no gun, no knife, and no courage to kill someone I had once considered family. Hatred for him conquered my whole body; I could feel it run through my veins, turning my red blood black with grief.

"I swear that you will pay for this, Samatar. Aunt Zainaba and Uncle Ali trusted you so much, thinking that you were their brother. Uncle Ali thought you were his friend. He helped you so much and respected you so much, but you killed him and his family. How can you be so cold and heartless that you killed your own cousin and her family with your own hands?" No words came out of my mouth, but I responded to him without an ounce of satisfaction. I responded to him in my head—my tongue and lips failed me.

I couldn't come up with any logical explanation for why he would do that to his own family. I couldn't find any way to explain why anyone would kill another human being.

Did he kill them because of the tribal disease? No, that can't be. His whole family is mixed with every imaginable Somali tribe. Did he kill my family because of his ego? Why? Why would he kill another human being? Why would anyone kill another human? My head was giving me more questions than answers.

Had he been from a different family, I might have assumed that he had killed my family because he was infected by the tribal disease sweeping through our nation. However horrifying it sounded, that would have made some sense to me. Killing Uncle Ali and everyone else would have made some sense. He would have been like any one of the millions of Somali people that were infected with the tribalism and the hatred disease. But he killed his own cousin, a cousin who had trusted him and who had loved him more than anyone else. The cousin who had looked up to him and the children who had known him as their beloved uncle.

Nothing made sense anymore; our home was turned upside down. Chaos and brain-damaging disease had torn our home apart. Like our teacher had said, may Allah bless her soul, all we could do was pray to God, so I just prayed.

He locked the gate and left with a group of men who were with him. I listened to their chatter and footsteps as they quickly disappeared into the distance. They laughed as if they had just won the lottery. They laughed as if they had just left a celebration, a wedding, or maybe a birthday party. Soon enough, everything seemed eerily quiet. The air stood still, the blood stopped gushing, and the guns were silent. For a moment, it felt like time had stopped altogether.

Is it the end of the world? Is it the day of judgment? Am I dead too? I thought, staring into a dark hole.

But as I opened my eyes, our world was still burning. Our country was being destroyed by the minute. And I could do nothing but stand there as if all the blood and all the energy were drained out of my body.

9

We did not know what to do. We did not go in the house right away. No one said a word. We remained still, as if our bodies were cemented to the ground. Eventually, Grandma told us to go into the house before it got darker, because wild animals would come with the darkness.

"Soon enough, the lions, hyenas, cheetahs, foxes, and vultures will come into the city, attracted by the smell of human blood and flesh. Let's go into the house. I cannot handle seeing our family eaten by another wild animal!" Grandma cried.

No one responded to her; it was as if our blood had frozen. But Grandma would not stop telling us to go in. She told us to go into the house again and again. She waited for a little bit, collected her strength, and then repeated herself until we got up.

Mohamed moved toward the gate. The gate was locked, and we didn't have keys. He climbed over the wall and opened the gate from the inside. We helped Grandma up and walked her toward the house, slowly and fearfully.

We then helped Halima up and helped her go into Grandma's room. When Halima saw the situation Grandma was in, she instantly found energy. Halima helped Grandma to clean the blood. We went outside and brought our family's bodies into the house, one by one. We put all their bodies in the living room, where we used to chat and have our family meetings. There had been so much life and laughter in this room. No one smiled this time. We couldn't bring ourselves to look at them, so we covered them with bedsheets. We locked the gate and all the doors. We ran to Grandma's room and sat on her floor, not saying a word to each other.

The room no longer smelled of Somali incense—the smell of our family's blood took over the air. I detested breathing. Every breath reassured me that they were all gone.

After a while, Halima said, "Ayan, go get me the first aid kit and Dad's surgical toolbox from their room."

I went to the room, but I couldn't find anything. Halima and Mohamed came to help me look. We looked everywhere but could not find any of the first aid kits or any of Uncle Ali and Aunt Zainaba's surgical tools.

"Just get me several towels, a knife, a candle, a match, and a fork," Halima said in a very low voice filled with pain.

"What do you need those things for?" I asked, looking at Halima through my tears.

She had no energy to explain and scolded, "Just go get them for me! Do you have to know everything? God!"

Halima was in no mood to tell me anything. I went out of the room and got her what she had asked for. Then Grandma told me to leave, but I refused. I wanted to see what they were doing to my grandma. I was scared that Grandma might die if I left the room or closed my eyes for a second.

I cried and sat on the floor, refusing to leave. Grandma told them to let me be. They made me promise that I was not going to interfere, that I wasn't going to cry, and that I was not going to yell or ask any questions until they were done helping Grandma.

"Ayan, we love Grandma just as much as you love her. We are going to remove the bullet from where she was shot in her back. Please do not interfere, and do not look!" Halima said as tears rolled down her cheeks. She wiped her tears, clenching her teeth in anger. I had never seen so much anger, pain, heartbreak, and sadness in anyone's eyes before.

There were no hospitals or clinics that we felt safe enough to take her to. And the two doctors in our family were in the living room, their blood decorating the white marble floor.

Mohamed and Halima sat on the bed near Grandma. They removed the sheet Halima placed on her to hide her wound. As I saw the bullet entrance, I gasped for air and started crying.

"Ayan, stop looking! Hold Grandma's hand," Mohamed said.

They helped each other to remove the bullet. Grandma was not crying or screaming; she tightened her teeth and clenched her fists. Halima cried throughout the procedure.

I sat on the ground in front of Grandma's face, looking into her eyes. My forehead touched her warm and sweaty forehead. Grandma clenched my hands, her nails digging into my skin. I felt her pain; no words came out of my mouth. I looked into the whites of her eyes as her pupils dilated from the pain. Tears rolled down our red cheeks. It felt like hours of unending agony.

Halima and Mohamed finally removed the bullet fragments from Grandma's back. They then wrapped the towel and a piece of cloth around her waist, trying to stop the bleeding. It was painful to watch the bullet being removed from her back with their hands and a fork. Grandma was very weak, tired, and sad, but she pretended to be fine and healthy for us. We could see the pain on her face. We were worried that she might not make it, and we prayed to God as we sat on the floor between her bed and the wall.

That night, Grandma asked us to listen to her carefully. We attentively listened to the words that she quietly spoke. She told us that in the morning we had to wash the bodies and bury everyone in the yard. We looked at each other and then back at Grandma as tears filled our eyes. We didn't want to bury them. We were hoping that they would just wake up in the morning and everything would go back to normal. Burying them meant that it was real, that our family was no longer with us, and that we were all alone in this world. It was a reality that we were not ready to face. But what choice did we have?

We were hoping that it was all just a bad dream, but our hopes were very far from our reality. Our reality killed every bit of our hope and drowned us in its vast darkness. Grandma told us we had to properly bury our family. She gave us step-by-step instructions for the burial ritual.

It was very late, so we all went to sleep in Grandma's room; it made us feel little bit safer.

That next morning, I tried to make breakfast. We needed strength to bury our family.

"I will go cook something," I said to Halima.

"Don't burn yourself," she said.

I entered the kitchen without saying a word. I started making tea and eggs; they were the only things that I knew how to make. I opened the cupboard to get some sugar for the tea, and I started screaming at the top of my lungs. I screamed with surprise, fear, worry, and relief all at the same time. Mohamed and Halima ran to the kitchen.

"What happened? Did you burn yourself? Where?" Halima and Mohamed started searching for a burn on my hands.

"I didn't burn myself!" I cried. "The kids are in the cupboard! Ayaanle, Siman, Siham, and Hussein are in there. I don't know if they are dead or alive, but they are not moving."

"What?" Mohamed and Halima said at the same time.

They took the kids out of the cupboard and checked their pulses to see if they were still alive. Fortunately, they were alive, but they were in a bad shape. Slowly, they started to wake up and speak. We gave them water and food and washed their faces. We then asked them what had happened. They told us that Suad, our maid, had given them a pill and told them not to make any noise or they would get in trouble.

Ayaanle said, "Suad said that Dhagdheer would eat us if we made any noise. She then put water, bread, and snacks in there and told us to eat quietly, but only when we got very hungry. And then she closed the cupboard doors, and we heard lots of bad noises. But we fell asleep, and when we woke, we couldn't open the cupboard."

"She must have given them sleeping pills," Halima said. They were unaware of the new world around them. They didn't even know that their parents, their sisters, and their brothers were no longer in this world with them.

That morning, that dark morning, we started digging graves for all our family members who were massacred. It took us two days to dig enough graves for everyone. Two days of no rest, no talking to each other, no eye contact, and no conversations outside of, "Hand me that." We occasionally ate and broke into tears.

We first buried Aunt Zainaba's body. She was killed pregnant, which gave her the status of martyr. I would rather have seen her die of old age. We didn't have to wash her or put a white cloth on her. We buried her with her clothes, exactly how she was. As we put her in the shallow grave, we remembered all the good times that we had shared with her. We remembered the things she had said and the many things that she had done for us, all the times she had made us smile.

I couldn't help but think of her beautiful smile and laughter as she sat on a mattress one afternoon, holding a cup of tea. I kept remembering when she brushed my hair and tied it back together with her beautiful, gentle hands. I kept seeing her swinging on the swing as the wind made her hair dance. I kept smelling her sweet perfume. I kept seeing the moments when she taught me how to read, the days she told us stories, the times she kissed my forehead and told me that I had done well.

It was hard for me to believe that the aunt who I had loved so much was gone. It was hard to believe that the aunt who had told me about college, schools, the importance of education was lying inside a shallow grave. It was a bitter reality that I couldn't swallow. I could not imagine what life would be like, never speaking to her and never seeing her beautiful smile again.

After burying Aunt Zainaba, we carried Uncle Ali's body to another shallow grave next to hers. I remembered all the stories he had told me about the prophets: the stories of Adam, Jesus, David, Moses, Isaiah, Solomon, Noah, and Muhammad (peace be upon them all). The stories he told me about the heroes of Islam and the stories of great women who made the world a better place. These were the stories that I loved hearing more than anything else, the stories that made me love coming home. I remembered how he had smiled at me and had given me gifts. All that was gone and would never come back. The thought that Uncle Ali was gone and that I would never hear his voice again made my heart heavy with grief.

I remembered when he had told me that he was like my father and the time that he had given me a necklace and a journal. I ran to my room and took the necklace out and returned with it in my hand. I wore it as if it would make me closer to him.

"May God have mercy on your soul, Uncle! I love you, and I will miss you. I promise you that I will become a great doctor, and I will get justice for you! Why did this have to happen to you? Oh, God, why are you taking my family without me? You took my family in Ruuraan, and now you have taken my family in Mogadishu. Why? Why not me? Why does everyone I love have to die? Why don't you take me with them!" I broke down in tears as I sat on the hot, dirty ground near his grave, while Mohamed and Halima shoveled the dirt on him.

Once they had completely covered him, Halima sat by me and hugged me as she cried silently.

"Come on, please get it together!" Mohamed said. "I know you are sad and heartbroken by what happened to our family. They did not deserve what happened to them, and we do not deserve it. But we have to be strong. That is what our parents would want us to do. The least we can do is give them a proper burial. Let's get going."

We got up, still crying, and we finished burying them. We prayed for them and read the Quran for them. Grandma was still sick and getting weaker by the minute.

In a weak voice, she said, "Ayan, come here." I held her hand, which brought back the feeling of family. She reminded me of the last story she had told us when we were all laughing and smiling, believing we would always stay together.

As I looked at her, tears filled my eyes. She saw the hatred and the sorrow right through me.

"Don't hold it back, dear," Grandma said. Her eyes looked so sad that I could not bear to look at them anymore.

"Grandma, I will not cry anymore. I will not cry again until I become a doctor and until I make Samatar pay for what he did to our family," I replied in a voice so filled with hatred that I could not recognize it as my own.

"Ayan, you saw something you shouldn't have seen, dear. Do not hate your uncle, sweetie. He killed our family because of greed and jealousy. Satan got into his head, dear. He will pay for what he did to our family in the hereafter. Everyone is killing each other in our country, and he thought he could get away with it because no one will say that he killed his own pregnant cousin and her family. And there is no government to hold him accountable. But God is all-seeing and all-hearing. Samatar will certainly pay for what he did. But you have to let go of it, and you have to forgive him. Not for him but for you. You have to make sure that you do not hate his tribe because of him. They have done nothing to you. I know it is hard, but you have to find it in your heart. Holding that anger and hatred will only destroy you, my dear. Remember that what he has done has nothing to do with his tribe. He didn't kill our loved ones because of a tribe, and even

he wants Ayon to forgive him & his tribe because she recognises this etc as a disease that would change Ayan's mindset.

if he had, his tribesmen are not responsible for what he did. Make sure the disease does not touch your pure heart."

"Grandma, there is no devil bigger than he is. Why are you telling me to forgive a man who took everything from us? Look at you, Grandma—he shot you! You would not be in this situation if it were not for him. Our family would not be buried beneath the ground. He killed your son, your grandchildren, and your pregnant daughter-in-law, and you want me to forgive him?" I shook my head with anger, feeling my head constrict.

"Ayan, I know you are angry, dear, and you have every right to be angry. I understand why you hate him so much, but promise me that you will never try to take revenge on him. Ayan, you would be no different from him if you took revenge. You don't want to be him. You should never want to hurt his family or his tribesmen, who have done nothing to you. Ayan, you are so young, my dear; you cannot let hate consume you, and you cannot let what he did destroy you. You have to be very strong, you have to grow strong, and you have to become a great doctor who will make me proud!" Grandma cried.

"Grandma, I can't promise you that. I am sorry. I will not hurt an innocent person, but I will make him pay for what he did, I promise! I will never forgive him, and I will make sure that he does not destroy my life. I will become a doctor, and I will make you and Uncle Ali proud of me," I said and left the room in tears.

In the next room, I saw Halima sitting on the floor, sobbing, and I sat by her.

That night, I couldn't sleep. I stared into the darkness all night long. I prayed the entire night that when the sun rose, everything would be fine and back to normal. I kept seeing the blood on the streets, the chaos in the city, the bodies lying everywhere. I tried to make my mind wander elsewhere, but it kept running back to the bodies of my loved ones, burying the people we thought would always be in our lives. It was the collapse of our world. It was too much and too sudden for my mind to process. I kept seeing flashes of the images, and I was sweating with pain. I started being afraid of my eyes. Closing them did not abate the pain and the strength of the flashing images.

The next morning, Halima and Mohamed woke up early to make breakfast for us. I woke the kids up and told them to wash their faces and brush their teeth.

I also went out of Grandma's room to use the restroom. Once the food was ready, Halima told me to take the tea and the breakfast to Grandma's room so we could all eat there together.

I went into Grandma's room. Grandma was usually a light sleeper, but she didn't wake up to my noise.

"Grandma, Grandma, Grandma," I said as fear instantly overtook me like the shadow of a cloud. "Grandma . . . Grandma, Grandma!" I repeated, but there was no response from her.

My heart started racing in terror.

"She must be in a very deep sleep," Halima said as she came into the room. "She has been through a lot. Let her sleep, Ayan."

I didn't listen to her. Grandma was not the type to not respond. I gently shook her shoulder to wake her up, but she didn't respond at all. Halima and Mohamed ran to Grandma and tried to wake her with me, but she wouldn't wake up. She was gone too. Just like that.

"Grandma! Not you too, Grandma!" I screamed as tears flowed down my cheeks, and we all started crying.

I have never felt so alone, so isolated, and so lonely in my life as that day. We had lost every adult in our family—we lost our grandparents, parents, uncles, aunts, sisters, and brothers. Everything was happening too fast; the people who were important to us were all gone in a matter of days. It felt like the blink of an eye.

I remembered what Uncle Ali had once told me: "God told us that everything will die when their time ends, so we must work hard for our hereafter before that day comes." I understood that everyone of us will die someday, I just couldn't process why they all had to go so close to each other. I couldn't understand why God decided to give all my family members a time so close to each other and why I was left behind.

Halima calmed the kids down and took them to the living room. Mohamed and I started to dig a grave for Grandma.

Once we dug a grave that was deep enough, the three of us wrapped her body with a white bedsheet and buried her with the rest of the family in the yard.

We could no longer stay in our home. We didn't feel safe, and our hearts were pounding with fear. We went to Uncle Ali and Aunt Zainaba's bedroom. The scent of their sweet perfume mixed with the smell of Somali uunsi incense still lingered. It felt comforting and painful at the same time.

We moved all the furniture that we could to barricade the door so no one could break in. None of us dared to sleep on their bed, as if we believed they would come back the next morning, so we all slept on the floor. The kids fell asleep with empty stomachs as we stared into the never-ending darkness.

We were alone for the first time in our lives. Alone with no elders to respect and love. Alone with no one to complain to. Alone with no one to smile to. Alone with no one to protect us. Alone with no one to tell us stories. We were alone, alone, and all alone. Alone as we shivered with the fear of the nonstop missiles, the gunshots, and the chaos all around us. We did not know when one was going to hit us.

10

The next morning, we wandered the empty house that was once filled with laughter. No one was sitting on the white chairs in the yard. The wind seemed to stand still, the swing did not swing. The smell of the air had changed from a fresh ocean breeze to the stench of blood, fire, gunpowder, and death.

Halima made breakfast while I helped the kids take showers and change. Mohamed went to search for money or anything valuable that we could take with us. We knew that Samatar could come back anytime. We had to leave our home and the graves of our family behind to save our lives. Our lives were all that was left of three generations of our family.

Halima gave me breakfast, but I couldn't eat it. I tried hard not to cry, but the tears wouldn't stop even though my face and eyes hurt. My eyes were red, and my nose was swollen. The kids ate a little, but neither Mohamed nor Halima could eat anything. We went to help Mohamed collect valuables around the house.

We opened saving boxes that Uncle Ali, Aunt Zainaba, and Grandma had kept. We found money in all of them. Halima said that it was enough to keep us safe for a year, but she was worried that we might not find a place to exchange it or that someone might loot us. We wore the shoes that Grandma had bought for us and some clothes. We each packed a few items to wear and all the food that we could carry in our school backpacks. We didn't know where to go, but we knew it wasn't safe for us to stay at our home anymore. It no longer felt like a home.

We knew that if Uncle Samatar learned that we were still alive, he would hunt us down and kill us all. We had to leave our city and go anywhere safe. It didn't matter where we went as long as we could survive. As we were about to leave our home, a neighbor woman came looking for us.

We told her what happened, and she started crying. She told us that some people were going to the Middle East, some people were going to

Ethiopia, some were going to Kenya, some to Europe, some to America, and some people moved to different, safer parts of the country. We did not know where to go, so we asked her where she was going. She had told us that she was going to Yemen and asked us to come with her. We were happy that some people in Somalia were still nice enough to help us. We told her that we would go to her house in a few minutes, and she left.

Something was fishy about the way she was crying. It didn't seem natural, but I didn't say anything. I told myself, *It's just your imagination, Ayan. Not everyone is Samatar.* Uncle Ali used to say, "People are like our fingers; no two people are the same." Perhaps she was genuinely being nice to us.

We finished gathering our things and prepared to leave as fast as we could. And then we went to our neighbor's house, feeling a little sense of safety. They all came out to greet us, and they had weird smiles on their faces. I felt uneasy, but I told myself that I should not lose my trust in all of humans because of what Samatar had done.

The women said, "Let's go. We are ready to leave for Yemen!" My suspicions were getting stronger, but I had to ignore my feelings and go with the flow.

Halima replied, "We can't leave now! What if Samatar and his men see us and kill us?"

Looking at the ground, the woman said, "It's all right, dear. We do not have to leave right now. How much money do you have?" She looked at us and smiled. "You probably have a lot since your family was loaded."

We haven't even sat down, I thought. *Why is she asking us about money? She didn't even offer us tea.*

I could see that Halima and Mohamed were also growing suspicious of the woman's behavior, but none of us listened to our instincts. We were so desperate for some good and for help that we were willing to overlook her actions.

Halima looked at her and said, "We don't have any money."

I was surprised by Halima's lie. I had never seen Halima look someone dead in the eyes and lie.

"Okay, that's fine. You can stay with us. Come with me," the woman said as she walked us toward one of her rooms. "You can stay here until we decide to leave."

The room was filthy, but that didn't matter to us. At least we had a room and someone willing to help us.

"It smells bad here! Can we go back home?" Siham cried.

"We will go home soon," Halima said, hugging her.

I was feeling a little guilty that I had doubted the nice people who were helping us out. After a while, Halima took out our money to hide it where the family could not easily find it. As she did so, we heard the woman say, "Wow, that is a lot of money! Rich people always have a lot of money with them." The woman entered the room with her husband close behind.

We jumped with fear. We didn't know what to do.

"We are sorry," Mohamed tried to explain. "We didn't mean to lie to you. It's just we didn't know how much or what we had, so we had to count it and be sure before we told you."

"No problem. That's totally fine. We understand," the woman's husband said. "Keep your money, and make sure no one else sees that you have it. People could get greedy, you know. We were just checking up on you." They walked out of the room very fast.

Halima locked the room from the inside and quickly divided the money, putting a part of it in each of our fanny packs. She then told us to hide our fanny packs underneath our clothes and not to tell anyone that we had it. She then put one small part in her backpack.

A few minutes later, the husband and the wife came back to the room with a big gun.

"All of you, line up and put your hands up!" he screamed at us. "Hand me the money!"

"Please, don't do this to us," Halima begged him. "We have no one left, and this is all the money we have. Please don't take it from us."

He said, "Shut up. Hand me the money, or I will shoot all of you."

Halima shook and cried as she handed him the money in her backpack.

"You are little innocent kids; may Allah protect you from harm and the evil eye. We don't mean to hurt you, but we don't have a choice. We have to get our family out of here, and we don't have any money. There are no nice people on this planet anymore. We are sorry, but we have to do this. God might never forgive us, but I can't see my kids suffer. I knew your parents. They were very nice people. Your sister Fathi was a rare gem. I am so sorry to hear that they are gone. She gave us money and food so many times when our own relatives had turned their backs on us. For the sake of your sister Fathi and your parents, we will let you go," he said as he lowered the gun and pointed to the door.

"Take this and hide it somewhere so that no one will be able to find it." He handed some of the money back to Halima. "It's not the old friendly world that you knew. Don't trust anyone. Please leave before we get greedy again and hurt you."

"Thank you!" Mohamed said. "And don't say that there are no nice people left on this planet while you are still walking on it. Thank you so much for letting us go, and may Allah help you and protect your family."

We ran out of the house and along the side of the road. There were bodies in the street with their throats cut like goats and cows. The smell of blood took over the smell of the nice winds that used to flow through our city. The road ahead seemed like an endless procession of bodies and bullets. There were hands, legs, and heads lying on the ground. I wondered where their bodies went. I wondered who would bury all these people.

I then thought that lions and hyenas would come and be happy eating all these dead bodies. Bullet casings covered the ground like leaves on a windy fall day. Buildings were demolished, with all their windows broken. It seemed as if our city had never been inhabited.

The whole city seemed as if it had been burned down or destroyed by a severe earthquake. Missiles had knocked down parts of tall buildings and beautiful houses. Some of the most beautiful buildings were no longer recognizable. Some of the houses were burned so that only a little bit of them stood. We walked and walked, stepping over dead bodies. At the beginning, it was hard to step over the dead bodies, but soon enough that became normal.

We were very tired and afraid. We didn't know when the shooting would start again. We kept walking to escape from the fear in our hearts and our beloved city, even though we didn't know if we were walking toward danger or away from it. We just had to walk to feel a little sense of hope.

Then Siman cried, and when we asked her what was wrong, she told us that she was hungry. We had to get somewhere safe, or at least to someone's house. All the kids started complaining and crying. They said that they were very tired and couldn't move anymore. We walked from the big road into a little alley, spreading Halima's scarf on the ground. We took out some food and gave it to the kids. We also ate a little. I nervously looked around, scared that someone would see us and kill us.

"Ayan, relax and eat some food. We will be all right," Halima said as she tried to calm me down. But I could not relax. My heart never stopped pounding with fear.

As we sat there eating our food as fast as we could, Mohamed suggested that we go to the Middle East, but Halima said that we should go to Europe.

"We cannot go to Europe," Mohamed said. "We need plane tickets, visas, and a lot of money. The government is no longer here, and the airport is shut down. There is no way for us to get to Europe."

We went through the whole world, talking about each country and the reasons why we couldn't go there. It all came down to three choices: go to Kenya or Ethiopia, stay in our country, or cross the sea into the Middle East. We finally agreed with Mohamed's idea to go to Middle East, particularly Saudi Arabia. To us, Mecca and Medina were the holiest and safest places on earth. After all, Medina was the city that had opened its doors for our prophet and the first Muslims. We hoped that Medina would open its doors to us like it did for the Muhajirun, the first Muslim emigrants. And we believed that we could not be turned away from Mecca, as all Muslims had equal rights to the city. We had learned in our Islamic studies class that the people who did not live in Mecca had the same rights as those who were native of the city.

After finishing the food, we decided to go to the harbor to find a ship that would take us to Medina, Saudi Arabia, even though we had no passports and no family or relatives there.

11

Although we were miles away from the place that we had called home, we still knew how to get to the harbor and the ships that would depart for the Middle East. Halima, Mohamed, and I took turns carrying the kids. We had to walk as fast as we could to get to the harbor before we were killed by someone, or hit by a stray missile, or darkness fell.

We knew that we might never make it there, but we had to try; we had no other option. We walked and quietly sang a song that we used to sing joyfully from school to home or when walking around the neighborhood. We sang it with a heavy heart, which made Halima choke on her words and brought tears to my eyes as I remembered Fathi singing it with us on our walks home.

> Gurigeeni aaway? Madhawoo ma dheera
>
> Where is our home? Neither close nor far
>
> Gurigeeni aaway? Madhawoo ma dheera
>
> Where is our home? Neither close nor far
>
> Gurigeeni aaway? Madhawoo ma dheera
>
> Where is our home? Neither close nor far
>
> Gurigeeni aaway? Madhawoo ma dheera . . .
>
> Where is our home? Neither close nor far . . .

We took turns quietly singing it so we wouldn't attract unwanted attention. It had no other words to it, just the question, "Where is our home?" And an answer, "Neither close nor far." Our home was neither far nor close; we no longer knew where it was.

Our feet started hurting and felt heavy as if rocks were tied to them. But we kept pushing and walking to get to the harbor. That was the only way we could see to escape, the only hope we could think of at the moment.

"Halima! Mohamed! Wait!" The voices were coming from some people in a car behind us. My body grew cold with fear, and my heart started beating so fast that I worried it might just stop beating altogether.

We thought it was Samatar and his men. I closed my eyes, and we all turned around slowly. As I opened my eyes little by little, I saw that it was not Samatar.

However, my brief happiness shrank like a plastic bag in a fire. I had lost my trust in people. I thought, *Our uncle killed our family. These men were Uncle Ali and Samatar's friends and coworkers. What if they kill us? What if they are no different from Samatar?*

I tried to find some courage in myself to hold my fears back. We stood there without moving while the men walked toward us. As they came close, I recognized one of them as a man Uncle Ali had worked with at his clinic. He had been friendly to me when I'd met him before, but I did not know whether I could trust anyone now. The sickness had spread to the entire city.

"Hey! How are you guys doing? Where is the rest of the family? Where are Ali and Zainaba? Why are you guys walking alone?" They questioned us with curiosity and concern.

"The rest of our family is not with us. They have all died," Halima said.

"To God we belong, and to him we shall return! May God have mercy on their souls. When did they die, and what happened?" The man's voice was low and filled with sorrow.

"They were killed," Mohamed replied.

"Who killed them? Where are they buried? And where are you going?" one of the men asked. I tried to answer them, but Halima stopped me before I could say anything.

"We don't know what happened," Halima said to them. "We were not there. They were killed while we were at school."

I looked at Halima's face, and her eyes said, *We can't trust these men!* I wasn't going to tell them either; no one could be trusted anymore.

"Where are you headed?" they asked.

"We are going to the harbor to catch a ship to Saudi Arabia, and we don't have any money," Mohamed told them.

"Why are you going there? Do you have anyone there?" they asked.

"Yes, our aunts and uncles live there. We called them earlier today, and they will be waiting for us there," Halima lied to them.

They would have never let us travel across the sea to a foreign land with no money and no elders. Halima didn't want them to make us stay with them. We were scared of them.

"Get in the car. We will drop you off at the harbor. It too dangerous for you to walk around the city like this at this time. The shooting could resume any moment. Your parents were our dear friends and coworkers. For their sake, we will help you. If you want, you can stay with us until the situation changes for the better." They sounded a lot like our neighbors.

We couldn't trust them and didn't want to go with them.

"Thank you, but we are all right. We will manage to get there. Thank you," Halima said, rejecting the men's offer to help even though we were walking so slowly from the pain in our feet.

But they insisted. They said that they would walk with us if we refused to ride in their car. They refused to let us go alone.

Mohamed and Halima started arguing about whether to go in the car or not.

"Halima, stop being a child," Mohamed said. "It is not the time to argue. We do not have anything to lose. Come on, let's get in. They are just trying to help."

"They are going to help?" Halima angrily responded. "And why would they? Our own family member killed our family, took our home, and now we are running away. How can you just trust them? We are not going in that car! You can go if you want, but the kids are staying with me."

"Come on, Halima. You know it's more dangerous roaming around the city with a bagful of gold and money. It's too dangerous. We could run into the militia groups ambushing and killing innocent people. You have seen the bodies and blood in the streets," Mohamed said, trying to convince her. But Halima was not buying it.

Mohamed got mad at her and yelled, "I am the man here, and I am responsible for all of you. And you are going to listen to me and get in that car. I don't want to argue with you, and I don't want you talking back to me. Now get in the car." I had never seen Halima and Mohamed argue. It was scary to see Mohamed so furious, but it got Halima into the car.

A shift in her mindset of trusting people.

We all crowded in. We avoided looking at the men and distracted our-selves as much as we could. We didn't want them to talk to us. They tried, but we replied with short answers and showed them that we had no interest in talking to them. They sensed that and stopped talking to us. It was a long, awkward ride to the harbor, but shorter than the walk.

"You are here," the men said to us. "May God be with you and guide you in every step. We wish you the best, and we will keep you in our prayers. Don't forget your home, your identity, and your roots. Hold on to them tightly, and be the kind of people your parents would have wanted you to be. Work hard and hold your values tightly." We said good-bye to them, and they handed us some money and prayed for us.

I felt bad for thinking they were bad, for suspecting nice people who were just trying to help us. I could tell that Halima did too.

At the harbor, crowds of people were trying to leave. The harbor was filled with boats of all sizes and shapes. People carried their children and belongings and tried to get on the boats, any boat, just one to take them out of Mogadishu. Some people were yelling, some were crying, and some were frozen by the horrors they had witnessed. People were yelling, sometimes fighting. A number of people looked around them at every second, scared of an attack.

Why is everyone running away from their home? Why are we leaving the only place we have ever known? Is it really that bad that so many people are fleeing their country?

In my heart, I knew it was very bad, that something terrible was hap-pening all around us. *Oh, God, please restore our home to what it was before the war. Please, God, bring peace back to our country,* I prayed as we walked toward the dock where people were trying to board the ships.

There were several midsize boats. I didn't know how they were going to fit all those people into them. There were so many people in front of the boats pushing each other, everyone trying to get on before the other. Some were screaming and using force. The owners of the boats were standing at the gangplank and collecting money from people. Those who did not have enough money couldn't get on.

I felt a little relief that money could get us onto the boats and that we had money with us. We wanted to leave at once and tried to go through, but it was so crowded that it was impossible. We waited until the crowd got smaller to make our way to the boats. We were worried that they might fill up before we got on them, but we had no choice but to wait.

Some people were rejected. They begged the boat owners to let them on, but the owners never let anyone on without paying a large amount of money. A lot of women with children and very old people were rejected. The mood grew tense, and the cries of desperate women grew louder. We were finally able to make our way to the man at the gangplank.

We stood in front of the man and hoped that he would let us on. We had no parents, no home, no family, and we were leaving behind the last thing that we could call ours—our country. I always thought that sugar was the sweetest thing in the world, but I learned that life was indeed the sweetest thing. So sweet that many people would give up anything to hold on to it.

"Where is your money? How much do you have?" the man screamed loudly.

Halima took out a handful of money and put it in his hand. "This is all we have. Can we please get on?" Halima asked with a low voice as if she were about to cry.

He counted the money and said, "How many people?"

"Seven people. Two teenagers and five kids," Halima told him.

He put the money in his pocket and said, "There is no space. Get out of here!"

"Can we get our money back?" Halima asked.

The man looked baffled. He smiled, leaned close to Halima, and said, "What money?"

"The money we just gave you!" Mohamed said defensively.

"How about I put five bullets between your eyes and see if you still need money!" the man replied, pointing his gun toward us.

"We are sorry," Halima calmed him down. "It is my mistake. I thought I gave you money, but I was wrong."

Disappointed and heartbroken, we walked away. We had lost the rest of the money in Halima's backpack and couldn't get onto the boat. Fortunately, we still had a little money in our shoes.

We walked and walked without direction and without a clue what to do. It got dark. Wandering the streets of Mogadishu deep into the night during the most active time of the war wasn't a situation anyone would want to be in. We didn't know what to do, but we knew that guests were always welcomed in our culture.

We went to a door and knocked. We didn't know what to expect. It could have been Samatar's house, someone we knew, or a complete stranger's house. Whoever's door it was, we had to take that risk. We prayed to God and hoped that someone nice would let us stay at their house for the night. A woman opened the door; she seemed like a nice person. She was wearing a red shawl and black dress.

She looked at us so curiously and said, "Hi, who are you looking for?"

"Auntie, please let us in! We don't have anywhere to go, please!" Halima cried.

"What do you think this is? Our house is neither an orphanage nor a shelter! Who told you to come here? We are struggling to take care of ourselves, and you want us to help you? Sorry—we can't help. Please leave!" The woman slammed the door in our faces.

We just sat in front of her house, helpless and unsure what to do. She then opened the door and said, "God will never forgive me if I let you sleep outside. Come in!" She held the door open for us.

We ran inside as if she would change her mind if we were not fast enough. When we entered the house, she took us to a small room and said, "Come out; it is just some lost kids." A man and three kids came out. Incredibly, they had been hiding from us.

No wonder she was mad. She thought we were dangerous people who were out to kill her family. The woman introduced her family, and we introduced ourselves. She told us to stay for the night and leave first thing in the morning. She didn't know where anything was, and there was barely anything in the whole house; it seemed as if they were just hiding there. It couldn't have been their home.

They told us to sleep in a room with nothing in it. We had to sleep on the floor without a pillow, mattress, or blankets. The floor was cold and dirty, and the kids refused to sleep on it.

"I can't sleep on the floor! It's too uncomfortable!" Siham cried.

Halima took out a hijab, Mohamed took out a shirt, and I took out a hijab. We put them on the floor, and the kids slept on them. Mohamed, Halima, and I lay on the floor with nothing between us and the floor except our clothes.

A week before that night, it would have been impossible for us to imagine all that had happened to us and the situation we were in at that moment. We were all scared and cramped in an empty room, staring at the dark walls.

Mohamed was shaking and wrapping his hands around him to keep himself warm. My two little sisters and two brothers fell asleep very fast. We were all tired from the endless walk.

I couldn't close my eyes; I was afraid of seeing all the horrible pictures that were stuck to my memory like a glue. I couldn't take what I had seen out of my head. I kept getting flashes of the images of our family. I didn't know how to turn it off, and I felt the pain every time.

Halima quietly asked, "Can't go to sleep?"

We then sat up and started talking quietly about all the memories we had of our family—all the good things we had and how life had changed in a matter of days. We said how we thought we were dreaming. We blamed Somalia, our country, and our people for our misery. We blamed them for catching a disease, and we blamed them for ruining our home.

We were so depressed and confused that we could no longer tell what we were feeling. It felt as if the night was longer than years, an hour longer than months. But in another way, we did not want the night to end. We knew that when the night ended, we had to face our tragic reality again. We had to face the horrible new image of our country. Without the night, we would be walking from one street to another street, hiding from one corner to another as if we were criminals.

What crime have we committed? I asked in my head. No answer came to mind.

We felt like criminals of an unknown crime. We had lost our family, our country, and thousands, maybe millions, of people for no apparent reason. At least not one that I could understand and accept.

Were we always like this, just waiting for the right moment to massacre each other? Or is our country being invaded by outside forces that are trying to destroy us? Did aliens invade us?

We couldn't make sense of what was happening to our country.

The whole night, I kept thinking and trying to make logical sense out of what was happening around us. I couldn't come up with a single answer. Nothing made sense anymore.

12

In the morning, we prayed our morning prayer, and we drank some water. Then the family came to tell us that we had to leave as soon as possible. The woman told us that there was no way they could shelter all of us; we were too many. We wore our shoes, and we put on our backpacks as we got ready to leave. Then the family told us that we could stay for breakfast. We were starving.

The woman and her daughter made Somali pancakes, called *anjero,* and tea. They gave each of us three anjero and a cup of tea without milk. I had never drunk tea without milk before that morning, but I gladly drank it.

I could see sadness in the woman's eyes.

She must feel bad for kicking us out.

She told us to take some anjero with oil and sugar on them for our journey. We thanked God and the family for helping us, and we went out the door.

We looked at both sides of the road to see if there were any people. There were few people, but none looked dangerous. We started walking without a direction or a destination in mind. We knew that our country was no longer the one we had known and called home. It looked as if some alien force had taken over. The change was so drastic that it looked nothing like the city I had dreamed of living in. It looked nothing like the beautiful blue-and-white city with palm trees and a beautiful ocean, full of modernity and new technologies. Mogadishu was crumbling to the ground.

We couldn't go back home; we knew Samatar would kill us without hesitation. We were homeless in a war-torn city where missiles and guns were firing all around us. We couldn't be wandering around, and we couldn't go back home. The only option was to get out of Mogadishu. So we decided to leave our home behind and find a place where we could feel safe and maybe call home someday. It might never be the same, it might never feel like home, but that was all right as long as we survived.

We finally reached a bus station, and we asked where they were headed. The people on the bus told us that they were heading toward the border with Kenya. They were driving to a city that was two days away, and then they would take a boat into Kenya. They told us that the route to Kenya was dangerous because it lay between militia groups, wild animals, and the Kenyan military. It was difficult to make it to Kenya safely. They told us that there was a refugee camp in Kenya for displaced people where we would get protection by the United Nations, but getting there was difficult. We boarded the bus and paid for our tickets.

We did not know what lay ahead of us, what destiny had in store for us. We started a new journey and decided that we were going to find a home and pursue our dreams regardless of what was in store for us, and we would do this with happy hearts and smiles.

We were going to find the smiles that had been wiped off our faces by the unfortunate tragedy that took away our family and everyone we loved. We didn't know where we were headed or what was waiting for us. We had only the hope of survival, and that hope was good enough to help us keep going.

It got dark, and the bus driver drove away from the road so we could rest for the night. We slept in the middle of nowhere on unknown sand, but I was aware of the wild animals all around us.

The more I thought about my family—both in the city and in the countryside—the heavier my heart grew with grief. The moon was full, just like the night I had wanted to run away, but this time the moon looked dull. I didn't look at it with a smile but rather with a heavy heart. I looked at it with a different kind of hope than I had on the night I'd run away from Ruuraan. That night, my hope had been one for education and success. But tonight, it was merely a hope for survival.

The darkness was fading away a little when everyone woke up for the morning prayer. There were no bathrooms to use, so everyone just walked away from where they had slept and went behind the bushes. We didn't have enough water, so we used sand to do our ablution.

We all got in a line, just like the line we used to form when we'd had a home, and we prayed together with our loved ones. The men stood in the front and women stood behind them; with one man leading, we stood shoulder to shoulder.

After praying, we went back to the bus and continued our journey to an unknown home. People started to chat and loosen up a little when we came to a roadblock. There was a long rope stretched across the road. Some men with guns sat in a little hut on the side of the road, and some of them stood on the side of the road with their guns ready to shoot at any moment.

The driver stopped the bus, and the men with guns told everyone to get off. Some of the men with guns were sitting on a mat in the makeshift room, chawing khat, a drug that grows in Kenya and Ethiopia. Little insects buzzed around a lamp in the small hut.

I could hear the birds chirping, and that sound soothed my heart for a moment. It was windy, and I could smell the cigarettes the men were smoking.

One of the men was praying. I found it ironic that he was part of a militia group blocking the road, looting people, killing people, and he was praying. I looked at him and wondered why he was praying, because praying was for righteous people. Prayer was for good people. He shouldn't be praying our beautiful and peaceful prayer while doing these forbidden acts. I hated the sight of everyone with a gun. I was angry at guns and everyone who had them. I was angry at him because I felt he was mocking my religion and my beliefs. He was praying yet doing everything that God told him not to.

Our religion didn't allow raping, killing, or harming people. That was exactly what these men and all the other evil men, of every tribe, who had destroying our country were doing. It didn't make sense that a person would pray and also commit such unforgivable sins. I couldn't say he wasn't Muslim, because it was not my job to judge who was Muslim and who was not; that was God's job. I kept all my thoughts to myself and avoided eye contact with any of them as if they could read my mind.

The men with guns then approached us. "Get in line and take out everything you have with you!" one of the men demanded.

Should have joined because of this militant context significance

We all got in line obediently like captured soldiers and walked out of the bus one by one, holding our hands up as they searched us. The first person they searched was a man. They searched him everywhere from his hair to his underwear to his shoes.

Then they asked the man who his tribe was, and the man told them a name that I had never heard. Our family never thought of what tribe we were until our family in Ruuraan was killed by a different tribe. Before the war, it hadn't mattered. *Tribe* was a superficial label. But now all the different tribes were killing each other. And we did not know what clan or tribe was the right one to claim at that moment.

Halima told us not to say a word and that she and Mohamed were going to take care of it. After telling them a name, they told the man to stand aside. They searched the second man the same way, and after searching him, they asked him who his tribe was. He told them a different name, but they told him to stand behind the first man.

The majority of the people were on one side, and we memorized the name of the tribe one lady had given them. Luckily, the men with guns didn't suspect us, and they let us join the majority of the people. There were seven guys and four girls who were separated from the rest of us.

One of the guys put a gun behind them and told them to walk toward the bushes behind their little hut. They cried and begged to be let go. The woman next to us said they were from the wrong tribe. Three armed men followed them. We could still see them behind the bushes, where the men with guns lined them up like they were praying and executed them one by one. I saw them fall to the ground like dominoes. They kept firing until there was no movement. And then it was silent again.

We covered the kids' eyes so they would not see the horrific scene in front of us, but I couldn't close my eyes. I saw what the men with guns were doing. I saw their faces and the colors the women were wearing. I got another flashing nightmare that day, in addition to the nightmare of my family's bodies.

After they executed the people, the men with guns took our possessions into the hut. But everyone was happy that we had not been mercilessly killed like our fellow passengers. Material goods didn't matter as long as we were alive. They told us to go back to the bus, but they stopped the kids and me to ask us more questions. My heart started beating. I started crying because I thought I was going to end up like the people they had killed behind the bushes. But Halima talked to them.

Halima told the men that we were all together, so they told us to all come together. Then they started searching us again. It was uncomfortable to see how they were searching Halima, but she couldn't say anything. No one could utter a word.

Mohamed couldn't watch what they were doing to Halima, so he looked away. A man came to Halima and pulled her close to him. He took his rough, ugly hand and put it between Halima's breasts. He started touching her breasts and squishing them as if they were stress balls for him to play with.

We could all feel the pain and see it in her eyes, but we stood there helplessly. The only man in our family had no power to defend his sister who was being sexually violated right in front of him. Then the man touched Halima all over her body. The worst of it was when he put his hands under her underwear right in front of everyone. No one said a thing. I wanted to kick him and yell at him, but he had a gun. It was clear to him that she had no money with her, but he continued touching her with his dirty, ugly hands. He kept smiling as he lustfully looked at her with his red, ugly eyes.

He then questioned her again. He asked her again who our tribe was, where we were going, and who we were. Halima told him everything, repeating what the woman had told us to say. We were terrified, and I could see that everyone on the bus was worried for us. I could see it in their eyes, but no one had the courage to say a word. They had seen what these men were capable of. Finally, he let go of her and told us to get back on the bus.

The whole bus was silent. We were overtaken by emotions, and no one said a word to each other. We could hear the fear and the frustration in our breaths and the cries of our hearts.

Halima did not talk; she was looking out the window, trying to find relief in the wide blue sky. But she couldn't hold it together and started weeping loudly. Mohamed hugged her and tried to calm her down.

"It's all right, Halima!" Mohamed said as tears fell down his cheeks. "We will get through it! You will be fine; you are still alive, and you have lost nothing. Please stop crying; everything will be all right. This is nothing but a test that will end soon. Please stop crying, Halima. You will be all right. I promise we will get through this!"

She kept crying, and several other women on the bus started crying with her. Her eyes and nose were red. Her hair and her scarf were a mess, but she was in such pain that she didn't notice that most of her hair was showing.

Hussein turned to Halima, put his small hands on her cheeks, and said, "Halima, please don't cry. Everything will be all right. I will beat that man up when I grow up! Please don't cry."

Halima hugged him tightly and said, "I am sorry, baby! I will stop crying." She smiled in spite of the tears in her eyes and the pain in her heart.

Halima held back her tears, and the bus became dead silent except for the occasional cry from a baby. After hours of driving, we arrived at a small village. There was only one road for cars to use, which divided the village into two parts. The houses were small and lined the sides of the road. All the houses were the same design, as if they were copied and pasted from one house.

There was a lot of soil on the ground, beautiful red soil that filled our shoes. The houses were not made from rock and cement like the one we lived in; instead, they were made of dirt and wood and had aluminum as a roof to protect them from rain.

There were a couple of small shops, and some people were selling goods outside. Except for one tree, there was nothing green for as far as our eyes could see.

The tree was half-alive and half-dead. It reminded me of us. I looked at the tree and wondered what made it half-alive and half-dead. I had a negative feeling about this village. I looked around more. There were no trees, no green vegetation, not even little weeds or grass.

I wondered, *Is this place so bad that the grass and trees decided not to grow here? The green must have dried up when the bloodshed started.*

We stood along the side of the road and tried to figure out what to do. Two red dust devils blinded us. We held each other and tried to cover our eyes and mouths. The red dust turned us red—our faces, our clothes, and our eyelashes. We looked as if we were buried and then taken out of the grave.

I inhaled a lot of dust, so I tried to breathe through my mouth, but my mouth was filled with sand. I spit it out; it tasted familiar but also terrible.

The dust devils abated, and everyone started moving again. Everyone in the village knew to hide from the dust devils. We were caught off guard and had sand for dinner.

There were a lot of kids in the village with big bellies and skinny bodies wearing ragged clothes. Some kids wrapped a worn-out scarf around their small bodies. Some of them wore shoes, and others did not. Their hair had turned reddish blond with the dust and malnutrition.

Most of them had big eyes, but they kept squinting. Maybe they were trying to prevent the red sand from getting in their eyes. They joined the crowd around the bus as if they had never seen a car before. Some of them came near us and stared at us as if we were some sort of aliens in a zoo. The whole place looked strange, and the people there were worse. They were speaking Somali and they looked like Somali people, but they spoke differently.

The bus driver told us that he couldn't go beyond this village. He told us that we had to wait for another car to take us where we wanted to go. We didn't know where we wanted to go, but we certainly didn't want to stay in that village. We didn't even know its name. We didn't know anyone, and there were no hotels. Our only option was to ask the villagers if we could stay with them until we found another car to take us away.

13

We knew that people would let us in and help us as much as we needed. We had seen that all the time when we had a home. But we felt embarrassed, and none of us were willing to knock on a stranger's doors and ask for help. The shame of begging was not something we were ready to face again.

We didn't know what to do, so we just sat under the half-alive and half-dead tree to relax and figure out what we were going to do. As we sat there, I couldn't help noticing the people in this small village.

There was an old woman struggling with several bags. She could hardly walk, and she was carrying much more than she could handle. A young man about Halima's age walked quickly toward her and offered to carry all the bags for her. They didn't seem to know each other. She prayed to God to give that young man whatever he wished for and thanked him. She had a smile on her face as he relieved her burden. He smiled and thanked her for praying for him; they disappeared into the distance.

Maybe, maybe not everyone is bad, I argued with myself, unable to decide whether the world had any light left or if it were black with no kindness left in it. *Maybe there is some respect for humanity left in this world. Maybe the world isn't as dark as you think, Ayan. What am I thinking? There is no respect for human life in our country. No, Ayan, maybe it's just the city. But it's not the city only; I heard Grandma and Uncle Ali say our whole country was taken over by the disease. How could that be?*

I saw six or seven women walking together at a medium pace like they had no worries. I was mesmerized by the way they were walking, so peacefully and elegantly.

"Stop staring at people, Ayan!" Halima woke me with a nudge.

The women were wearing traditional Somali dresses just like all the Somali women I had ever seen. They were wearing big colorful shawls with floral patterns and dresses that matched. They were the most common, the cheapest clothes that were available in Mogadishu. Their clothes were almost identical except in different colors.

That must be a new style of fashion for them, I thought.

The women were all tall and slim with long necks. The reminded me of gerenuk strolling through the grassland with no fear of lions, cheetahs, or hyenas. Their hips swayed ever so gently like a fashionable lioness.

As the women got closer, I could hear what they were saying. I was surprised by their talk, which was Somali but with an accent that I had never heard before. I did not understand some of the words they were saying. They were loud—anyone within a mile radius could hear them, and at times, they would burst into laughter. I realized that I had forgotten how to laugh or even smile.

They came toward us and greeted us. They didn't ask us where we were from; they knew where we came from by our accent. I was surprised by how friendly they were and how nice they were to us. One of the women asked us where our parents were.

We were numbed with a terrifying memory. I tried to say that they were no longer with us, but the words would not come out of my mouth. We didn't want to say it because saying it was the first step to accepting it, and I was not ready to accept that yet.

Siham answered them in an innocent voice, "We are playing hide-and-seek with them. Our parents will come here later when the game is over. They will come and find us."

Tears filled Halima's eyes, but she tried to hold them back so the kids didn't see her crying.

They looked at our faces and knew exactly what happened. "May God bless their souls!" one of the women said in a humble voice. "Do you know anyone here?" she asked.

"We don't even know where we are!" Mohamed answered her.

"We should take them with us," one of them suggested.

However, almost all of them made excuses as to why they could not take us with them.

Oh, God, why are you doing this to us? I don't want to be a beggar. Please help us, I prayed to God in my head. I was losing the little hope of humanity I had found by observing the young man who had helped the old woman.

One woman said that she did not have any kids and there were not that many people in her household. She told us that she lived in a big house with her husband and her in-laws. But she said that she would only take us if we agreed to her conditions. She made us promise that we wouldn't make any noises, that the kids would not cry at night, that we would behave and do what she told us to. She had a similar name as our Aunt Zainaba—her name was Zainab.

We were desperate and in no position to say anything except to thank her and agree to her conditions.

Thank you for answering my prayers! I thanked God for listening to me and answering my prayers quickly.

We were relieved when she said that she would host us until we found another car to take us where we wanted to go. We thanked her and followed her to her house gratefully.

I was looking for a big house, more like the one we had lived in in Mogadishu with our family. However, the house she lived in and called "a big house" was nothing like a big house. It was a small, short house, and it looked like burned red clay. She took us to one of the rooms.

Mohamed and Halima were tall; they had to duck to get in the room. She told us to wait there and that she would come back.

We had been sitting there for a while when Zainab came in with a big plate of food. We almost ran to the plate and ate like hungry beasts, but we had to behave and act civilized. The kids tried to run toward her too, but Halima said, "Don't you dare!" Everyone sat back.

Zainab put the plate in the middle of the room, and we stared at the plate. It had been a while since we had sat around a big plate that could abolish our hunger. I remembered the laughter and the jokes in our home when we'd eaten food together. There were neither laughter nor jokes this time.

Zainab left the room, and we started to eat. As we were eating, a man came into the room. He looked at all of us and left the room without talking to us.

After eating, Zainab showed us the bathroom, and we took a shower with a bucket of water. Mohamed took a shower first, and then Halima helped Siham, Hussein, Siman, and then Ayaanle. I was the last one to take a shower.

Their bathroom was different. They had dug a hole in the ground and sealed the top with cement while leaving a little hole for waste to enter. I looked inside the hole; it was full of feces and urine.

They must have been using it for years, I thought.

As I poured the last bit of water on my head, I heard Zainab arguing with the man who had come into the room earlier. They were arguing about us.

He said, "Are you crazy? You know that cars rarely come to this small village. It could take weeks or months if not years until they find a car! You are so jealous because I married another woman and she had two boys. You think bringing other people's kids to your house will make them yours and that I will love you more for it? Wake up, woman! Return these kids to wherever you got them from. This is my house, and you have no right to bring others here without my permission." Hurtful words poured out of his mouth.

I had never heard a man talking to his wife so harshly and disrespectfully like that before. For a moment, I regretted coming with her and I felt bad for her, but we didn't have another choice. Zainab wasn't yelling; she was quietly trying to make him understand.

"They are little kids without parents in the middle of nowhere," Zainab said. "They don't know where they are, let alone anyone in this village. I am not trying to make them my children, and I am not jealous of that lousy woman you married or her kids. I couldn't walk away from little kids on the street who needed help. God would never forgive me if I did that. I couldn't leave them helplessly sitting under that tree."

He started talking again, getting louder with every word that came out of his mouth.

"What do you mean you couldn't leave them? You could have made excuses and left them there. You don't know them. They are not your relatives, and you don't owe their parents anything. For your information, you are under no obligation to care for them." He was angry and mean; he didn't want us in his house.

"They are innocent, helpless kids," she replied. "It's not their fault they are in despair; this is a test, not just for them but for every human being they come across. How can you be heartless and say that? Don't you remember what God has said? He told us to be good to orphans and to those in need. He also said that he doesn't like arrogant people."

He did not answer her for a while, and then he said, "I understand what you are trying to say, and I know that we have to help those in need, but you know we don't have much money left. I just had a son, and I spent a lot of my money celebrating. They can stay until they find a car, but they have to leave with the first car no matter where it is going. I hope you are happy! And don't you dare turn my house into an orphanage!" He stormed out.

I got out of the bathroom and went to the room where the rest of my family was. We sat in the tiny room until nightfall.

We were tired and wanted to sleep. There was a small mat in one quarter of the room. The kids slept on the mat while Halima, Mohamed, and I slept on the sand. I couldn't sleep that whole night. Sleeping on the sand reminded me of my family in Ruuraan.

I remembered my mom and her gentle fingers as she tied my hair back before I went to bed. I remembered when we sat by Grandma as my older sisters milked the goats and my older brothers and cousins milked the camels. I remembered as my mom and aunt made tea for everyone. I remembered the laughter in Ruuraan and the laughter in Mogadishu with my family.

We all lined up parallel to each other and used our arms and our backpacks as pillows.

"Ayan, are you still awake?" Mohamed asked me.

"Yes. I am having a hard time falling asleep," I responded.

"Stop worrying, Ayan. Everything will be all right, and we will live through this. Go to sleep," Mohamed said softly.

"I can't stop thinking about our family members. I keep thinking of Grandma telling us stories, Mom brushing my hair, and me massaging her legs. I can't stop thinking of Uncle Ali and Aunt Zainaba and how they always showered us with love. I can't stop thinking about our sisters, brothers, uncles, aunts, and grandparents. I don't know what to do!"

"Just go to sleep. I can't stop the thoughts either, but thinking of them will not change anything; it will only make us hurt. They would want us to be strong, they would want us to survive, and they would want us to be safe. Now go to sleep and tell yourself that everything will work out. I promise you, everything will be all right soon."

"Thank you, Mohamed. I will try to go to sleep. You should do the same."

"I can't sleep either," Halima added. "But we should try."

It got very quiet as we fought with our own memories. I tried to sleep, but my memories were too vivid and strong to let me drift off. I couldn't sleep no matter what I did. I decided to stop trying, and I lay there in the dark room feeling the sand beneath me. I eventually fell asleep but was woken by the terrible sound of roars.

Siham started crying, and all the kids followed her. Halima and Mohamed tried to calm everyone down. They told them that there was no reason for them to be afraid, as the door was locked. I tried to be brave, but I wasn't. I was shaking with fear because I knew that the roar came from a lion.

"We are here, and as long as we are here, no one and nothing can harm you," Mohamed said. "If anything tries to harm my siblings, I will punch and kick them so hard that they will hide from your shadows."

Hussein held my hand and said, "I . . . I . . . I am still scared. I don't want to go back to sleep. Can you turn on the light?"

Halima wiped the salty tears from Hussein's face and hugged him. "I will sleep in front of the door. If anything comes in, I will fight with it, and it won't be able to get to you. I promise I will protect you." Halima felt her way to the door.

Mohamed told her that she should sleep by the kids and that he would sleep by the door. After all, he was the man in our household.

I was scared that something might happen to Mohamed. Millions of questions were going through my head.

What if someone shoots him? What if someone stabs him? What if the roaring lion's long claws hurt Mohamed through the cracks on the door? The door is too weak to protect Mohamed from bullets. I started crying.

I didn't want anything to happen to Mohamed. I decided to stay awake, as if my eyes somehow had the power to protect him. I couldn't even see him. I felt my way to the door and quietly slept right next to him.

"Ayan, what happened? Why don't you sleep? Nothing will happen to you. Please go back to sleep by Halima and the kids," Mohammad said. He noticed that I was crying.

"I don't want anything to happen to you," I said as he wiped my tears in the dark and told me not to cry.

"Ayan, I know we have been through a lot, but God has always been there for us. Nothing will happen to me or to us. We will get through this and learn to laugh again. Don't cry. You have to be strong; we all have to be strong for each other. Crying is for losers who have no hope. Besides, it won't change anything. When you cry, you are putting more pain in everyone else's hearts. Please be strong for us and stop crying," he said.

"I promise I will never cry again!" I said. "I will not for as long as we have each other!" I cried as I accidently felt his wet face and his tears. I was surprised to see Mohamed crying. I suppose he was in pain just like everyone else, but he hid his tears from us to be strong for us. I decided to do the same too.

I thought of our family members as I lay there. I kept getting flashes of burying them, flashes of their bodies outside our house, and flashes of their blood mingling.

"Ayan, why do you keep turning and tossing? Please, go to sleep."

"I can't sleep. I tried, but nothing is working!" I said with frustration.

"How about we read the Quran together? I will start by reading a verse, and we will alternate reading them until we fall asleep," Mohammad suggested.

"That's good idea. Where should we start?" I asked.

"Let's start from chapter 93," Mohamed said.

Mohamed, Halima, and I took turns reading one verse at a time.

I don't know when I fell asleep; the last thing I remembered was starting chapter 40. We got up to pray the morning prayer the same way we had with our family. After praying, we sat in the room until the sun came out. Then Zainab knocked on our door and told us that breakfast was ready.

Halima went to the kitchen with Zainab. She came back with a plate filled with anjero soaked in tea, and Zainab carried in cups and a thermos filled with tea and milk. We washed our hands and ate the anjero and then drank the tea with milk. We thanked her.

"Who was reading the Quran all night last night?" Zainab asked.

"Mohamed, Ayan, and I couldn't sleep, so we read it until we fell asleep," Halima said.

"You are good kids. Your parents taught you well, and I am sure they would have been very proud of you had they been here today."

My heart dropped when the word *parents* came out of her mouth. Tears filled my eyes, but I held them back. I'd promised Mohamed that I wouldn't cry again.

"I have never seen stronger kids than you," Zainab said. "God never puts a burden on people that they cannot handle. You will get through this. Always remember that there is nothing in this world you cannot handle."

I knew that she had no problem with us staying with her, but her husband didn't want us to be at his house.

"Thank you so much, Zainab. How can we ever repay you?" Halima asked.

"What are you talking about? You don't have to repay me," Zainab said. "We have to help each other and be there for each other. What kind of humans would we be if we didn't help each other? Just pray that God will bless me with good kids like you."

14

We spent the next week keeping our hope alive, which wasn't easy. Aside from helping Zainab around the house, there was not much else to do. We had walked through the village from one side to the other—nothing grew there. Zainab's husband would occasionally visit and get angry that we were still around. I hated being at his house.

As each day passed, it grew harder and harder to imagine that we would ever make it to Kenya. But then, one day, a truckful of people and stolen goods came to the village. We thought we were dreaming. When we realized it was not a dream, we jumped up and down with joy and hugged each other. We thanked God and breathed a huge sigh of relief.

Mohamed ran to the truck as fast as he could. We ran behind him holding our hands. Everyone got out, bought food and milk from the village, and went back to their seats. Mohamed talked to the driver, and he let us get on the truck. Halima climbed first, and then Mohamed handed the kids to her one by one, and he then told me to climb. Mohamed got on last.

We settled our backs against the wall of the truck. There was a man with a gun sitting right next to us. As soon as we saw him, we started shivering. We remembered all the terrifying images we had seen and all the people who had been killed by guns. Our brief happiness shriveled. We kept staring at him. Mohamed got up and sat right next to him to show us that there was no need for us to be afraid of him. Mohamed then started chatting with him. It turns out, he was the security guard and was on the truck to protect it. Mohamed then got up and came back to sit by us.

"Mohamed, why doesn't he look different?" I asked. "He has a gun and probably killed people. Why doesn't he look sick?"

"What do you mean?" he asked.

"Grandma said that Somali people were infected with a disease, which was why they had weapons and started killing each other. He does not look sick, though, does he?"

I didn't realize how loudly I was speaking. Everyone started laughing, and I felt embarrassed.

"Don't say bad things about people!" Mohamed exclaimed.

"She is funny!" the man with the gun said. "I have not killed anyone. I have this gun to protect this truck and myself. And the disease your grandmother told you about . . . you will understand it when you grow up."

He asked me if I wanted to touch his gun. He noticed that I was staring at it a little too much. I didn't respond. I kept thinking that if Samatar didn't have a gun, he wouldn't have been able to kill all my family. I hated guns, and I was staring at it to show it how much I hated it, as if it had eyes and could feel my hatred. I wanted to melt all the weapons in the world so there would be no wars, so there would be no families killed, and so other kids would not go through what we were going through. He pulled a lever on his gun, and it made a terrible noise. Everyone was terrified, including me. Sweat started rushing from my skin. We had all learned to fear guns since the war had started.

"Sorry, everyone. I didn't mean to scare you," the man with the gun apologized. "I was just getting my gun ready in case we face any problems. This area is known for ambushes. But don't worry. I am on this truck to protect it and to protect all of you. I am not here to kill anyone."

Everyone let out a loud sigh, but the tension was still there. The driver drove through the sand away from the road. He then turned off the car and told everyone to sleep until the morning. Two men with guns were on guard duty to watch out for militia groups and wild animals. I couldn't fall asleep that night. I had not slept well for a single night since we left Mogadishu. In the morning, we prayed the morning prayer and drove away.

After two days of driving safely, we came to an unsafe region. The driver said that this region had the largest concentration of wild animals in Somalia and the most militia groups. He said that we would have to drive through the night or else we would become a dinner for lions or we would be killed by the tribes who lived here.

The driver took out the lights, including the brake lights, and kept driving on the dirt road in the dark. We only had two flashlights. He told us not to use them, as it could attract attention and get us killed. The driver stopped the car so we could pray. Some people started complaining because they were scared.

"Why are you stopping the car? You were just saying we have to drive no matter what! How can you stop? We don't want to die here!" the people cried.

"You are not the only ones scared. We are all scared, but we have to pray," one of the gunmen said.

"We could pray when we reach a safe place! We are traveling through danger. We are under no obligation to pray. We can even pray on the truck," one woman said.

"There is no safe place in this country. We could die any moment," the driver said as he took out a little mat and started praying by the car. "I am praying. It's your choice whether you want to come down and pray or stay there scared."

"Prayer is important, but our lives are important too!" an old man said.

"You don't have to pray if you don't want to. But trust me, death will not leave you if it is your time. Stop being cowards and pray so we can get going," one woman said, getting off the truck to pray.

People started getting down one by one and prayed very fast. Soon we were all back on the truck. The driver drove the entire night until it was morning again.

As the sun rose behind us, we came to a city. The driver told us that this was as far as he could drive. He said that anyone going farther would require a boat from this city to go to Kenya. Taking a boat was the safest way to get there.

We were tired, and every inch of our bodies wanted to rest. But we didn't know if this city was a safe place to rest. We could see tension everywhere. Men with guns and heavy weapons lurked about, ready to fight at any moment. We knew there was no time to rest.

We ate breakfast in a small restaurant. The restaurant was made from tree branches, and the sunrays came through the tree branches on the roof. The chairs and the table were carved from wood. Most of the silverware was either carved from wood or made from metal. Young boys, ten years old at the most, were serving people. Most of the people eating at the restaurant were travelers running away from the war like we were. When we were done eating, we walked down to the harbor.

We boarded a crowded large wooden canoe. Every inch of it was filled with people. The boat launched out into the water and to Kenya.

One more shot at life, one more chance of finding home and our smiles again. And just like that, we left Somalia, our home. We left our home, the graves of our family, and our lives. We carried nothing with us but a hope for a better future.

15

I could not hold on anymore. My numb fingers could no longer hold the weight of my body, though I fought for them to. Against my will, my fingers let go.

Is this it? Is this the end? Have you been through all that just to drown in these foreign waters, Ayan? Is this what buoyancy feels like? I thought as the foreign waters wrapped their arms around me, swallowing me like prey.

I felt a sense of calm, maybe because death was so close to me or maybe because the water was hydrating my dehydrated and malnourished little body. I didn't fight the water; I sank deeper and deeper, thinking about my mom and her hopeful words. She once told me that God sends angels to children to protect them when they fall down. I prayed to God and hoped that an angel would stretch out his hands for me.

Part of me wanted to fight, to swim, to scream, to save myself. But I had no fight left in me. It was over; it was time for me to join my family. I could see them—their beautiful faces smiling at me. I saw Uncle Ali, his perfect white teeth and his jet-black beard, and his radiant face. He extended his hand to me, and I extended mine. He started pulling me up into the light.

The light hurt, but I opened my eyes. I was in a hut made of sticks. I could see the rays of the sun through the cracks.

Why is heaven so ugly? I asked myself.

"Mom! Dad! She is awake!" a child screamed and ran out of the hut.

A few seconds later, a group of people came into the hut and looked at me with a mix of emotion. A lady helped me sit up.

"Hi! I am Khadija. What's your name?" she asked.

"Ayan. Where am I? Who are you?" I said, looking at these strangers with fright.

"My husband, Khadar, saved you from the ocean while he was out fishing," she said.

"I am alive! Where is Mohamed? Where is Halima? Where is my family? Are they outside?" I spoke as fast as I could get the words out of my mouth, my heart racing.

"I am sorry, dear. It was just you," she said. I tried to get up, but I was too weak to stand on my own.

"Please, help me get up! I have to find my family. I have to find them!" I said.

"Where will you find them? Do you know where they are?" she asked.

"They were on the boat with me. I have to go to the ocean!" I said.

"Honey, there was no boat, and there was no one with you. My husband found you all alone out in the ocean."

"I was not alone! My family was with me! Please help me find them!" I cried.

"Where do we find them? Sweetie, you have been in a coma for two days," she said.

"Where did you find me? Take me there! My family is waiting for me!" I cried.

"Khadar, let's take her to the beach," she said.

They helped me up, and we started to walk. On our way to the harbor, I felt like the snail that walks ever so slowly.

"I wish I had wings to fly!" I cried.

There was no sign of my family at the beach. I sat there and cried my eyes out. For the next two months, I went there every morning and stayed there until the sun set. But there was no sign of my family anywhere.

As time passed, I grew to know Khadija and her family. She brought me food and water while I sat by the ocean every single day for two months. She often sat with me in the hot sun. I barely said a single word to her for the first two weeks, but slowly I started opening up to her. I told her everything about my family and what had happened to them, both in Ruuraan and Mogadishu.

Eventually, I started to accept the reality that maybe they were never going to come back. I prayed to God every morning and every night to protect them and bless them with a good life. I started helping Khadija around the house.

Six months later, I told Khadija that I wanted to work and go to school. I told her that I could no longer sit around and wait for my family to find me. She told me that she knew a family in Nairobi that was looking for a maid. And without hesitation, I told her I would take it. I wanted to be able to support myself and not rely on anyone. I felt like a burden to Khadija and her family who were already struggling to survive.

"They want someone to live with them," Khadija said. "You will be responsible for all the house chores; they will provide you with food, a place to sleep, and they will pay you."

"I will take the job," I said.

"I will take you to Nairobi next week," Khadija said.

The following week, we got on a bus that carried us to Nairobi.

Khadija told me to watch out for the daughters. She told me that the mother and the sons were nice but the daughters were mean to the maids. She told me that they had chased out every girl who had ever tried to work for the family. But I was not worried too much about them.

"I will be nice to them," I said and smiled. "I am sure we will get along just fine."

Khadija took me to their house late that afternoon, a couple of hours before the sun set. They lived in a nice part of Nairobi in a gated area filled with beautiful, big houses. The closer we got to their house, the richer the area looked. They had a watchman at the front and a big paved front yard. They had a garden on the side of the house, and the grass looked ever so green.

I was a little scared and had to swallow my pride. A few years ago, I couldn't have imagined working as a maid. I was in this family's position, with my own family and Suad, our maid, and Dayib, our watchman. And now, I was going to work as a maid for girls my own age. It didn't matter what I did, though; I just needed food and a roof over my head. It was not the time for ego; it was time for survival.

The mother greeted me warmly. She seemed like a nice person and smelled really good.

I am in trouble. She smells like a neat freak! I thought.

I had heard the horrors of working for women who were neat freaks—women who expected the impossible from their maids. I hoped that she wasn't one of them, that she was a faithful person who would treat me well. She called her family together and introduced me to them.

"Welcome to our house, Ayan. I will treat you like one of my daughters, and I want you to treat us like your own family. These are my children: Hibo, Haboon, Hoodo, Hodan, Awale, and Mahamed . . ." As she said the names of her children, tears filled my eyes. I recognized her.

I remembered the day Nura had knocked on our door and begged for food and help. Now the tables had turned. I couldn't cry in front of them. I had to be strong. I swallowed and tried to hold back my tears.

"Hi, everyone. My name is Ayan. Nice to meet you all," I said in a weak voice that was filled with the pain of the open wound bleeding in my heart. Oh, how I wished I were standing in front of my own family.

She showed me around the house, the kitchen, and where I would sleep. I couldn't tell if she didn't recognize me or if she didn't want to acknowledge me. I didn't ask her, and I pretended that I had never met her.

What if she makes me sleep in the kitchen alone? I wondered.

I was very pleased when the mother told me that I was going to share a room with Haboon, Hodan, and Hibo. I could see on their faces, though, that they felt disgusted that the maid would share a room with them.

I felt so small and so disgusting, as if I were demoted from being a human being.

I put my plastic bag in the room and started making dinner.

As I was making dinner, Nura came into the kitchen. She looked at me and shook her head.

"Are you Dr. Ali's niece?"

I looked up at her with tears filling my eyes. "Yes."

"Don't tell anyone that you know me. Don't tell them that you have seen me begging in Mogadishu," she whispered.

"Don't worry, Aunt Nura, I won't tell anyone," I said, fighting my tears.

It was tiring physical labor, day in and day out. I was usually the last person to go to sleep at night and the first to wake up in the morning. Only one of the family of ten helped me out, their middle daughter, Hibo. She was very nice to me, and we became good friends. I didn't talk much to anyone else. I just took their orders, answered their questions, and gave them what they asked for.

One day, while I was making breakfast and Hibo was doing the dishes, she asked me, "What happened to your family?"

My heart was filled with pain at the memory. "What do you mean?" I answered, getting defensive.

"I am sorry. I didn't mean to upset you. You were crying in your sleep last night, and you called out some names. I assumed they were your family members. Where is your family?" she asked apologetically.

"I am the only one left," I said. "Most of them were killed in Somalia, and I lost the rest of them on my way to Kenya."

"I am sorry," she said and hugged me as tears rolled down my cheeks. "I didn't know. May God bless their souls. Don't worry; we are your family now. You have us."

I smiled and wiped the tears from my eyes. I was quiet for a few minutes, and then I started telling her about funny experiences I'd had in Kenya. I could tell that Hibo was trying really hard to brighten up the mood and cheer me up. I was glad that I had met her and thanked her for being friendly to me.

Then Awale came out of his room and headed for the kitchen. For some reason, I didn't like Awale. He was very cocky and had a terrible attitude. He was so full of himself and always made fun of me. Somehow he always found a way to pick on me and get under my skin. He always criticized anything I did.

He would say, "The food is salty," "You always make everything late," "You don't know how to cook," and "You didn't wash my clothes properly." And he also teased me about my looks. He said that I had goat eyes.

I disregarded his comments and focused on getting along with everyone except for him. He knew how to push my buttons more than anyone I had ever met.

"I can't even sleep in this house anymore! Why are you two laughing so loudly? You are girls; have some respect for yourselves," he said, standing over us.

I held my anger back and promised that I wasn't going to let him get to me. But I also wasn't going to take it quietly!

"Here we go again! Why are you always yelling like an old man?" I said as Hibo and I laughed together. "What happened? Did you have a fight with your imaginary wife?"

"You wish you were my wife!" he said. "I have news for you. I will never marry a stupid woman like you! No one wants a goat for a wife."

"What do you know? You are such a brainless idiot!" I said in English, forgetting that their school was an English-based school just like the one I used to go to in Mogadishu.

"*Wow!* You speak English?" he said, surprised.

"Better than the broken English you speak!" I responded.

"Seriously, how did you learn English? You are a maid! I didn't know you went to school," he mumbled.

"Why am I not surprised? Only an idiot like you would think like that about other people. Aren't maids people too?"

Hibo interrupted us and said, "Guys, please stop arguing. It's five in the morning! Just wait until the sun rises if you have to argue. Awale, she is from a family of doctors, and she used to go to an English private school."

"Oh, what happened to your family? Did you run away, or did they kick you out?" he said, laughing at his own corny joke.

I couldn't hold the tears back, so I ran to the restroom without saying a word.

I heard him ask Hibo what was wrong with me, and she told him what had happened to my family. I washed my face and came back to finish making breakfast.

"Ayan, I am really sorry," he apologized. "I had no idea. I didn't mean what I said."

Our fights slowly turned into a friendship. I told him about my dream of becoming a doctor, but how that dream had died with my family. He started to help me around the house and no longer criticized the work I did. He also started helping me to resume my studies. He gave me math, English, and science books. At that time, he was going to high school in the mornings and teaching English and math school at night.

Awale told me that I could come to his classes for free and learn more math and English. He said that I could help tutor the other students, and in return, he would teach me. At first, I refused because I didn't think his mother was going to let her maid go to school. But Awale convinced Nura to let me go and give me the supplies I would need.

He told Aunt Nura that his class was getting very crowded and he needed some help. He told her that I was very educated and fluent in English and my math skills were very good. Nura said that she would let me help him, but only if I finished my work on time. I started waking up a couple of hours earlier than normal and did my work as fast as I could. I was ecstatic now that I had something to look forward to. I hadn't realized how much I had missed school. Although my days were very long, my dreams were reignited, and I looked forward to learning. I felt blessed and thanked God often.

I started going to Awale's class and learning. I was getting my hope back, and the dark clouds that hid my dream were clearing up. It felt good, and I felt a lot less helpless. I enjoyed helping students and seeing that aha moment in their eyes when they finally understood. I started making friends, feeling a little normal, and believing that life wasn't so dark after all. I learned to smile and sometimes laugh at myself for the constant smile from my heart. It felt good to smile—not a fake smile to look normal to others but a genuine smile from my heart.

I didn't realize the power of a smile until that time. Sometimes I felt guilty for smiling so much, because there was a part of me that knew a smile would only end in tears.

16

Everyone liked Awale. Some of the girls liked him more than just as their tutor. I heard some of them whispering about him. Some of them even asked me about him. I didn't like it, but I didn't know why.

"Are you Awale's sister?" one of Awale's students asked me one night.

"No," I responded.

"How are you related to him?" she continued.

"How is that any of your business?" I said.

"Don't bite my head off; I am just asking. Are you his wife or something?"

I walked away from her without a response and felt angry for some reason. I told myself that I had no reason to be mad at him or any of the girls. I could only be mad at myself. I told myself that he would never see me as a woman who could become his wife.

You are their maid! A maid who has no family, no money, and nothing special about her, I scolded myself.

I tried to talk my heart out of this weird new feeling that was growing. But no matter how much I scolded my heart and how much I tried to remove any sort of hope, my heart was not listening to me. The feelings were getting stronger and stronger as time passed. I found myself getting jealous every time I saw a girl flirting with him, but I hid it, as I didn't want to lose my friendship with him. I never told him how I felt, and I denied every accusation that my friends or his sister Hibo made about my feelings for him.

Awale and I grew closer as time went on. Without us realizing, we started spending much more time together.

He would wake up at three in the morning with me and ask me to help him with the lesson plan while I made breakfast. He would also teach me extra math, science, and practice English with me. And sometimes he would help me with my work.

"Let me make breakfast today," he said, smiling.

"Do you want your mom to kill me? Have you made a cup of tea in your life?" I asked.

"No, but how hard can it be?"

"Okay, here, make a canjeelo," I handed him the bowl with flour, and he made a crooked one. I started laughing.

"Why are you laughing at me? You made it look so easy. How am I supposed to make it?"

"Practice makes perfect! Give it back before your mom sees you making it," I said as I grabbed the bowl and the cup from him.

The more time I spent with him, the more I developed feelings for him. He was my first love, and I wasn't sure what to do with my feelings.

One Friday morning, I decided that I was going to tell him. I didn't want to leave any regrets behind and wonder what it would have been like if I had told him. I didn't get much sleep that night as I planned and thought of what I would tell him and how I would react to all the possible responses. I had a concrete plan until he came into the room.

I forgot everything that I had planned to say. This was because there was a voice in the back of my head saying, *Ayan, stop dreaming. It will never be possible between you and Awale. He is everything a girl would want, and you are their maid. He just sees you like one of his sisters. Get over these feelings before you ruin your relationship with him.*

"Good morning, Ayan. You seem a little lost today. What's up?" he asked.

I giggled and said, "Good morning, Awale. Nothing really. I was just thinking of something."

We started talking about the lesson plan and then random things until the sun rose and he had to get ready for his school. I made several attempts to tell him how I felt just so that I could get over it and not think of him every minute of the day, but I failed to say anything that day.

Two weeks after my first failed attempt, things took a 180-degree turn.

After class ended and everyone had left that night, I was heading home when Jama approached us.

"Ayan, can I talk to you alone for a second?" Jama asked me politely.

"Sure. What's up?" I said to Jama.

"Awale, you can go ahead; I will walk her home," Jama said.

Awale looked at me, waiting for me. I felt like he wanted to be there with me and was reluctant to leave me alone with another boy.

"It's okay, Awale. You can go ahead," I told him.

Awale walked very fast and disappeared into the distance.

"Jama, what do you want to talk to me about?"

"I know you are not the type of girl to mess around with, and I am sincere. I really don't want to waste your time or mine, but I have to tell you something. You are beautiful, smart, nice, respected, and the most amazing girl that I have known in my entire life. I hope you will consider what I am asking you tonight. You don't have to answer me now, take all the time you need, and think about it," Jama said.

"It's late," I said in a hurry. "I have to go home. Can you please stop beating around the bush and get to the point?"

"I like you. I really do. I don't like to waste your time and mess around, but I like you, and I want to marry you. I have been observing you for a while, and I really like you. Could we get to know each other to see if we are compatible? Would you please give me a chance?"

Jama was a good man. He was from a good family, educated, nice, very handsome, and stable. But my heart was already taken.

"Thank you, Jama. I don't know what to say. I won't lie to you and waste your time. I am really sorry, but I can't help you in that matter," I said to him.

"Ayan, just give me a chance. Get to know me; that is all I am asking from you. You don't have to reply to me. Just think about it and tell me when you are ready."

"I am sorry, Jama. I really can't help you," I responded to him.

"Just think about it, Ayan," he insisted.

"I will think about, but if I were you, I wouldn't hold my breath."

"Why? Are you seeing someone?" he asked.

"No, not at the moment."

He walked me home, and we said good night at the door. I was surprised to see Awale pacing around the yard.

"Hey, Awale. Are you okay?" I asked him quietly.

"Okay? Huh? Ayan, I never thought you were like that! How could you disrespect me in front of him? Why didn't you tell him to meet you some other time? You were walking with me, and you just told me to go—just like that!" He was furious.

"Excuse me, Awale. We were just walking home. There is nothing wrong with me talking to Jama for couple of minutes."

"Everything is wrong with it! The least you could have done was acknowledge I was there. You could have asked him to meet you some other time or asked me to wait for you instead of telling me to go like some kind of unimportant person."

"Why would I tell him to meet me some other time? We were not talking about anything important, and I would have seen you at home anyway."

"I don't want you talking to that guy. I don't like him. He is a player, Ayan, and I don't want you being played. Stay away from him," he warned.

"Awale, I am not a little kid. And you are in no position to tell me who I can talk to and who I cannot talk to. Just because I work for your family doesn't mean you own me," I said and walked into the room.

I went to bed. That morning, he didn't wake up at the early time. I cooked and cleaned all alone. It was boring and little lonely. I missed him and felt bad that I had yelled at him. He woke up a little before school and left without eating or saying hi to anyone. He was still mad at me from the night before.

Hibo was helping me do the laundry when I saw him walk in from the gate.

"Hibo, isn't it funny how some people think they own you because they helped you?"

Hibo looked at me, puzzled.

And then Awale said to Hibo, "Hibo, you know it's true what they say, never do any good and nothing bad will ever happen to you! Some people just don't know how to respect people." Our eyes met, and having eye contact with him was electrifying. He then walked toward his room without saying anything else.

"Ayan, what's going on? Did you guys have a fight?"

"Yeah, a little. Last night, Jama said that he had something to tell me. So I told Awale to keep going and that I would follow after I talked to Jama. And when I got home, he started acting like I had done something wrong.

But Awale doesn't own me! I am free to talk to whoever I want and do whatever I want!"

"Aww, that's cute!" Hibo said, laughing.

"Hibo, we had a fight, and he is not talking to me! What is cute about that?"

"Ayan, you are so slow! Don't you get it? He likes you. He is jealous of Jama." Hibo smiled.

"You and your wild thinking. You know that's not possible between us," I said. To be honest, though, hearing that from Hibo was like music to my ears.

"Why not? You are smart, strong, and beautiful. Any man will be lucky to have you," she said.

"Thanks! But did you forget that I am also your maid?"

"Stop thinking too much about being a maid. Your job doesn't define you. There is a lot more to you than your work," Hibo said.

I went to the kitchen and started cooking. I didn't go to his school that night; I just went to my room and tried to sleep. The next morning, it was the same. He didn't eat breakfast, and he didn't talk to me.

The third day, Awale woke up a little bit after I did. He walked to the kitchen, and we looked at each other and smiled.

"I am sorry, Ayan. I didn't mean to yell at you. I overreacted. I don't know what happened to me. I had something important to tell you, and he just had to ruin it. I don't own you, and I don't help you so that you can be in debt to me. I help you out because I am your friend." He was looking at my eyes, and I couldn't turn away from him. His eyes were like a magnet.

"I am sorry too. I overreacted because I thought you didn't trust me. I am sorry."

"Apology accepted. Are we cool now?" he asked.

"We are always cool. You are the one who was acting up like a toddler," I said, and we both laughed.

"So what did he want to talk to you about?" he asked.

"He wanted to marry me," I said.

"You cannot marry him!" Awale said. "Sorry, I mean, what did you tell him?"

"I told him that I would think about it," I responded.

"What you mean you will think about it? Do you like him?" he asked anxiously.

"Okay, enough about me; what's the important thing that you were going to tell me that night?" I asked.

"What was that? Um, nothing. It was nothing important. Don't worry about it," he said, chuckling nervously as he scratched the back of his head.

"Nothing important? You just said it was important. Come on, you can tell me anything. Tell me!" I said.

"Jama ruined my chance to tell you. I had to collect so much courage for so many days, and at the exact moment I was about to tell you, he ruined it," Awale said.

"Don't worry about him. Just tell me. I am still here!" I insisted.

"First, promise me that this will have no effect on our friendship and that it will not change anything between us, regardless of how it goes," he said.

I was getting butterflies in my stomach when those words came out of his mouth. So many thoughts flooded my mind.

"Yeah, I promise. What is it?" I said, looking at him with hopeful eyes.

"I have feelings for you," Awale said, looking directly into my eyes. "I don't know when or how it happened, but I cannot stop thinking of you. I really like you and see you as more than a friend. I tried to tell you so many times, but I failed each time."

I was stunned. I was breathing hard, looking from left to right and wondering what to do.

"Awale, this is not something to joke about," I said.

"Ayan, I am serious. I would never joke about such a thing."

I don't know what happened to me or why I said it, but I said, "I am sorry. I don't feel the same way about you."

"Oh, it's okay. I was expecting that," he said, disappointed.

I loved him and wanted to say it, but I turned him down. I was scared of love. Love was causing me a lot of problems. I figured that if I stayed away from love, I would never be hurt again.

As time went on, my feelings grew harder to deny and suppress. I couldn't help but fall in love with him, even though I didn't want to love him—or anyone, for that matter. Part of the wall around my heart broke every time he looked at me with those eyes. I finally understood why we had to lower our gazes—eyes really are the gate to the soul.

I didn't want to face him, but I missed him and found myself running to wherever he was. He was constantly on my mind, and I couldn't figure out a way to get him out of my head. I always found distractions, but somehow he always found a way back into my thoughts.

"Ayan, stop torturing yourself and Awale," Hibo told me one day. "I know you really like him. Why don't you just tell him how you feel? What are you scared of?"

"Love! Bad things happen to everyone that I love, and I don't want anything to happen to Awale. I love him, but I don't want to get hurt. Not again, never."

"Ayan, life is not always like that. Nothing will happen to him just because of your love for him. This love could be a gift for you from God to rebuild the family you have lost, the house you lost, and the loved ones you have lost. You can have a great family and achieve all your dreams and goals with him. Everything happens for a reason, Ayan, and your family's tragedy had nothing to do with you or your love; it was meant to be. Their time in this world has ended," Hibo said.

"Thanks, Hibo. I wish it were that easy. I am not ready for that yet."

"I am telling you, you will not lose anything by accepting your feelings. Please stop torturing my friend and my brother," she said.

"I wish I could do that," I responded to Hibo.

Hibo walked out of the kitchen. I sat there thinking for a while. Maybe she was right and I had nothing to lose. As selfish as it sounded, I had considered saying yes to him because the family was going to America. If I were his wife, they would certainly not leave me behind.

I wanted to go to America, the land where every dream came true, where everyone had a chance, and where everyone was rich. I had heard so many people talking about it as if it were heaven. Everyone wanted to live the American dream, and I did too. But I knew that was wrong, especially after all that he had done for me, so I got that thought out of my head as

[handwritten marginal note: The American Dream is associated with wealth & opportunity]

soon as it came to me.

I didn't know what to do. I really liked Awale, but I was scared of losing the little hope I had of achieving my dream of becoming a doctor. I wanted to become educated and help people. I wanted to have a better life, as I was the only one I had to worry about. I really wanted a family, even more than the American dream. I wanted love, but I felt that I was not worthy of it.

What do you have to lose, Ayan? I asked myself for what felt like the millionth time.

I made my decision and called Hibo. "Hibo, you are right! I can actually achieve my dreams and goals with him. I have nothing to lose. I will talk to him, and if he agrees to my conditions, then I will say yes to him."

Hibo hugged me, saying, "I am glad you decided that. Good luck, and let me know how it goes."

I anxiously waited for the class to end that night. When we closed the class, I told him that I had something important to discuss with him.

We walked to home slowly.

"What did you want to talk to me about, Ayan?" he asked.

"Uh . . . I . . . I . . . like you too. But I am worried that I cannot have a relationship with you. We are from two different worlds. I want to achieve my dreams and goals. Love is something that exists and just happens, but I don't want to love anyone," I mumbled. I turned toward him.

He looked into my eyes and said, "I love you too, Ayan. Thank you for telling me this. We are not from two different worlds; even if we were, we can unite them to make our own world. I will never get in the way of your dreams and goals. I promise you that I will help you achieve them. I want to think of you, I want you to think of me, and I want to live in your heart forever. We can make this work! We are almost at home. Let's think of how we want to do this tomorrow."

"What about your family? Will they let you marry a maid?" I asked nervously.

"I already told my mom that I was interested in you, and she is completely fine with it. I am a man, Ayan. I can marry whomever I want to marry. I promise you that I will never hurt you. I will be there for you, and I will help you achieve every one of your goals and dreams. Just give me the chance to do so."

"I don't know! You are right; let's finish talking about this tomorrow," I said.

"Sounds good to me. Thank you so much, Ayan. You made me very happy tonight. This will be a night that I will remember for the rest of my life."

His face lit up, and his smile was the most amazing smile that I had seen. We got home, and he went to his room and I went into mine, blushing red.

"So how did it go?" Hibo asked me.

"I told him! But we didn't finish talking. I didn't promise him anything," I told her.

"Ayan, you are still scared. I won't let him go if he hurts you one bit. I promise," Hibo said.

A few days later, Khadija came to visit me. I was very happy to see her.

"Khadija! How are you? How have you been, and the rest of the family? I missed you so much." I hugged her.

"Ayan! We are doing well, and the family is doing well. How have you been? Have they been treating you well?" she asked.

"I am doing well, Khadija. Thank you so much. Yes, they have been very nice to me. I was actually going to come see you soon. I need advice on an important matter," I told her.

"What's the matter?" she asked.

"Awale proposed to me! I like him, but I don't know if I should say yes or no. I want to achieve my goals and dreams. I don't want marriage to get in the way of my dreams. You know that I don't have anyone in this world, and I am all I can depend on! I want to make something out of myself first," I said.

"Congratulations! That's good news," Khadija said loudly.

"Shh, lower your voice, Khadija. They don't know it yet."

"That's good news, Ayan! You should say yes! Opportunities knock on your door once in a lifetime. You should grab it and hold on tightly! His family is very nice. Plus, they are rich, and they are going to America soon. You will be set for life. Don't be stupid. What is there to think about? Don't you know that America is the place where you can make all your dreams come true? If I were you, I would marry him even if I didn't like him. Why do you think so many girls from our refugee camps marry ninety-year-old grandpas? Certainly not for love or looks. Even if you don't like him, you can use him to get to your dreams. America is a free place; you can divorce him when you get there. A lot of women did that and live happily in America now." Khadija's words sounded selfish, but they made sense to me.

"You are right, Khadija, I was thinking of that too. But to be honest, I really love Awale, and I don't want to marry him just because I want to go to America. Awale is a very nice guy. But I am just so scared," I said.

"Ayan, you will be fine as long as you don't trust him too much and as long as you don't forget your goals. Approach this matter cautiously, and think of how you can get the best out of it. But be careful. Don't dig too deep of a hole. You never know; you might be the one who falls in it."

"Thank you, Khadija. I will keep that in mind," I said.

"Well, I am glad to see you happy and doing well. Let me know if anything comes up, and remember we are always here for you," Khadija said, hugging me.

"Thank you, Khadija. I will forever be indebted to you. Thank you!" I hugged her tightly.

I walked Khadija to the door and said good-bye to her. I then walked into the kitchen and found Hibo sitting on a chair and looking angry.

Oh no! She must have overheard my talk with Khadija's, I thought.

"Ayan, I never knew you were so selfish! I thought you loved my brother! But you are just using him to get to America? How can you be so selfish and cruel?" Hibo asked.

"Hibo, you are misunderstanding me. I really love him, but I also care about my future and my goals. I was just trying to be polite to Khadija. She has done a lot for me. I really didn't mean it that way," I said.

"Ayan, if you try to play my brother and use my family, I swear you will see the worst of me," Hibo said.

"Hibo, you know I would never hurt your brother or your family. You have been nothing but good to me, and you have helped me so much. I would never hurt Awale's feelings. I love him," I said.

Hibo calmed down a little and left the kitchen. I got back to my work, feeling ever so guilty.

How could I even entertain such an idea? It's good opportunity, though, I thought, troubled and conflicted by my feelings.

17

A couple of nights later, I told Awale that I would marry him, but on one condition.

"I will do anything to be with you, Ayan. Anything, just say it. I will agree to it," he said, stopping and looking deep into my eyes.

"I will marry you, but we will not have that kind of relationship," I said.

"What do you mean?" he asked, puzzled.

"What I mean is that we will legally be husband and wife, but we will not behave with each other like a husband and wife until we get to America."

"Ayan, don't you trust me?" Awale asked. His gaze piercing through my soul.

"Yes, I do trust you, Awale. It's just that my goals are important to me, and I have to look out for myself," I said.

"Ayan, you don't have to look out for yourself anymore. You are not alone. We are your family now," Awale tried to reason with me.

"I know that, and I really do love and trust you. But I want to make something out of myself. I don't want to get pregnant before I achieve my dreams," I said.

"Okay, Ayan, I agree to your condition, but you have to promise me that you will not ask me to divorce you once we get to America," Awale said.

"I promise you that I will never ask you for a divorce, whether we get to America or not. Awale, I am not using you to go to America. I love you and I want to be with you, but just as much as I want to be with you, I also want to be successful. I want to become a doctor," I said.

"I agree to your condition, and I will tell the family to prepare our wedding. Thank you for loving me and accepting me, Ayan. I love you."

He told his family that night. I hid in the room, pretending to be asleep. I could hear the chatter, the congratulations that Awale was getting, and his mother singing with joy. There was laughter everywhere. I wanted to be part of it, but I was shy, so I stayed in my room.

The next morning, I woke up at my regular time to make breakfast, but his sisters and mother kicked me out of the kitchen.

"Good morning, bride. You are not allowed to come to the kitchen anymore. Now go back to sleep," Nura told me as his sisters pushed me out of the kitchen. I smiled and blushed. Then Awale came out of his room.

"Look at this! The groom woke up this early to see his bride. How sweet!" his sister Haboon teased him.

He blushed, saying, "I was just going to get some water."

"Who gets thirsty this early in the morning? You are thirsty for something else, huh?" Haboon teased him.

"Shut up, Haboon!" Awale said and hustled back to his room.

Two weeks later, we got the news that we were going to America in two months. Nura had added me to their family list several months back when Awale had first told her that he was interested in marrying me. I was happy to hear that we were going to America so soon. I had thought it would take longer.

As the wedding date got closer, we started the preparations. There was something to do every minute of the day. I felt a little sad that my family was not there and that there was no input on the wedding from my side. It was the norm for the groom's family to pay for the wedding expenses and the bride's family to organize it to their liking. There was no one from my family, but I was happy.

Awale's family booked a wedding hall in a nearby luxury hotel. The decorations, the food, the music, and all other details were organized by Awale's family. I just went to the shopping center with them one day to get fitted for a bridal dress, and then it was picked up by my mother-in-law. I didn't even try it on before the wedding day. It was beautiful.

My wedding was very different from what I had imagined as a child. My wedding felt empty without my family there. I had never missed my family more than I did that day. I had never wished more that they were there with me.

The bride's father, uncles, grandfathers, brothers, or other male relatives give the bride's hand to the groom. I didn't have any, so they had to look for a man who was from my same tribe. I had never met this man before, but he gave my hand in the ceremony.

The bride's and the groom's families invite people and have fun dancing together to the tunes of traditional and modern music. But my wedding was organized by Awale's family, so only one family was dancing. The food was amazing, and everything looked extremely beautiful. The dancing was quite amusing too.

Though everyone seemed to have enjoyed the wedding, I did not. I was missing my family and felt like an imposter. I felt that at any moment my wedding was going to be canceled and that all of this was going to be revealed as a cruel joke. People danced all kinds of traditional Somali dances throughout the day. I forced myself to smile.

When the wedding ended, it was time to go home to my new husband. That was scary. I had never been alone with a man. I knew Awale was very nice and would never break his word, but I was worried that something bad might happen to him. We entered our newly decorated room, which held a bed.

It felt good to sit on a bed and be in a house that I could call mine. The bed was beautiful and comfortable—not as good as the bed we used to have back in Mogadishu, but it was a nice one. It had been years since I had last slept on a bed.

Everyone wished us a good night and left Awale and me alone.

"I will sleep on the floor," Awale said in a sweet voice that made me feel guilty. "You will sleep on the bed."

"No, I will sleep on the floor. I am used to sleeping on the floor," I replied, looking down at the carpet and hoping to avoid his gaze.

"No, I cannot let my beautiful wife sleep on the floor. What kind of man would I be?"

We both smiled at each other, our eyes meeting. It was electrifying. It felt really good to know that I was not alone in this world anymore. I finally had a family and someone that I could hold on to. It was the most amazing feeling that I had felt in years. I spread our new blanket for him on the floor, and I slept on the bed.

I woke up very early in the morning; I hadn't sleep much. I looked at him for what felt like a thousand times, just to make sure I wasn't dreaming and that he was real. He was peacefully sleeping. I couldn't help but stare longingly at him. I wanted to get up, pray our morning prayer, and make breakfast for him, but something was telling me to just keep staring at him. And even though I'd made him promise me that we were not to be husband and wife until we got to America, I longed for him. I wanted to be in his arms.

I was lost in my daydream when I heard, "Staring much?" I was startled and embarrassed at being caught by him.

"No, I wasn't staring at you. I was just checking to see if you were up," I replied, blushing.

He laughed and said, "It's all right, dear. I am your husband. You can stare at me all you want. I am all yours!" he said, teasingly winking at me.

I smiled and put my head back on my pillow. After a little bit, we got up and prayed. I couldn't go back to sleep, so I awkwardly lay on the bed, feeling his presence near me.

I took a shower, wore a beautiful dress, and came back to the bed. After a little while, his sister and my bridesmaids brought us breakfast. I opened the door for them and took the breakfast from them. I put it in front of him and tried to go back to my bed, but he held my hand, saying, "You are not going to make me eat alone on our first day of marriage, are you, my love?" I smiled shyly and sat with him.

It was very hard to eat breakfast with his vivid stare, but I tried. His sisters, my sisters-in-law, came back and took the plates. As newlyweds, we had to stay inside for seven days. The thought of staying inside with him for seven days was daunting at first, but he made it very easy.

I could tell that it was very hard for him to be around me twenty-four hours a day and not be able to touch me. I was feeling guilty, and as time went on, I wanted to be his wife. We had many deep conversations and talked about everything humanly possible.

On the fifth day, I decided that I wanted to be his wife because I realized that there was no one like him on this planet. He was a rare type of man. He was locked in a room with me for five days, and he held himself to his promise to me. I was his wife, he had every right to touch me, every right to change his mind, and every right to end our relationship. But he didn't even attempt to kiss me.

On the sixth morning, after morning prayer, our eyes met as we sat on the carpet in our bedroom. I couldn't turn away from him, and neither could he. We just stared at each other with the biggest smiles on our faces. I don't know what we were smiling about. I guess happiness is sometimes expressed through a deep smile.

I couldn't torture him and myself anymore. I got up and walked over to him.

"Ayan, how was your slee—" he asked, but I didn't let him finish.

I sat by him and kissed him before he could finish his sentence. He kissed me back, but then he stopped himself.

"Ayan, I don't want to break the promise I made to you. I am not saying that I don't want to kiss you. I do! Are you sure this is what you want?" he asked, looking at me with eyes filled with mercy and love.

"Yes, my love, this is what I want. I want to be your wife. I want to be your family, I want to hold your hand, and I would rather have you than all my other dreams in this world." I held his hands and looked deep into his eyes.

He got up and opened his bag. I looked at him curiously. He took out a small box that I had never seen before.

"What is that?" I asked him curiously.

"Protection," he said, smiling.

"What?" I asked.

"They will prevent you from getting pregnant. Ayan, we are both very young, and we have so much to achieve. I don't want to put you in a situation that can make it harder for you to achieve your dreams and goals. Life has been hard enough for you. I am here to be your right hand and to support you," he said.

I looked at him and felt puzzled and amazed at the same time. I started laughing.

"Why are you laughing?" he said, tickling me.

"You are the best husband anyone could ever wish for. Thank you, Awale!" We passionately began to get intimate, but it was painful because of my circumcision. And as much as I wanted to be in his arms, I was hurting and I started bleeding. I didn't want to stop him, so I tried to bear the pain. Awale saw that I was in tears and stopped.

"Ayan, are you all right, dear?" he asked.

"I am in so much pain. I think I am bleeding," I said, with tears in my eyes.

"I am so sorry, dear. Why didn't you tell me you were circumcised? I would have taken you to the hospital to have your circumcision opened up," he said, wiping my tears away.

"I didn't think you would understand," I said.

"Let's go to the hospital and have you treated," he said. He hugged me and kissed my forehead. Het got up and got ready to take me to the hospital.

"It is too early? Is the hospital open now?" I asked.

"My friend's older sister is a doctor. I will call her to meet us at the hospital," Awale said and helped me get ready.

We went to the hospital, and I had the surgery to reverse my circumcision. This time, anesthetics were used, and Awale took care of me while I healed. And after I was healed, we were able to be intimate without the pain and the bleeding.

I opened my heart and let love in. I was finally able to love, I was finally able to trust, and I was finally able to genuinely feel that I was not alone in this world for the first time since I had lost my family. I still felt a dark cloud hovering over me as if the other shoe were about to drop, but I ignored it and enjoyed my time with Awale.

I missed my mom. I finally felt like I was a woman. I didn't agree that circumcision made me a woman, but I didn't resent my family. It was their way of giving me the best they could in the world they had lived in. I have no doubt that if I had stayed in Ruuraan, it would have been very difficult for me to find a husband had I not been circumcised. I know my mom and Grandma were trying to set me up for success within the culture they lived in.

18

The last year had brought a great change, and then in just two months, all our lives changed again. We were going to be resettled in America. Refugees didn't have much choice about where they were resettled. You just waited until someone was willing to let you into their safe home. Nura was able to add me to her family list just in time. Awale, though, had arrived in Kenya after the rest of his family and was part of a different resettlement program. Unfortunately, his resettlement did not come out yet, so he was not coming with us. I felt very sad that he wasn't coming with us.

"Awale, I love you, and I don't want to leave you," I said, hugging him.

"I love you too, Ayan! Don't worry, sweetheart; my process will come through soon, and I will come shortly after you."

"What if the process doesn't come through?" I asked, tears filling my eyes.

"You are going to be there! If this process does not come through, you will bring me to America," Awale said, putting his right hand under my ear and brushing my hair back with his left hand.

On the day of our flight, I prayed to thank Allah for all that he had blessed me with, and I prayed for my family and asked God to forgive them and bless them.

Awale entered the room when I finished my prayers, and I hugged him tightly.

"Thank you, my dear. Thank you for being there for me, thank you for being patient with me, thank you for teaching me how to love and trust again, and thank you for being my wonderful husband. I can never ask God for anything better. I am truly blessed to have you. Thank you." I hugged him tightly and cried.

"I am the one who's blessed to have you as my wife. You smell really nice! I will miss seeing your goat eyes every morning," he said, hugging me tighter. "Ayan, don't cry! You will always be in my heart and on my mind. I will call you and email you every day. And I promise you that I will never break your heart, I will never make you cry, and I will never look at any other woman. I love you more than words can express."

"I love you more, Awale! I don't know how to say good-bye and leave without you. I will miss you so much!" I cried.

"It is only a matter of days, a few months at the most." Awale hugged me as if he were never going to see me again.

Aunt Nura knocked on the door and said, "Lovebirds, it is time to go."

"We are coming, Mom," Awale said.

He grabbed my luggage, and we drove to Jomo Kenyatta International Airport. We held hands all the way to the airport.

"These two are shameless," Hodo teased us. "They keep flirting with each other and holding hands in public."

"Are you jealous? Go get your own husband," Awale teased her.

"Ewww, shut up," she said.

"They are still in the honey month," Aunt Nura said. "Leave them alone."

I tried to pull my hand away from him, but he wouldn't let go of me.

As we got to the security door, Awale said good-bye to everyone. I waited for them to finish.

"Let's go. Let the lovebirds say good-bye to each other," Aunt Nura said.

They started walking toward the security check. Awale hugged me tightly. I felt a little uncomfortable because we were in public, but a part of me did not want to let go of him. I wanted to be in his arms forever.

They were calling for me, as our departure time was close.

"You should go, honey," Awale said. I took one last good look at him to console my heart, which was breaking into a million tiny pieces.

"Don't I get a good-bye kiss?" Awale said.

"We are in public, Awale," I said, walking close to him. I kissed him, closed my eyes, and then walked toward the security gate. "I love you, Ayan!"

"I love you more, Awale!" We waved to each other. As I walked onto the plane, my tears began to pour like rain. I wanted to get out and run to his arms, but I also wanted to go to this dreamland and have a better life. I felt as if my heart wanted to break free from my rib cage and take a flight to Awale.

I sat by the window, giving up every attempt to hide my tears. A few minutes later, the plane took off to America, where every dream comes true. As we soared above the clouds, I started writing in my journal.

I am hopeful that maybe America will be the place where I can finally call home. I hope it's the place where all my dreams will come true and that I will make a difference. I've heard that American is an accepting home, free of oppression and war, a place where I won't have to worry about getting detained for no reason or killed. I hope that America will be my adopted home, my second chance at life.

Eighteen hours later, we landed at MSP International Airport in Minnesota. I was in dreamland. I knew there were no guarantees for tomorrow, but I was still filled with hope and gratitude.

The American Dream

19

"Good morning, Mother. Thank you for waking me," I said to Nura.

I got up to get ready in the small bedroom that I shared with my sisters-in-law, Hibo, Hodan, and Haboon, in America.

"You are always late," Nura said and huffed. "One day, I will just let you miss your bus."

If only her words were as beautiful as her face. My mother-in-law, the most beautiful woman I have ever seen—externally, of course. Her big amber eyes shone under the light with her lashes curling upward like peacock feathers. It was easy to see her natural beauty, but for some odd reason, she reminded me of a snake.

Since we'd left Kenya, Nura had been cold toward me. Awale wasn't brought to America with us; he had to stay back in Nairobi. During our first week in America, Nura started looking for information on how I could bring Awale over. We found out that I was underage and could not bring him; I had to be eighteen to do so. Nura asked me to drop out of school and work to support the family and to save up enough money to bring him to America once I turned eighteen, but I refused. I was not willing to throw away my future and my life, so I continued going to school while working part-time.

Nura blamed me for her son not coming with us, as if I had something to do with it. And the more she missed him, the colder she became toward me. Every little thing I did irritated her. One day, she yelled at me for walking by her in the kitchen.

We had been in America for about six months at that time. I was still adjusting to living in this country. Before we came to America, I thought that we were going to live in a mansion, a gated house with a white fence and huge backyard. We thought we were going to be rich because money was easy to make in America and everyone in America was rich. We thought there were no bugs, no diseases, and no hardship. In my mind, America was heaven.

Minnesota was great in many ways, but it did have bugs. All kinds of bugs came out in the summer. We were not living in luxury or anything close to a mansion. We shared a two-bedroom apartment between nine of us.

There was no privacy in our home. I couldn't even say, "I love you," and other sweet words to Awale. We would pour our hearts out to each other only on days and nights when we were lucky enough that no one was at home or the nights when I stayed up until everyone was asleep. The rest of the time, we talked like we were just friends. Every morning, I missed him and wished he were there with me. I knew he would have never let Nura treat me like she did.

"Really, Mom?" Hibo muttered from her bed. "This early in the morning? Would you please give her a break? I honestly don't know why she puts up with your bullshit!"

"Hibo, don't talk to your mom like that. It's disrespectful," I said.

Nura snapped at me, "Who do you think you are to decide how my daughter should talk to me?" She never missed an opportunity to get under my skin.

On the school bus, I sat beside Nasteho, my only friend and the only person in the world who knew what was going on with me.

I met Nasteho on the bus on the first day of school. She was sitting by the window, the wind playing with her long hair, and she reminded me of Aunt Zainaba. I stood by the seat she was sitting in and lost myself in a memory of the wind playing with Aunt Zainaba's hair as she sat on the swing and gently swung back and forth.

"What is wrong with you? Either sit down or move so people can come into the bus!" Nasteho snapped me back into reality.

"I am sorry!" I said in Somali, quickly sitting by her.

"I am sorry; I didn't mean to yell at you. I talked to you, but you seemed lost," Nasteho said.

"It is okay. You reminded me of my aunt Zainaba. You look so much like her. She loved letting the wind play with her hair," I said with a lump in my throat, trying to hold back the tears.

Somehow, Nasteho sensed my pain, and without saying a word, she hugged me. It was nice to be hugged. I hadn't been hugged in so long, but I felt little weird, as I did not know her. I sat back.

"She must have been beautiful if I reminded you of her!" Nasteho said, laughing.

I laughed with her.

"Hi, I am Nasteho," she said.

"Hi, I am Ayan," I replied.

Nasteho was my age. Her mom was from the southern part of Somalia, close to Kenya, and her dad was from the northern part of Somalia, close to Djibouti. She spoke a mix of southern and northern Somali accents and almost sounded like two different people. From the day that I first met her on the bus, Nasteho became my best friend.

"Thank God for school," I sighed as I sank into the brown leather school bus seat. "Eight hours of peace!"

"I have never seen someone who likes school more than you. You are one weird human," Nasteho said, squinting her dark brown eyes while tapping her pointer finger on the side of her pink lips.

"Nasteho, other people don't live my kind of life. They live normal lives. Seriously, though, how do you plan to counsel people?" I teased her. Nasteho's dream was to graduate from high school, get married, have a baby, and then study psychology so she could become a therapist—she had laid out her plans in exactly that order.

"That's what college is for; you learn how to do actual work," Nasteho said. "It's not as useless as high school. I hate that we have to get through high school to get to college. Who made those stupid rules? And did the witch get to you today?"

"Yeah, she never misses a day," I said.

"Don't worry, you are almost free from her! Six more months and you will be going to college! You will bring Awale to America as soon as you turn eighteen, and you can move to your own place with your husband. You won't have to live with that beautiful snake-eyed woman!" Nasteho hugged me. She always made me feel like everything was going to be all right.

"Hey, that's my mother-in-law you are talking about!" I said, and we laughed. "It is mind-boggling how you can insult and compliment someone at the same time."

"I have good news that will cheer you up for the rest of the year," Nasteho said as she handed me a letter.

"What is it?" I asked her.

"I don't know. I'm just the messenger. Open it," Nasteho said.

"But it's already open." I smiled and took out the letter, which read:

Dear Ayan Raage,

Congratulations! You have been nominated to apply for the S. E. Hogenson Scholarship. It is an honor to invite you to submit the rest of your application to be considered for this scholarship . . .

"Who nominated me?" I asked Nasteho. I couldn't believe that I might receive a scholarship to study at college and then medical school.

"Dr. H. and I did. No one deserves this scholarship more than you," Nasteho said, looking at me with a big smile on her face.

"Your name describes you well; you really are a blessing from God. Thank you!" I hugged her.

Nasteho always knew how to cheer me up. Our school bus pulled up to the front of our school.

"Ugh, why is it so cold! I love Minnesota, but this damn winter, ugh!" I said, shivering.

"What are you complaining about? It is only November. Winter hasn't even started yet. Things will only get colder from here," Nasteho said as she ran with me into the school building.

20

As Christmas turned into the new year, Minnesota's winter grew harsher, much like my mother-in-law. I felt like my mere existence frustrated her. One day, she got upset at me and said that my heavy breathing was distracting her from the news she was trying to watch. She didn't even understand English and had no idea what the newscaster was saying. I just kept silent.

Time was not moving as fast as I wanted it to move, but things were kind of coming together for me. I was getting closer to my dream. It was almost near the end of the four years of high school.

That evening when I came back from school, I found two letters for me in the mailbox—one was from the University of Minnesota, my first-choice college. The other was from the full-ride scholarship that Nasteho and my science teacher, Dr. H., had nominated me for.

I took the smelly elevator to the thirteenth floor; it always smelled like urine.

Why would anyone urinate in public? I thought as I left the elevator and walked down the long, dim hallway to get to our apartment.

Truly, it was my mother-in-law's apartment, which I shared with eight of my in-laws. It was a little crowded, but we made it work. I lived by the Somali saying that a family's love made any situation bearable.

I was glad that I was the first person to arrive home, because it meant I had a moment of peace. I walked up the metal stairs to the bedroom that I shared with my sisters-in-law. I sat on the lower bunk bed, holding the two letters in my hand.

Why are you so scared? Just open them. I tried to convince myself to open the letters.

What do you have to lose? If it's a yes, it's a good thing, and if it's a no, it's all right. You got into four other good schools, and you already received six of the thirty-two scholarships that you applied to. Plus, there are probably more on their way. Just open it. What's the worst that can happen?

I stood up and walked back and forth in the room and did several pow-er poses to help myself feel more in control.

Open it, Ayan. Whatever happens is what's best for you. God will help you. Just open it; everything will be all right, I convinced myself.

I opened the scholarship letter first, my heart pounding, I read the first line. It read:

> Dear Ayan Raage,
>
> Congratulations! We are honored to inform that you have been selected as this year's recipient of the S. E. Hogenson scholarship . . .

Tears filled my eyes. I hadn't been that happy for a long time. Wiping my tears, I opened the other letter from the University of Minnesota. It read:

> Dear Ayan Raage,
>
> We are pleased to inform you that you have been accepted to the University of Minnesota, college of biological sciences . . .

I put my forehead on the floor to prostrate to God to thank him for all the blessings. My tears flooded the floor. For the first time in years, I cried because of happiness.

I heard the door open. It was my mother-in-law; I knew her footsteps and the sound of her key chain. I ran down the stairs to her, holding my papers. Thrilled, I said, "Mom, I got in! I got into the school that I wanted to go to, and I received a full-ride scholarship!"

She looked at me with aversion. "But what about getting a job? You need to start saving money so you can bring Awale here. Why don't you start working full-time now and then go to college later when he gets here?" I knew she didn't understand me, but I couldn't help but wonder why she couldn't fake a smile and congratulate me.

"Don't worry, Mom, I will work very hard. I will go to college, and I will work at the same time to save up enough money to bring Awale here. And since I don't have to pay for college, I will be able to save up. I promise you, I will get him here as soon as I can."

"I know ungrateful women like yourself. You want to enjoy life in the United States while my son—*my son*—is in a refugee camp! College, college, college, is that all you care about? Do you care about anything besides yourself? You have a responsibility to this family, to me, and to Awale. Where are your priorities?" She was nearly crying. I had never seen her so distraught.

"I am sorry, Mother. I am sorry that it is taking so long for Awale to get here. I know you miss him, and I promise you he will get here soon. But he is going to college in Nairobi. You don't have to worry about him. He is doing fine. I talked to him this morning," I tried to calm her.

"What are you trying to say? Are you saying that I don't know what my son is doing or where he is?" she yelled at me again.

"I am sorry. That's not what I meant," I whispered.

Slowly, I walked back to my room. I wished, not for the first time, that Awale had come to America with us. I cried in frustration.

Through my bedroom door, I could hear Hibo, Hodan, and Hoodo as they entered the apartment. Nura was sitting in the living room, waiting for them.

"Where are you coming from at this hour?" she asked them.

"We were studying at the library," Hibo said.

"Other people your age are getting into universities and getting scholarships. What are you waiting for?"

To Nura, I had become "other people" instead of family. A harsh realization took over my body as I wiped my tears.

"We are going to community college first. Financial aid will cover most of it, and it's cheaper than the four-year university. We've applied to some jobs too," Hodan said.

"Jobs! Why are you applying to jobs? Who told you to apply to work? I don't want work getting in the way of your education. I will give you everything you need; just focus on your studies and finish school." She made it clear that she wanted them to go to college and get a higher education.

What have I done that she wishes to keep me in the dark without an education? I asked myself.

They started chatting about their dreams, goals, marriage, boys, and so many other things that I couldn't be part of. I listened to Nura talk and laugh in a way that she never did with me. I couldn't take listening to them anymore, so I got up and closed the door quietly.

21

It was my senior year of high school, a few months before graduation, when I told my mother-in-law that I was going to go to college. We had been in America for three years at that time. The immigration office had declined my application to bring Awale to America. I filed the paperwork for him the day I turned eighteen, but I didn't have enough income to sponsor him, and I couldn't prove to the government that I could take care of him financially. To be honest, I didn't blame the government. I didn't even have my own place, so how could I prove that I could take care of him financially?

I even thought of putting college on hold to work three jobs so I could make enough money and bring him over, but deep down, I knew I wouldn't be able to live with myself if I made that kind of sacrifice. I knew that if I put my education on hold, I would lose my scholarships and I might never get the chance to go to college. It was too big a price to pay. I knew that if I delayed college, I would eventually resent Awale, and that would be the end of our relationship. I knew that I had to continue with college, which meant that it would take me that much longer to bring Awale to America.

I was making dinner for my in-laws that evening, and they were all sitting in the living room waiting for me. I was trying to make dinner quickly and had all four burners on. I had tea on one, flatbread on another, beans on another, and soup on the last. The kitchen was hot and small, just enough space for one person to quickly walk behind me. There was a white fridge on my right by the wall. I was sweating, tired, and trying to make the food as fast as I could.

"What is taking you so long?" Nura yelled from the living room. "Bring the food. You are always so slow!"

It reminded me of when we were in Kenya and I would be in the kitchen cooking for them while they waited for the food together as a family.

"So, Ayan, what's your plan after graduation?" Haboon asked.

"I have been thinking a lot about this," I said. "I've decided to go to a four-year college. I got into my first choice, the University of Minnesota. What about you?"

"We are going to community college first and then transferring to four-year schools," Hodan said.

"You are going to college?" my mother-in-law said to me before I could reply to Haboon. "Didn't we talk about this? You have to save up enough money to bring Awale here. You have to work a lot. There won't be time for college."

"I will work and go to college at the same time. I have a full-ride scholarship. I will lose it if I am not full-time student. I cannot afford to lose it, Mother; I need to get an education so I can become a doctor." I had told her all of this before, and I hoped that she would not get angry with me this time.

"What's the point of you going to college? You are a woman. When my son gets here, you will be a wife. You will give birth to children, and your education will be wasted. You will get a high school diploma soon. That's good enough for a person like you." She tried to convince me to not go to college. At least she thought she was reasoning with me.

"I am a woman; that's more of a reason for me to get education," I said, suppressing my emotions. "I will be a wife and I will have kids someday, but God willing, I will also have a career. It's all about time management, Mother. I promise I will bring Awale here soon."

"You make promises you can't keep. There is nothing you can do right. I knew you were useless and good for nothing. I don't know why I keep asking you to bring him here. If you hadn't tricked my son into marrying you, you would have been rotting in a refugee camp, raped, maybe with a few kids and a husband who shows you your place, unlike my pathetic son."

"Really, Mom? You are such a hypocrite!" Hibo shouted. "How can you try to talk her out of college? She is the valedictorian. She got into one of the best colleges in the country on a full-ride scholarship. If anything, you should be proud of her or at least supporting her. We all know that you don't like her, but that doesn't mean you can abuse her. And you, Ayan, grow some spine!" Hibo stormed out of the living room.

"Keep disrespecting me and talking to me like that in front of other people. I should have slept the night I was giving birth to you!" Nura yelled after Hibo.

"What other people?" Hibo shouted from the other room. "Your daughters? Or do you mean Ayan? She is your daughter-in-law. Fear God and stop abusing her. I honestly don't know why she respects you so much."

"Had my son Awale been here, you wouldn't have been talking to me like that!" my mother-in-law cried.

"Had Awale been here, he wouldn't have let you talk to or treat his wife like that." Hibo closed the door with a loud bang.

"Are you happy with what you have done?" Nura yelled at me. "You have turned my son against me and now my daughters."

"I am sorry, Mother." I continued cooking dinner. Once I finished cooking, I put it on the table for them and went to my bedroom. I didn't feel like eating.

Hibo soon came into the bedroom with a book and lay down on her bed. I could see that she was angry.

"Hibo, go eat some food. And don't worry. She is just having a hard time. It's rude and disrespectful to talk to your mother like that."

"She is so mean to you, and she has always been mean to you since we came to America. But you never say a word against her. Don't you have a spine or any blood in you? She doesn't deserve your respect. I honestly don't know why you put up with her," Hibo said, upset.

"She is the closest thing I have to a mother," I said as tears filled my eyes.

"You are the best daughter, sister, and daughter-in-law anyone could ever wish for. I really hope she sees that before it's too late. I am sorry that you have been through all that and now you have to go through this. You should have married to a better family that would have loved you unconditionally." She came to me and hugged me.

"She will come around once Awale gets here," I said. "Don't worry. I am happy and very blessed to be in this family. Awale loves me, you love me, and everyone else does. I would not trade our family for the world. Life is not perfect, Hibo; every family has its weakness and issues. We will work through ours."

"I love you. It just makes me so upset how she is treating you and how you don't ever say anything back to her. I am sorry, Ayan."

"I love you too, Hibo. Now go eat some food before it gets cold."

"Ayan, tomorrow, I want to take you to a very special place, just the two of us. You can bring Nasteho too if you'd like. I want to do something nice for you."

"Okay," I said, "but what is it?" I felt the tingle of a surprise all over my body.

"It's a surprise," she said, smiling. "That's all I'll say until tomorrow."

Hibo went downstairs, and I got ready for bed.

I heard my phone vibrating as I was drifting into sleep.

"Hi, Ayan. How are you, my dear wife?" Awale said in a sweet tone that made me realize how much I missed him.

"I am doing fine. How are you, honey?" I greeted him, pulling the covers over my head.

"I am good, but I miss you terribly. I miss seeing your smile every morning and eating the food you cook. I miss holding you in my arms and smelling your perfume."

"I miss you too, Awale. I miss you so much and wish you were here. I think in a few more years I will be able to bring you here. May God bless us both with the patience to wait for each other," I said as tears rolled down my cheeks.

"How is Mom treating you?" Awale asked. "I heard she is giving you a hard time. I will talk to her."

"Mom is good to me. She treats me like her own daughter. I am so blessed to have her as a mother-in-law. How are you? Did you decide on a major yet?" I asked.

"Are you crying?" Awale asked.

"No. Tell me what's new with school and life." I tried to distract him.

"Are you all right, darling? I know you are crying. What happened?" Awale asked.

"I just miss you so much."

"I miss you too, my love. God willing, we will be reunited soon." He kissed me through the phone.

"Did you decide on a major yet?" I asked him.

"Yes, dear, I decided on computer science. How is high school? You are almost done. I am so proud of you!" he said.

"Thank you so much, my love. I am very grateful and excited to go to university on a full-ride scholarship."

"That's my wife! What did you decide? And did you tell Mom?"

"It's not much of a decision, but I am going to the University of Minnesota. I submitted the deposit yesterday. I haven't told Mom yet. I don't know how to tell her. She is so worried about you, and she wants me to work and bring you here before I go to college."

"No, dear, go to university and get your education first. I will always be here for you. I am going to a university, and I am living in a safe place. There is no need for you to worry about me. Focus on your school and achieving your dream. God willing, we will be together soon."

"Thank you, Awale; your support means the world to me. I love you more than my words can describe. I want you to be here with me more than anything, but it's really hard to pay half the rent, electricity, water, and everything else in the house and try to save up," I said.

"I want you to succeed and achieve your goals," Awale said emotionally. "Don't worry about me. And I want you to know that I love you no matter what."

22

In my third year of college, I came home from work one day exhausted. It was around 11:00 p.m. when I walked into the building. It had been a really long day, going from school to work. My feet and body were aching. I was worried about my midterms the following week, and I had homework due the next day.

I walked quietly into our apartment. It looked like everyone was sleeping. I put my backpack on the floor by the sofa and went to the kitchen to see if there was anything that I could eat. I got some oranges and water. I sat on the sofa and started working on my homework as I ate the oranges. After about thirty minutes, the phone rang. I picked it up, but before I said hello, Nura picked up the other phone in her bedroom.

"Hello?" Nura said.

"Hello, Mom; it is Awale." I was so happy to hear his voice. I hadn't talked to him for about four weeks at that time. I missed him so much.

"Hi, Awale. How are you doing, my son? We miss you so much!" Nura said.

I quietly stayed on the line, listening to their conversation. I just wanted to hear his voice.

"I am doing well, Mom. I miss you too! How is everyone doing?" Awale said.

"We are doing well, my son. Everyone is doing well—everyone, that is, except Ayan," she said.

"Is Ayan all right? What happened to her? Is—"
Nura cut him off before he could finish his sentence. "Relax. Nothing is wrong with her! Why do you care so much about that horrible woman? She doesn't even care about you!" Nura said.

"Mom, please be nice to Ayan. She is my life, and she means the world to me," Awale said.

"She does? When was the last time she called you?" Nura said.

"I haven't talked to her for a while. That's why I called tonight. I was hoping that it was late enough for you and that she was at home. Is she at home?" Awale asked.

"You are so innocent, my son! That woman has you wrapped around her finger! She doesn't care about you! When will you wake up!" Nura said.

"Mom, please don't start this again. Why do you dislike her so much? What has she ever done to you?" Awale asked.

"She is a selfish person who only cares about herself! She has been in the US for six years, and she doesn't want to bring you here with us. All she cares about is her education!" Nura said.

"Mom, please, we both know that is not true. Ayan does more for you than any of your daughters do. Please be nice to her," Awale said.

"You are trying to side with her now! It is true. If she wanted to bring you here, she could have! How many people who have come after us have brought their spouses over to America? Just think and tell me I am lying!" Nura said.

"Mom, our circumstances are different," Awale said.

"Is that so? Okay, when was the last time she contacted you? When was the last time she answered your phone? She has been working for years. If you can't come to America, did she ever bother to come visit you? She is an American citizen and can travel to Kenya," Nura said.

"You have a point, Mom, but I am sure Ayan has her reasons."

"I am sure she does have her own selfish reasons! She doesn't care about you, Awale; she just used you to come to America. If she wants you with us like she says, why isn't she bringing you here? Why is she not calling you or answering your calls? Why isn't she coming to visit you?" Nura said.

Awale was silent.

"Also, this woman that you care so much about has friends who are men. She is hanging out with other men. And she comes home late every day," Nura said. "What kind of good wife hangs out late with men who are not her husband? Awale, you are my son, and I want what is best for you. This woman does not care about you. You need to start thinking for yourself."

"What men are you talking about?" Awale asked.

"Ask her who Ahmed, Ali, and Max are!" Nura said.

"Who are they? How do you know about them?" Awale asked.

"I tried to open your eyes many times, but you are blinded by love! Wake up, my son!" Nura said.

Awale was silent. My heart dropped. *I hope Awale is not starting to believe her lies.*

"Anyhow, I think she is home. It is midnight, and she just got home. Do you want me to give her the phone?" Nura asked.

"No, it's okay, Mom. I will talk to her some other time. Tell everyone I said hello," Awale hung up the phone.

I tried to focus on my homework, but I couldn't. I became so restless. I put away my homework and went to bed. I tossed and turned but couldn't fall asleep.

The next morning, I got out of the house extra early to stop by a nearby halal store. I bought two calling cards for ten dollars to call Awale. I called his phone, but Awale wouldn't answer. For the next two weeks, I continued trying to call him, but he didn't answer.

I went to Wilson Library on the university campus, took out my journal, and started writing a letter to Awale to explain to him. I wanted to tell him how I felt and how much I missed him.

Dear Awale,

It hurts me how much we have grown apart. I know how hard it must be for you to live in Nairobi without your family, especially without me. I know that I don't always get a chance to talk to you on the phone every day like we used to when we first moved to America. I miss you more than my words can describe, and I love you more than anything else in this world.

I have never looked at any other man. I have never dated any other men, and I have never loved any man but you. You are the first and the last person on my mind. You are the only man that I long for, the only man that I truly love. I wish I could open my chest just to show you my heart. I wish I could take your hand and put it on my heart just to show you how much of my heart beats for you.

Without you, every day is a battle for me. Sometimes, I feel like I am being punished for something that I don't understand. I am not in heaven, and you are not in hell. I don't get a chance to speak with you much, not because I don't care about you but because I am struggling with all the responsibilities on my shoulders. I know it is hard for you to understand what I am going through in America because you are not here to experience it with me. But know that I am not ignoring you, and no one means more to me than you do.

When we got to America, I started going to high school. As you know, the legal age to become an adult in America is eighteen years, and I was fifteen. I couldn't file a petition to bring you to America as my husband while I was still a minor. I had to wait for three years to even be able to file a petition for you. I wanted to bring you to America, I wanted to be with you more than anything else, but I couldn't violate the law. Those first three years were the longest years of my life. I missed you so much that sometimes I felt like someone was holding a flaming torch under my heart.

Once I turned sixteen, I started working part-time after school to financially support our family. I often had to stay up late to do my homework and study for classes after work. I was physically and mentally tired. Your mom still blames me for not bringing you to America. She gives me a hard time and makes my life harder every single day. I never told you how much pain and hurt she is causing me because I don't want to strain your relationship with your mother. I never complain, I never talk back to her, and I never say anything against her.

The hope of you someday coming to America keeps me going. She is my legal guardian, and I don't have anyone else in America. I quietly listen to her daily taunts. I am grateful to your sister Hibo and my friend Nasteho; they are the only people who keep me going. At times, I feel like I can no longer breathe, but then I remember you and I get up again, I gain my breath again.

I filed a petition to bring you to America the day that I turned eighteen, but I wasn't making enough money to sponsor you. My application for you was denied. I took another job and started working longer hours. I was barely getting four hours of sleep each day. I fainted at work and at school due to exhaustion several times, but I never complained. I kept working, kept my head down, and hoped for a better tomorrow.

I have been filing petitions again and again to bring you here with us, but my applications have been denied. I don't make enough money to bring you to America, and I cannot quit college to work full-time or I will lose my scholarship. I cannot afford to pay for college without the scholarship. I cannot afford to sacrifice everything for you and your family.

I tried saving money so I can come to Nairobi to see you, but supporting you and your family makes it impossible for me to save enough money to travel. All I wanted was your love and a family to belong to, but your mom has never accepted me as part of your family.

What hurts me the most is not your mother's harsh words, not even my struggles at work and at school, but the fact that we are growing apart each day. What hurts me is the thought of you moving further away from me. What hurts the most is hearing you believe the lies that your mom is feeding you. It is the thought that you think I don't care about you and that I don't love you, when the truth is that there is nothing on this planet that I care more about and love more than you. Not even my own soul.

I feel like I am burning my soul for you and for your family, but none of you even notice. I cannot afford to lose my mental health and my well-being. I am going to decide for myself from now on. I will still support you and your family, but I need to make some changes to take care of myself. I have sacrificed enough.

Yours,

Ayan Raage

Three weeks later, Awale called the house, and I answered the phone.

"Awale, how are you, my dear?" I said.

"I am okay. You?" Awale said, and his voice sounded far away. I felt like someone stabbed my heart. The distance between us seemed so big.

"I am doing well, my love! I miss you! I have been trying to call you. Is everything okay, my heart?" I asked.

"I am okay. How is school and life?" Awale asked.

"School is good, and life is hard without you. I wish you were here!" I said.

"You do? Then why don't you bring me to America? Or come visit me?" Awale said.

"Please don't talk like that, Awale; you know I have been trying to get you to America from the day I set a foot here. You know I can't afford to visit you. I support you and your family. I work two jobs, and I am going to school full-time," I said.

"You have been using those excuses for six years, Ayan. I am starting to believe that maybe you don't really care about me or want to be with me," Awale said.

"Awale, this is Nura's talk, not yours. Please don't make things harder for me than they already are."

"What is hard for you? I heard you are enjoying life in America without me. And who are those men that I am hearing you are hanging out with? You are a married woman. Why would you even be talking to other men?" Awale said.

"Awale, you are crossing a line. I am not that kind of woman. They are my college friends," I responded to him.

"I don't care who they are! You need to stop being friends with them. I don't want you talking to other men!" Awale said.

"Who are you to tell me who I can and can't be friends with? I am not going to drop my friends just because you said so and because you are so insecure. Do you even trust me?" I said.

"I don't know, Ayan! Should I be trusting you?" Awale said.

I hung up the phone and went to the bathroom to cry in solitude. After crying for what seemed like hours, I got out of the bathroom and went to sleep.

That next morning, I called Awale again. He answered this time.

"Awale, I am sorry. I shouldn't have hung up the phone on you," I said.

"I am sorry, Ayan. I shouldn't have talked to you like that," Awale said.

"How are you?" I asked.

"I am doing fine. I miss you a lot! How are you, my soul?" Awale said.

"I am doing fine. I miss you too. Awale, I hope you didn't believe your mom. You know I am not that type of woman. I would never do anything to hurt you," I said.

"Ayan, I know you will never hurt me. But is it true? Are you really friends with all these men?" Awale asked.

"They are my friends from school. There is nothing between us. We just help each other out at school," I responded.

"Ayan, I know, but please don't give society anything to doubt. Why don't you find women friends at school? Why do you have to be friends with men?" Awale said.

"Awale, I am not going to explain to you why I am friends with my friends; please stop this."

"Ayan, I am your husband. I have a right to tell you not to hang out with strange men just like you have the right to tell me not to hang out with strange women," Awale said.

"Awale, I am not a child for you to tell me who I can and cannot be friends with. I can't believe we are even having this conversation. I don't tell you what to do; please don't tell me who I can and cannot be friends with," I responded.

"Ayan, do you even care about me? I am not even sure I know you anymore. You don't call me for weeks, you are always busy when I call you. You don't want to bring me to America. You don't want to visit me. Why don't you just tell me what you really want," Awale said.

"Awale, I have to get ready for my second job. I have to go. Have a good night!"

"Exactly my point! Have a good night," Awale said and hung up the phone.

I went to the bathroom and called Nasteho.

"Nasteho, I feel like I am losing my mind. I don't think I can take this anymore. I need to get out of this house," I said in tears.

"Is everything okay, dear? What happened?" Nasteho asked.

"Nura keeps taunting me, and now she is trying to poison Awale against me. Awale is starting to doubt me. He thinks I don't care about him. He had the audacity to tell me that I cannot be friends with Ahmed, Max, and Ali. It is one thing for her to be mean to me, but to try and get between me and Awale!" I cried.

"I am so sorry, dear! What are you going to do?" Nasteho said.

"I am moving out!" I said.

"It is about time, Ayan. You have put up with them long enough," Nasteho said.

"I have, and I can't take it anymore. I feel like someone is holding a torch under my heart. I feel like I'm being suffocated, Nasteho."

"We have a spare room. Do you want to move in with us? You can have the whole basement to yourself. There is a living room, bedroom, and bathroom there. You don't have to worry about paying rent. This would be a good way for you to save enough money too. Maybe you can finally go see Awale," Nasteho offered.

"Thank you, Nasteho. You are such a wonderful friend, but I don't want to burden you and your husband. I will try to find a cheap place, maybe with a roommate," I said.

"Come on, Ayan, you know we see you as family. You will never burden us. This is what family and friends are for. Come, move in with us. I am pregnant, and you know how much my husband works. I could use your help too. Please move in with us," Nasteho said.

"I don't know. I would love to help you, Nasteho, but I work a lot and I have to study a lot. I might not be able to help you much, and I don't want to be a burden to you and your family. You have helped me a lot!" I said.

"You don't even have to help me! Ayan, I care about you and your well-being. You need to get out of that house," Nasteho said.

"Let me think about it," I said.

About four weeks later, I decided to move in with Nasteho and her family. Nura made a big deal out of me moving out. She called Awale while I was coming down from the stairs with my luggage in my right hand.

"Awale, this woman is out of hand! She won't listen to a word that I say. She doesn't respect me or you," Nura told Awale over the phone.

"Mom, hi, how are you? And what are you talking about?" Awale said.

"I am talking about your wife! She said she is moving out! She started hanging out with men, and now she wants to go live with people that I don't know," Nura said.

"Is Ayan near you? Can I talk to her?" Awale said.

"Yes! Here, talk some sense into her!" Nura handed me the phone and stared at me as if she could murder me with her eyes.

"Hello, Awale, how are you, dear?" I said.

"I am doing fine, my heart. What is going on? Mom said you are moving out?" Awale said.

"Yes, Awale, I am moving out. I can't put up with your mom anymore. I am sick and tired of her taunts and her coming between us. I am moving out right now," I said.

"You should have discussed this with us before you made such a major decision," Awale said.

"There is nothing to discuss. I have had enough of your mother! I have a right to live in a place where my well-being is not constantly under attack! I can't live with this woman!" I said.

"Ayan, that's your mother-in-law you are talking about. Where is your respect?"

"Awale, I've had enough. I am going to move out whether you and your mom agree to it or not. Bye!" I said.

"Ayan, don't you dare set a foot outside that house," Awale said.

"Come and stop me," I said and hung up the phone.

I grabbed my luggage and my backpack and walked out the door. I couldn't stop crying as I walked the never-ending hallway toward the stinky elevators.

The following weeks were very hard for me to adjust to living at Nasteho's house. I missed Awale and wanted to talk to him. I finally got a calling card and called him. We apologized to each other, but our relationship was not the same as before. I filed a new petition to bring him to America again and was waiting to hear back from the immigration office. I began saving money because I had stopped giving money to Nura, but I continued to send money to Awale.

Awale called me once a month. Our phone conversations went from once a month to once every two months. Instead of hours of chatting and laughing with each other, now we talked for just a few minutes as we checked in with each other. I missed Awale, and I didn't know how to get back to how we were.

About six months later, on a Friday, I received a letter from the immigration office. I went to my room and prayed before I opened it. When I pulled the letter out, I read that my petition for Awale was finally accepted. I screamed with happiness and thanked God. I ran to Nasteho and shared the happy news with her.

I called Awale, but his phone was off. I called Hibo and told her that I wanted to see her. Hibo, Nasteho, little Ayan, and I went to Mall of America that Saturday. Nasteho, little Ayan, and I carpooled. Hibo met us at the food court. I showed the letter to Hibo, who smiled.

"This is good news. Congratulations, Ayan," Hibo said, forcing herself to smile.

"Thank you, Hibo. Is everything okay? I expected a little bit more happiness from you. This means so much to me! I can't wait to share this news with Awale! He will be so happy! I can finally bring him to America! Oh, I can't wait to finally see him and hug him and fall sleep in his arms," I said with happy tears filling my eyes.

Hibo hugged me and said, "Let's go shopping!"

We went to Macy's, where I found a beautiful black maxi dress on the clearance rack.

"This is such a beautiful dress! Ayan, you should get this one! Maybe you can wear this for Awale," Nasteho said.

"Oh, no, I can't. I have to save every penny that I can! I will have to get us our own little place, a home for me and Awale. I will need to order furniture." I started imagining my little world with Awale.

"I agree with Nasteho," Hibo said, almost getting emotional. "I think you should take this dress and a couple of other beautiful dresses. You deserve it! You've worked so hard for years. It is time to think of yourself, Ayan."

"Thank you, Hibo, but I really can't."

We walked around the mall a little bit more, and I talked about all the things I could finally show Awale when he arrived.

"We should go to a spa!" Hibo said.

"The spa!" Nasteho said, laughing. "You think Ayan will go to the spa?"

"It is okay to enjoy a little! What do you work so hard for if you can't enjoy it!" Hibo said.

"How about this. We go eat lunch, and I will pay for us," I said.

"Oh my God! You broke her, Hibo! Ayan is willing to spend money on food," Nasteho teased me.

"Let's go before I change my mind," I said.

We went to the food court and had our lunch. I didn't buy any clothes or go to the spa. I wanted to save every penny that I had earned. I wanted to find an apartment for Awale and me. I wanted to order furniture for our home. I couldn't wait to share the news with Awale.

I couldn't stop smiling.

Hibo ate her food quickly and said that she had an appointment that she needed to run to. She avoided eye contact and quickly left the mall.

"What is up with Hibo today?" Nasteho asked.

"I am not sure," I said. "She seems a little off today."

"Maybe she had a fight with her mom," Nasteho said.

"I don't think so. I think something is going on. She will talk to me about it when she is ready. Hibo likes to take her time, process her emotions on her own, and then share them with people close to her," I said.

"I hope it is nothing serious."

I started to feel uneasy, like something unpleasant was going to happen. I ignored my gut feeling and reasoned that I was probably just worried about Hibo.

Nasteho wanted to go to the aquarium, so we went to the aquarium and then walked around the mall a little more before going home.

In the middle of the night, my phone rang, and I woke quickly. "Ugh! Who is calling me at this hour! I have only four hours to sleep! Why are they calling me?" I cursed the phone but forced myself out of bed to pick it up.

"Hello?" I answered.

"Hello, hi, Ayan. How are you?"

"Hibo? I am fine. Is everything all right?" I asked worriedly.

"Yeah, I am all right. How are you?" Hibo asked.

"I am doing great. It's two in the morning. Are you okay?"

"Yeah, I am. I just couldn't sleep. How is work and school?"

"It's a hustle, but I am getting the hang of it. I am almost there. How are you? How is the family?"

"Good, good, good! It must be hard to be a full-time university student and work two jobs. When do you sleep?" she asked.

"I sleep whenever I get a chance. I usually get about four hours, but I am very blessed and happy. How is Mom doing?" I asked her.

"She is good. How are you?"

"Hibo, what's going on? What's wrong?" I asked her.

"Nothing. Just saying hi."

"Come on, Hibo, I know you better than that. Please tell me what's going on."

"Well, it's nothing big. It's just one of my friends is going to get hurt, and I am really worried about her."

"Who? Why would she? What's going on?" I asked her.

"Well, her husband betrayed her, and she doesn't know about it. I don't know what to do. That's why I couldn't sleep." I could hear the concern in her voice.

"Are you sure? If you are not sure, don't get involved. Something like that could ruin their life even if it's not true," I advised her.

"I am sure!" she responded.

"If you are sure, then you must tell her. It's better for her to find out sooner than later," I suggested.

"I don't know. I don't want to see her getting hurt. I love her more than my own sisters. If you were in her shoes, would you want to know?" she asked.

"Yes, of course!" I said without giving it a second thought.

"Um . . . ," she hesitated, and then the line was quiet.

"Hello, are you there?" I asked.

"Awale came!" she said.

A mixture of happy, confusing, and surprising feelings took over my body. I was happy that Awale was finally in America, but I was confused about how he'd gotten here. I had only recently learned that the immigration office had approved his application, but we hadn't yet had a chance to make the travel arrangements for him.

"That's a nice surprise," I said. "When did he come? Why didn't he tell me?"

"He has been here for a few weeks," she said.

"What do you mean he has been here for a few weeks? I didn't hear from him."

"Because Mom, Awale, and his new wife wanted to surprise you." Hibo started crying.

"His new wife! What? That's impossible! Hibo, there are certain things you shouldn't joke about," I scolded her.

"I am not joking. He married Salma. She brought him here, and he has been living with her in Minneapolis for about three weeks now."

"Hibo, it's late. I have to go back to sleep. I don't know what to say right now. Good night." I hung up the phone on her.

I felt weak in my knees, and I slumped to the ground. My chest started constricting, and my breathing got harder. My head felt as if it were about to explode, and my heart felt as if it would escape from my chest.

"This can't be true! Awale would never do this to me. That witch wants to create problems between Awale and me. She must have put Hibo up to this!" I cried in denial and tried to convince myself that it was all a bad dream. I tried to shut out the thought that Awale could do such a thing to me, but I couldn't sleep.

I knew Hibo, and I knew deep down that she would never lie to me like that. I couldn't help but believe her words. I sat on the floor and cried silently.

The next morning, Nasteho knocked on my door. "Ayan, it's almost noon. Aren't you going to work and school today?"

I opened the door. "I am not feeling well; I can't go to work today. Could you please call them and tell them that I won't be able to come in?" I whispered as tears rolled from my eyes.

"Are you all right, dear? You are crying, and your eyes are all red. What happened?" Nasteho asked, holding her one-year-old daughter, little Ayan, on her side.

"No, I am not all right at all." I hugged Nasteho and started sobbing.

"What's wrong? Who died? Tell me what happened?"

"It's Awale," I responded.

"What about him? Let's sit down."

"Hibo called me last night. She said that Awale is in Minneapolis and that he has been here for a few weeks now," I said, sobbing like a child.

"Isn't that good news? Why are you crying?" Nasteho asked.

"He married Salma. That's how he got here!"

"That's impossible! I am sure that witch put her up to this. Don't let this get to you. Awale would never do that to you," Nasteho tried to comfort me. "I have Salma's number. I will call her. This cannot be true." Nasteho frantically looked for Salma's number, and when she called her, she put her on speakerphone.

After the second ring, Salma picked up.

"Hi, Salma, how are you?"

"Oh, hi, Nasteho, I am doing great! How are you and your little baby? I haven't heard from you in ages!" I could hear the evil happiness in her voice.

"We are doing great. What a nice surprise, though, I heard you got married. What's that about? You didn't bother to invite us to your wedding? I thought we were friends!" Nasteho chuckled, trying to conceal her feelings.

"I am so sorry, Nasteho. I wanted to invite you, but I got very busy. The family was handling the wedding invitations. It was nothing big, just family."

"Oh, that's fine, congratulations. Who is the lucky guy? Do we know him?" Nasteho asked.

"Well, you kind of know him. He is Aunt Nura's oldest son, Awale." Once his name came out of her mouth, a feeling I had never before felt took over my body. My chest constricted, and my breathing became ever so difficult. I felt like someone had pulled the rug out from under my feet and I was floating in space. My tears just disappeared.

"That's great. Congratulations. Wasn't he in Kenya?"

"Yes, he was, but I brought him to Minnesota a few weeks ago."

"Congratulations; I am so happy for you. Let me say hi to him. I want to congratulate him," Nasteho said.

"Awale, come here, babe! Come say hi to my friend Nasteho."

"Greetings, Nasteho. How are you, sister?" It was his voice.

My world became so small, it could no longer hold me. It felt like someone had sucked the life right out of my body. My heart shattered into pieces.

"Hi, Awale, I am doing great. Hope you are too. Congratulations," Nasteho said as tears filled her eyes.

"Thank you," he politely replied.

"Welcome to Minnesota. Um . . . I have to go now. It's nice to meet you." Nasteho hung up the phone before he could speak again.

23

I didn't know how to take it. I didn't know what to do. All I could think of were my mother's words when she told me to expect nothing from people and from the jungle. I should have listened to her.

I got up and smiled. "Nasteho, why are you crying? It's just a man. I buried my family and lost everyone who was related to me. This is nothing. Stop crying. Some people don't deserve tears." I patted her shoulder, and then I washed my face and got ready to leave.

On the inside, I felt like I was breaking and everything was falling apart. There was only one place I could go that would make me feel better.

I went to the spa at the Mall of America and booked myself four hours—two hours of full-body massage, one hour of facial, and one of waxing. After my spa, I went to the shops. I started with Macy's and bought the cutest dress I could find. I then went to a nice restaurant and had a full meal by myself. I spent the whole day treating myself.

I had never treated myself to the spa and never bought clothes unless I absolutely had to buy them. I had never spent any of my money to treat myself for the past seven years. I was a full-time college student and working multiple jobs since high school to save up enough money to sponsor Awale and financially support his family.

I returned home late that evening.

"Wow, Ayan, you are sparkling. Where did you go?" Nasteho asked me.

"I went to the spa and then shopping. It was a beautiful day for me." I could tell Nasteho wanted to ask me how I was feeling. I knew she wanted to put on her therapist hat. "Don't worry, Nasteho, I am fine. If there is anything I've learned in life, it's how to block and get rid of useless emotions. Now I can focus on me and treat myself right. I shouldn't have neglected myself for him."

"Ayan, it's all right to cry and be angry. I am here for you; don't bottle it up. Just let it go—cry, be angry, break things if you have to," Nasteho said.

"I promise, I am all right. Don't worry about me, Nasteho." I hugged her and went to my room.

The next day, I started looking for an apartment of my own. With all the money that I had been saving, I could live on my own without working for a couple of years. I put in my notice for my jobs and started focusing only on school. I started looking at medical schools and registered for the MCAT class.

Soon I found an apartment a few blocks from Nasteho's house. I ordered nice furniture and decorated my place like I had always wanted to.

Every morning, I looked at the mirror on my closet door and remind myself who I was and that I was going to be happy.

Every night, I looked at the necklace that Uncle Ali had given me that read *Dr. Ayan*. It reminded me of my goals, where I was headed, and what I had to do. It kept me going.

About a month later, the Saturday before finals week, my school friends came to my apartment to study. Max was lying on the sofa, writing a final paper for his technical writing class. Megan, Ahmed, and Alia were sitting at my dining table discussing and reviewing their notes for their biochemistry class. Ali was sitting on the floor, going through his notes for his math class, and I was on my love seat under the window, working on my last genetics homework for that semester. We had snacks, tea, pizza, and rice on the kitchen island. Coffee was brewing. My white curtains were open to let in the sunlight and to get a glimpse of the lake as we studied. All the lights were turned on—we needed all the light we could get for the long study hours.

I heard a knock on my door, and I opened it. Awale was standing there. He was right in front of me, tall and built. He had gained a lot of muscle since I'd last seen him. He'd grown a full beard that made him look a lot maturer than when I'd left Kenya. He was darker, and his hairline had receded a little; his Somali forehead was finally showing its true colors. It had been almost seven years since I had last seen him. His eyes were as mesmerizing as always, with his lashes curling up.

I felt so small standing in front of him. I was shocked at first, and I wanted to jump in his arms and hug him tightly. He looked so handsome! But I had to stay strong and hide those feelings. My heart started to beat fast, but after what he had done to me, I had to be strong.

I took a deep breath and smiled. "Hi, Awale. What a nice surprise! Come on in." I held the door for him to let him into my house.

My friends were still laughing about some joke I'd missed.

"Hey, guys, this is Awale, my ex-husband."

"What? When did you get divorced? Last time I knew, you were working two jobs to get him here. What happened?" Ahmed asked.

"Long story short, life goes on." I chuckled nervously.

"God blessed you with such a beautiful and smart girl, and you let her go?" Ali said, shaking Awale's hand. "Hello, Awale, I am Ali."

"What do you mean by *ex-husband*?" Awale laughed. "I am still your husband."

"Stop claiming to be my husband unless you want to go to jail," I said, looking at him furiously.

"Lovers' quarrel, huh? Hi, I am Max," Max joked and shook Awale's hand.

"Awale, these are my friends from school. That is Ahmed, that's Megan, and that's Alia." Awale shook Ahmed's hand and waved to Megan and Alia.

"Please, sit down. I will get you some tea."

Awale sat down uncomfortably, and I went to the kitchen to get him tea and some cookies. I didn't realize that I was crying until I saw a tear drop into the tea. I dumped the tea into the sink and poured him another cup. I reminded myself to be strong.

Ayan, Ayan, listen to me, don't break down now. Don't give him what he wants. Stay strong. You have lost everyone you have ever called yours; you can handle losing one person more. Get ahold of yourself! Breathe! I calmed myself down and wiped my tears. I went to the living room and put the tea and cookies in front of him.

He kept trying to catch my gaze, and I kept trying to avoid his eyes. My friends realized the tension and that we hadn't seen each other for over seven years. They decided that it was a good time to call it a day.

"We have to go. Thanks for letting us study at your place, Ayan. We will see you tomorrow," Ahmed said as they left.

Awale and I sat there for a while, with neither one of us uttering a word.

"Seven years, huh! You still look as beautiful," he started.

"Six years, close to seven years! Thank you," I responded.

"Nice place! How is school going?"

"Thanks. School is going well." There were more silent moments than words.

"So how have you been? How is life?" he asked.

"As you can see, life is beautiful. God is great; I am very blessed." I forced myself to smile. I accidently met his eyes, and I saw anger and hatred in the midst of the love that I remembered.

I guess distance doesn't make all hearts grow fonder of each other.

"I heard that you had forgotten everyone, including me," Awale said.

"Oh, well, sometimes you just have to do what you have to do. Life is short. Who can waste time waiting for other people?" I said, swallowing my emotions.

"I never thought you could change so much. You must have heard by now that I had gotten married."

"Yes, congratulations! I am happy for you. I hope she is someone who won't forget you like I did." I was trying to hold on to the last of my dignity.

"Thank you! So what's going on with you? Any wedding bells?" he asked.

"Well, now that you are here, I think so. I couldn't just get married whenever I wanted to. I have to get divorced from you first," I said.

"You are not remorseful at all, are you?" He chuckled in disbelief.

"Remorseful? No, why would I be? I haven't committed any crimes."

"You haven't? I will leave that to God. There really is such a thing as karma, you know."

"Well, be my guest and send all the karma my way," I said, looking into his eyes with a fake smile.

"I loved you, chose you over my family, stayed faithful to you for seven years, and married you when everyone else told me not to marry you. I was there for you when you had no one with you and supported you. I gave you my heart. I just cannot believe that I have been such a fool. I am glad that

God has blessed me with such a great mother who opened my eyes," he said as tears filled his eyes.

"Six years, almost seven years! May she live long for you! What is the real reason you came here? Did you want to give me a divorce? I have been waiting for it for a long time; I would appreciate it if you would divorce me right now. America is such a large country; we never have to see each other, and we can be happy with the people that we love." I was barely able to hold my tears back.

"I never knew you could be such a heartless person."

"There are a lot of things that you don't know, and you didn't care enough to ask. Why not make this easy for both of us? Give me all three of them. Just say you divorce me three times. Just divorce me right now!" I could feel the pain in my heart; it was as if someone were repeatedly stabbing my heart with a jagged knife. I wanted to hold him, kiss him on the forehead, and tell him that I cared for and loved him. I wanted to tell him that I loved him more than anyone else in this world. But it was too late. I knew that he would not believe me.

"I cannot divorce you right now; we need witnesses," he said.

"Give me your number. I will arrange for witnesses. All you have to do is to come and divorce me," I said.

Suddenly, he got up, angry. I stood up too. He came toward me and hugged me tightly. It felt so nice that I almost forgot everything that he had done. He held me tighter, and I wanted to be in his arms forever. I could feel his tears dripping on my shoulder.

"I will never divorce you," he said, pushing me away. "You will forever be bound by our marriage, and you will never be able to marry your lover. Not while I am still alive. I hate that I still love you and that my heart still aches for you." He went for his shoes and tried to hide his tears from me.

"You haven't given me a shelter or food, and you haven't taken care of me for seven years!" I told him. "There is no imam that will not grant me a divorce from you without your consent."

"Suit yourself! Go divorce yourself!" He stormed out of my apartment.

I closed the door and started sobbing.

A few weeks later, I was out grocery shopping with Nasteho when I saw them together—Awale and his wife. I just wanted to disappear into thin air. I stared at them for a good minute, longing to take my rightful place by Awale's side.

"Ayan, are you all right? Is everything okay?" Nasteho touched my shoulder.

"Yeah, I am perfectly fine. I will go get some cereal." I walked away from Nasteho and hid my tears.

"I will say hi to Salma and that bastard," Nasteho said.

As I was grabbing a cereal box, I heard, "Does it hurt to see me with my beautiful wife?"

"People don't get hurt when they see someone using the trash they have discarded. I am happy for you, Awale. By the way, I will remember to invite you to my wedding."

"I will never divorce you!" He got so close to me that I could feel his breath on my face.

"Like you have that kind of power!" I said, pushing him away. "I will get a divorce from you—just wait and watch. After all, I have three ways. Would you like to know them?"

"You cannot invent your own laws, and I promise you I will never divorce you," he said.

"I am not scared of being alone. I will get a divorce from you, mark my words! The only reason I am even talking you is because I am not an ungrateful person." I walked away from him.

I bit my upper lip and then took a deep breath. I faked a laugh, louder than necessary, so he could hear me as I walked away.

Shortly after that encounter at the grocery store, I received a call from Awale's mom.

"Hi, Ayan. How are you?" she asked.

"I am doing great, very blessed. How are you, Mother?" I replied.

"I am not your mother; don't call me that. I am doing great, never been better. I just called you to share some happy news with you." I could hear the evil happiness in her tone.

"I am glad life is treating you well," I said.

"I am finally going to be a grandmother! Salma is pregnant. My son Awale will be a father soon." I could tell she was smiling and waiting for my reaction.

"That's such wonderful news! Congratulations! Thanks for letting me know, and congratulate them for me."

"Thank you, dear. Say, Masha Allah, you never know who has an evil eye. I will do so, and please come by my house this Saturday. We are having a family party to celebrate their marriage. I am sure you will enjoy it," she said.

"Masha Allah, thank you for the invitation, Mother, I mean, Nura. Bad habits are hard to let go of. I am a little busy this weekend. Besides, I am not really your family. But since you took the trouble to invite me, I will see if I can make it." I hung up the phone.

I went to the mirror and looked myself in the eye. I could see the tears filling my dark brown eyes, but more than that, I could see the pain deep in my heart.

Don't let it get to you, Ayan, don't let it get to you. The first season is coming soon. Smile and be happy. Soon you will find a better life. Life where you will have a family and achieve your dreams. God is with those who are patient. Be patient, Ayan. Be patient.

I saw a light coming through my window, and I moved the curtains aside. I saw a blue butterfly wandering aimlessly, alone, as if she had lost her way. It looked as if her wing was broken.

I had no time to repair her wing, so I prayed for her. "May God heal your wing. May you find your place in this world!"

I closed the curtains and got ready for work.

That night when I got home from work, I checked on the blue butterfly. I saw her mending her own broken wing. She was stronger and smarter than I had thought.

24

On the day I graduated from college, I woke at seven in the morning. I had risen earlier for morning prayer, but then went back to sleep because it was still early. The best naps are the ones right after morning prayer. I opened my window to the lake to let in the cool spring air. I took a deep breath, every cell in my body quenching its thirst with the natural world. I watched the wind play with the water and the leaves. I saw an old couple walking carefully together, holding hands. A young man was running with his dog around the lake. *What a sight, what a blessing,* I thought. I then prayed to thank God for blessing me so much and helping me find a better life.

I twisted my hair in a bun just like my mother had done that night before I transitioned from a girl to a woman, at least by the measuring stick of my nomadic family. I put on some makeup and wore a black dress that I had bought for my graduation. I stood in front of the mirror and carefully put on my graduation gown, medal, and hat. I saw the blue butterfly flying over my head, spreading its wings, and I couldn't help but be mesmerized by the light beaming from it.

"You did it, Ayan!" I told my glowing soul and winked at myself.

I was walking to the car when my phone rang.

"Congratulations, Ayan! You did it!" Nasteho congratulated me. "I am so proud of you, and I am sure your family would have been proud of you if they were here today."

"Thank you, Nasteho. I am so happy! I can't believe I am graduating from college."

"I know! I wish I could be there, but little Ayan is not feeling too well," she sighed.

"What happened? Is she okay?" I asked her.

"She woke up feeling a little funny this morning."

"Don't worry, Nasteho, she will be fine. I am driving to my graduation. I will call you when I get out. Don't worry about coming."

I went into the arena and sat onstage with my summa cum laude medal. I looked around; the whole stadium was filled with people cheering for their loved ones. Thousands of people, but not a single one was there for me. I felt alone.

It's all right, Ayan. You have God with you. You don't need anyone else. Good job for making it this far! I patted my shoulder just like Uncle Ali used to do when I did well in school.

Once I received my degree and walked off the stage, I couldn't hold my tears any longer. A mixture of happiness and loneliness took over my body. Everyone was hugging their family and friends, while their loved ones took pictures to preserve that moment. I couldn't take a single picture.

I started rushing toward the parking lot to leave the celebration. What's a celebration without loved ones? My tears kept falling; I couldn't hold them back anymore, so I just let them be. I stopped fighting.

I was walking on the grass on my toes so my high heels wouldn't sink into the grass when I heard, "Congratulations, Ayan. I am so proud of you." I turned around and saw Awale wearing a black tuxedo and holding a bouquet of white roses and a gift bag.

"Awale, what are you doing here?" I asked, surprised.

"You didn't think I was going to miss the biggest day of your life, did you? I know how much this day means to you. So I came to celebrate with you." He handed me the bouquet of roses and the gift bag.

"Thank you. They look beautiful," I said, wiping my tears.

He hugged me and whispered, "You did it! Good job. I am proud of you!"

"Thank you, Awale, for coming! I am going to head home. It was nice seeing you." I wanted to be in his arms, but I stepped back.

"Come on, Ayan, it's your graduation day. Celebrate a little. Let's take some pictures." He took out his phone.

"Thank you. I appreciate that you came, but I don't want your mother and wife to get mad at me. They already hate me enough."

"Just one picture. Plus, you are technically still my wife. Come on, let's just take one picture, for old time's sake."

"No, I am not your wife. I have never really been your wife. What makes people husband and wife is the relationship of their hearts. For God's sake, stop claiming that I am your wife." I was irritated with his words.

"We can talk more about how I am not your husband while we eat. Can I just take one picture of you and one picture of me and you?"

"I am not hungry. But, yes, we can take one picture."

"Trying to take advantage of me, hon?" He laughed and asked a woman to take our picture.

Once she took the picture, we thanked her, and she walked away to her family.

I smiled at Awale and said, "I see your jokes haven't improved much."

"At least I made you smile."

"What a cliché," I said.

"I made a reservation at a restaurant for us. Let's eat and celebrate. We can also talk about your favorite things—how I am not your husband," Awale said.

"I am not hungry, and I have a headache. Sorry, but I have to go home. Thanks for the thought, though; I appreciate it." I turned down his offer to celebrate, not because I didn't want to but because I was scared of getting weak.

"Come on, Ayan, it's your graduation. You deserve a good celebration. Forget about everything that happened between us for once, please."

"Thank you, Awale, but I am not feeling well." Saying his name felt good and painful at the same time.

"You are still using that 'I am sick' excuse to get out of uncomfortable situations. Let's just go celebrate. We don't even have to talk to each other. I know how much this accomplishment means to you, and you deserve a celebration."

"I have to go home and change. My clothes are not exactly fit for a restaurant. It was for my graduation."

"You look gorgeous in everything you wear." He looked directly in my eyes, and my heart skipped a beat. "We can stop at your house if you would like," he said.

"I can't go to a restaurant with you. I don't want anyone to see us together and misunderstand. I have some sweets at home that I bought for myself. We can eat that at my house, if you don't mind."

By the time I got to my apartment, he was already standing in front of the door, waiting for me patiently.

Gosh, had you waited for me like this, everything would have been all right, I thought as I walked toward him.

"You are a fast driver, huh. Come in." I opened the door for him.

We went up to my apartment on the fifth floor. He sat on my sofa in the living room, and I went to the kitchen to get him some Somali sweets and tea. I sat on the love seat facing him.

We joked a bit and had some tea with the sweets. It had been so long since I'd sat with him, talked with him, both of us glancing at each other and laughing at his corny jokes.

"Ayan, let's just have an honest talk. How long are we going to avoid this?" He grew serious all of a sudden.

"Our case was closed a long time ago, Awale. There is nothing left for us to talk about. You are married, and you have a baby on the way. I want to work for a year and start medical school next year. I have what I wanted, you and your mom have what you wanted—a good wife and a baby. It's a little too late for a discussion at this point."

"It's better to talk late than never to talk at all. We both deserve closure, Ayan. Just give me thirty minutes. I promise that after we talk, I will never bother you again. Unless of course you want me to."

"Have some tea. I need to change out of these graduation clothes."

I came back out and found him staring at our wedding photo, which I had forgotten on the TV stand. I had laid it facedown but never had the strength to throw it away.

"Remember our wedding night? We talked and ate all night long," Awale said, smiling.

"Yeah, we also made so many promises that neither one of us could keep. Well, I kept mine, but you couldn't keep yours." I said this as he looked at me, his eyes piercing through my soul. "I am pretty sure I remember you saying that you would never marry another woman while I was alive. But it's all in the past. Why do you want to talk about this now?"

"I know I failed to trust you and your words. I am very sorry. I failed to trust you, and I broke my promises to you. I broke your heart and mine too. I shouldn't have listened to anyone else." He moved closer to me and held my hand as he looked into my eyes. "I just want to apologize to you for all the pain and hurt that I have caused for not believing you and for failing to keep my promises. I have always loved you, and I still love you. I might not deserve to be forgiven for what I have done to you, but for what it is worth, I still want to ask for forgiveness. Please forgive me, Ayan. I have wronged you and broken your heart in the most horrible way that I could." Tears filled his eyes.

"Awale, I forgave you a long time ago. But I don't think I can ever forget what you have done to me. I was a full-time college student working two jobs just so I could support your family and also make enough money to bring you to the US. I worked so hard to make things work, but your mom poisoned your mind, and you believed her."

"I know. I messed up big-time. It is all my fault. I am really sorry." He hugged me and started crying.

I cried with him. I had no strength to push him away. All the anger, all the hatred, and all my resentment were not strong enough for the love I felt for him. I cried in his arms and hugged him as if we were making up for all the missing years.

"Thank you, Ayan. Thank you for not getting a divorce from me. I want to be with you. I promise you that I will never let anyone come between us again." He hugged me tighter.

I pushed him away. "I forgave you, but we can never get back together. I am sorry, but I cannot share my husband. Besides, it's illegal in this country. Of all the people, you should know how I feel about that. You buried our love, and there is no way to revive it. Our relationship is over."

"Ayan, I am not asking you to be one of my wives. I want you to be my only wife. There will be no one else. Please, give me a chance to make it up to you. I promise I won't let you down again." He moved closer to me.

I moved back. "It's too late for us. You have a wife and a kid on the way. Our relationship broke the day you decided to marry her. I am sorry, but I will never be able to be with you again. I cannot break another woman's home to build mine." I got up as tears rolled from my eyes. "I have some things to do. Please leave."

He stood up and hugged me tightly. "Please, Ayan, just give me one more chance. I promise I will prove to you that I am worthy of you. I have never loved her. She teamed up with my mom to manipulate me and break us apart. I am so sorry for failing us."

He kissed my forehead.

My voice brought me back to the reality that I was living in. *Ayan, get ahold of yourself!* I heard my inner voice yelling at me. I then pulled myself together and pushed him away. "I am sorry, Awale, but in this world, we are going to remain a broken dream. Please leave." I opened the door for him.

"I will divorce Salma. I already told her. Hibo opened my eyes, Ayan. They trapped me in a loveless marriage. I want you. I still love you." He tried to hold my hand, but I flinched and pulled away from his hand.

"I don't care whether you divorce her or not; you made a conscious decision to marry her. You wanted to get revenge on me for supposedly forgetting you when I did nothing but work hard for you and for your family. I am sorry, but I am not someone that you can walk out on whenever you want and come back whenever you want. You have decided to walk away—please keep walking, and don't look back, because I have moved on with my life. We are over." I gestured for him to get out.

He stared in my eyes for a minute, and my heart was begging me to let him back into my life. I just wanted to hug him and be in his arms forever, but I didn't, I couldn't. I locked my heart in a box and threw away the key between the Indian Ocean and the Red Sea.

He left, and I locked my door. I then sat on the floor and started crying.

About an hour later, Nasteho called me.

"Where are you, Ayan? Everyone is here waiting for you. Did you not get my text?"

"No, Nasteho, I didn't. I got caught up and haven't had a chance to check my phone," I said.

"Oh, okay. My husband and I organized a party to celebrate your graduation."

"A party? Okay, I will be there soon. How is little Ayan?"

"She is doing better. Her fever went down, and she is sleeping. Dress really nicely—like you are going to a wedding. Or better yet, like you are the bride. That witch is here—Mom invited her," Nasteho said.

"I don't care about her anymore. Awale was at my graduation today. He asked for forgiveness and said that he wanted to get back with me." I told her what happened with Awale.

"What did you say?"

"What else? I said no. He said that he was going to divorce Salma, but I refused to let him back into my life. I cannot be the reason that child grows up without his dad, and I cannot break someone's home. There's no hope for our relationship," I told Nasteho.

"Ya Allah!" Nasteho said. "You and your outdated moral values. Seriously, she married him on purpose. She knew he was your husband. She knew how hard you worked to support him and his family. She knew how much he meant to you, but she married him regardless. You shouldn't even be thinking about her. For once, Ayan, just think of yourself and your happiness. That witch Nura and Salma tricked him into marrying her. She stole your husband. Now that he has found out the truth and wants you back, you should forgive him and get back with him. He is human, and all humans make mistakes. God created us that way."

"I appreciate your advice, Nasteho, but I cannot let him into my life. He is a grown man with a brain. He made a choice and has to live with the consequences. I forgave him, but I cannot let him back into my life. Not after what he did to me."

"That witch! I want to jump her. Let's talk about this some other time. Dress really nicely and get your ass over here. Everyone is waiting for you. This is your day—let's celebrate it."

"I will see you in a bit." I hung up the phone.

About an hour later, I arrived at Nasteho's house. It was difficult to find a parking spot. I didn't know they had invited the whole city. Nasteho lived in the suburbs just outside of Minneapolis with her husband. They had bought a house after they had baby Ayan.

Nasteho was living the American dream. She lived in a big house with a white picket fence and a large backyard. As I walked toward her home, I could smell the freshly cut grass in her front yard.

Nasteho and her husband had set up a tent in her backyard for the party. Salads, pasta, rice, pita bread, chicken, goat meat, lamb meat, soup, and several desserts were perfectly lined up on a long table. Some people were sitting in the tent, and some people were sitting in the grass and enjoying the sun's rays. People were chatting and laughing as they shared food.

I walked through the house to get to her backyard. Her TV was on, playing an old Somali song, one of my favorites.

Aduunyadu waa giraan
This world is like a ring

Galaba meel taaganoo
At a different station each day

Marbaad guudkeeda tahay
At times, you are at the top

Marbaad gondaheeda tahay
At times, you are at the bottom

Mar unbaad gaadhinee
You will get there someday

Ha goyn rajada ha goyn
Don't sever hope, don't sever

Ha goyn
Don't sever

Ha goyn
Don't sever

Ha goyn
Don't sever

Ha goyn rajada, ha goyn

Don't sever the hope, don't sever

I walked into my graduation party, and everyone congratulated me. There was so much noise and a crush of friends surrounding me, with Nasteho at my side.

"Nasteho! Thank you! I love you so much!" I said with tears in my eyes.

"I love you too! Congratulations! I am so proud of you. I know how much school meant to you. And you did it!" She hugged me.

"It looks so beautiful. How much money did you spend on this?"

"Ayan, don't worry about money; that's why we didn't tell you we were throwing you a party. Just enjoy your big day. It's your day, dear. Let's *party*!" Nasteho said ever so animatedly.

"You truly are a blessing from God, just like your name says," I told her. "Wait, isn't that little Ayan running around?"

"Yes, she is all fine now," Nasteho said, laughing.

"You liar! She wasn't sick! You were preparing this!"

"Guilty as charged!" She smiled.

I sat by Nasteho, her mother, and her sisters, two tables away from Nura, Salma, Hibo, Haboon, and Hoodo. The girls ran to me when they saw me, and they congratulated and hugged me.

"Congratulations, Ayan! We are so proud of you." They all hugged me at the same time.

"Thank you, guys!" I said.

"Seriously, though," Hibo said, "we thought we were your sisters. Why didn't you invite us to your graduation?"

"I am sorry; I just didn't want to create drama between you and your mother. You know how she feels about me."

"It's all right, Ayan. We just want to tell you that we are very proud of you and can't wait to be at your graduation from medical school," Hibo said.

"Thank you, Hibo. I've missed you guys so much. We should hang out sometime," I said.

"Yes, we should. Without Mom knowing, of course," Hibo said, and they laughed.

They went back to their table. I didn't realize how much I had missed them until that moment, especially Hibo. She had always had a special place in my heart.

As we were eating, Nasteho's mother, Hawa, complimented me. "You look so beautiful! You are a smart, beautiful, and very well-mannered young lady. You came to this country at such a young age, and with no mother or father to tell you what to do, but look where you got yourself! Your parents would have been very proud of you if they were here today. We are all proud of you, dear. I wish I had a son your age; I would have made you my daughter-in-law without a second thought. The family you marry into will truly be blessed. I pray that God blesses you with all the happiness in the world and with the things you desire the most—becoming a doctor and having your own family."

"Thank you, Aunt Hawa. May God bless you with the best of this world and the best of the hereafter. Don't worry, I will train my daughters to be just like me. I am sure you will have plenty of grandsons," I said, winking at her, and we laughed.

"Hawa," Nura said, leaning over toward our table. "Did you meet my daughter-in-law, Salma?"

"No, I heard about her, though," Hawa said as she got up from the table. "Some women just like secondhand things, don't they?"

Nasteho shook her head sharply at her mother in warning, but Hawa ignored her and went to get some water.

"Where were we?" Hawa said as she came back to the table. "Oh yeah, nice to meet you, Salma."

"Nice to meet you, Aunt Hawa," Salma whispered. I was holding my laugh.

Nasteho read a message on her phone and said, "Ayan, could you please get the milk for little Ayan? It's in your old room. In the meantime, go fix your hair," she said, untying my hair.

"Did you just untie my hair?" I asked her.

"No, I was hiding them. They are showing," Nasteho said.

"You are such a weird human being!" I said, laughing, and I went to get the milk.

I went downstairs to my old room in Nasteho's house. There was no milk bottle in the room. In fact, it was exactly how I had left it. I took off my scarf and started gathering my hair together so I could put it in a bun. I was standing in front of the mirror when I saw a man locking the door. My heart pounded with fear, but then I realized it was Awale.

"Awale? What are you doing here?" I asked.

"You look so beautiful! I forgot how beautiful your hair is." He walked toward me.

I grabbed my scarf and put it on head.

"You don't have to cover up from me. I am still your husband, remember?"

"No, you were my husband."

"I can still see your hair," he chuckled.

"I don't care whether you can see my hair or not. What are you doing here? Why did you close the door? I don't want your wife and mother to misunderstand me. Please get out." I took off the scarf and started rolling my hair in a bun vigorously.

"I am here to tell everyone that I love you and that you are my wife."

"Don't you dare say such a thing. What are you trying to do? You have already ruined my life once, and now you want to humiliate me in front of the whole community! I want to keep my life private. Please don't do anything stupid like that," I said.

"I don't care what anyone thinks or says. I love you and I want you back, and that is the truth, Ayan." He moved closer to me as I stepped back. He then put his arm around my waist and pulled me toward him, hugging me tightly.

"Let go of me, Awale, or I will scream. You whole family is sitting outside. Let go of me." I lightly pushed him, it felt so nice to be in his arms.

"Go ahead and scream. I will just tell them you are my wife. What can they do or say?"

"Please, Awale, stop your childish games and let go of me." I struggled to free myself from his grip.

Deep down, though, I wanted to stay in his arms forever. I didn't want him to let go of me. I wanted him to hold me closer.

"I just want a chance, Ayan, just one chance to wake up next to you for the rest of my life. One chance to prove to you that I will never hurt you again. Please, Ayan, I love you."

I stopped resisting. "This is not going to change my mind. Let's be adults about this. Please let go of me. Don't ruin the happiest day of my life," I whispered in his ear.

"I am sorry, Ayan." He let go of me. I fixed my hair and went back to the yard.

"You smell like a man's cologne," Nasteho whispered, teasing me. "Did you hug him? Damn, you are fast!"

"Shut up. You set me up! I thought you were my friend," I said to her.

"I am your friend. That's why I am doing this. You need to snatch your man back. He is your husband, girl. If a woman stole my husband, I would get him back even if I had to bury her somewhere," Nasteho said.

"You are terrifying!" I said, smiling.

"What's going on? What are you whispering about?" Aunt Hawa asked.

"Nothing, Mom, just talking about Ayan's lover." Nasteho giggled.

"She is lying," I said. "There is no such person, Aunt Hawa."

"Breathe, girl, no need to blush. We all know girls talk to guys. I used to be a girl too, you know," Aunt Hawa said, laughing.

"Like mother, like daughter. Ganging up on me, huh?" I smiled.

The party was fantastic, and everyone left by the evening. I couldn't carry all the gifts, so I left them at Nasteho's house.

"Thank you, Nasteho," I said. "I love you. You are the best friend and the best sister anyone could ever ask for. I don't know what I did to deserve such an amazing friend."

"You are more than welcome, dear. I love you so much. You don't have to do anything to deserve good people in your life. You are an amazing human being, and anyone would be lucky to have you in their life. I am so glad to have met you."

I kissed little Ayan and said good-bye to Nasteho and her husband.

25

The weekend after graduation, I decided to not leave my apartment. I needed a couple of days to eat, sleep, and binge-watch all the shows that I had missed in the last seven years. I made a traditional Somali breakfast for myself and planned to order pizza for lunch and dinner.

In my pajamas, I brought my pillow and blanket to the living room and lay down on my sofa. I put my tea and breakfast on the coffee table, pulled the blanket over my legs, and turned on the TV.

About an hour into my lazy Saturday morning, I heard a knock on the door. Hibo was standing outside.

"Hi, Hibo! How are you?" I said and hugged her.

"Hi, Ayan. Sorry I didn't tell you that I was coming to your place!" Hibo said.

"It is all right, dear; come on in. Sorry the house is a little messy. Please take a seat," I said, clearing away some papers and books.

Hibo sat next to the sofa, and I went to the kitchen to get her some breakfast and tea.

"Are you still making anjero for breakfast?" Hibo asked, smiling.

"I wouldn't be Somali if I didn't." I laughed and handed her a mug of tea. "Let's eat."

"Sorry I came so early to your place without telling you," Hibo apologized again.

"Come on, Hibo, you don't need to apologize. I am glad you came to visit me! I have missed you so much!"

Hibo and I talked while we ate breakfast. Once we were done eating, I cleared away the dishes and returned to the living room to chat with Hibo more.

"How are things with you and Awale?" she asked.

"There is nothing between me and Awale," I responded. "I haven't had a chance to arrange for witnesses to get my divorce from him."

"Divorce? Didn't Awale reach out to you?" Hibo asked.

"He came to my graduation, and we talked. I have forgiven him, but I cannot undo the choices he's made. I don't see any alternative to getting a divorce," I said.

"Ayan, I think the two of you need to have a serious conversation. Awale is getting a divorce from Salma. I told him the truth," Hibo said.

"What do you mean he is getting divorced from Salma? What truth are you talking about?" I asked.

"He is getting a divorce from Salma because he still loves you," Hibo said.

"Love! I don't care about his love!" I said.

"I know Awale betrayed you," Hibo said, "but you need to hear the truth about what why he married Salma."

"Hibo, he is an adult, and he married Salma on purpose. I don't care how he married her or why he married her. The truth is he married her, and he broke my heart. I have moved on with my life, and he needs to move on with his life too."

"Please, just hear me out, Ayan," Hibo said. "Do you remember the engagement party for Max and Alia that you went to?"

"Yes."

"Salma is Alia's cousin, and she was at the engagement party. While you guys were taking group pictures with Alia and Max, she took pictures of you and Ahmed. Salma and Mom sent the pictures to Awale and told him that you were dating Ahmed. Mom told Awale that you were in love with Ahmed and that it was the reason that you had moved out. She told Awale that you were using work and school as excuses to not talk to him on the phone," Hibo said.

"What!? Awale knows that I love him more than my own soul and that I would never do anything to hurt him," I said.

"I know you do! But you were so busy with work and school that you had no time for him. And that gave Mom the opportunity to come between the two of you. Ayan, seven years is a very long time to wait for someone you love. At least give him credit for all the years that he did wait for you. Awale called you and gave you months to call him, but you never did. It broke his heart that you wouldn't call him back or check on him, even after he gave you three months," Hibo said.

"It's not like he was the only one waiting," I said as tears filled my eyes. "I was waiting too! He should know better. I was living in hell at your mom's house trying to do everything I could to support all of you. I passed out so many times from exhaustion because I was pushing myself so hard to earn money to bring Awale here. I was busy because I was working hard for both of us. I didn't call Awale because it was cheaper for him to call me and I was trying to save every penny!"

"I know, Ayan! I am so sorry for all the things that you had to go through. But think about it. When we moved to America, you and Awale used to talk to each other all the time. You couldn't get enough of each other, and if he didn't call you for a day, you used to call him. Imagine how he felt when you wouldn't call him even after months had passed. The bottom line is Awale is miserable because he never stopped loving you for a second, and now he knows he was lied to. You are miserable without him, and I know you have never stopped loving him. Please, talk to each other and resolve this misunderstanding before it is too late for both of you," Hibo said.

"It is already too late, Hibo. I appreciate that you are trying to help us, but nothing can be done. Awale is already married, and he has a baby on the way. I cannot be the reason that this baby grows up without a father," I said.

"It is not too late, Ayan. Awale would never neglect his own child. He will provide for the child. But he doesn't have to be with the woman who manipulated him and tricked him into marrying her. Salma stole your husband! Don't give her a second thought," Hibo said.

"Hibo, this is a lot to process," I said. "I need time to think about this."

"That's all I am asking for. Just talk to each other, and try to clear this misunderstanding between the two of you. I have never seen two people who love each other more than you and Awale. Please don't lose that love because of my mom's ego," Hibo said.

"Thank you, Hibo! You are such a wonderful sister and sister-in-law. Awale is lucky to be your brother. I just wish your mom were more like you. I can't understand why she hates me so much!" I said.

"She was hurt by my dad's family after he passed away. Since then, she has become very protective of who she lets into our family. I am seriously terrified of bringing any guy home," Hibo said, laughing.

"I am sure she will be happy to meet the man that you bring home. She just doesn't like me for some reason. I don't know if it is because of my tribe or because I was a maid and she doesn't think I am good enough for him."

"It has nothing to do with your tribe. Her mom is your tribe, and half of her friends are your tribe. I don't think it is because you were a maid either. I mean, she was a beggar before we arrived in Nairobi. I don't remember because I was too young, but she told me how we first met you in Mogadishu. We had to beg because my uncle had stolen everything from us. She always talks about how you and your family helped us," Hibo said.

"I didn't realize she talked about that," I said.

"She does and she always prays for your family."

"That's news to me! So why does she hate me so much, then?"

"I don't think she hates you. She is a complicated woman, and no one is good enough for her mighty son. She doesn't even try to hide that he is her favorite. Maybe she is threatened by how much Awale loves you. I honestly don't know, but I hope you can work through this and put all of it behind you," Hibo said.

"She is a complex woman. I will think about it," I said. "I need a little time."

Hibo and I watched a movie and ate some pizza. She stayed with me that whole day. It was nice to have her company.

26

A few weeks later, I received a surprising call from Nura.

"You bitch!" she screamed through the phone. "You can't live without ruining my family, can you? You think you can turn my son against me and ruin my daughter-in-law and grandchild's life? I will not let you do that, you low-life piece of shit!"

"Relax, Nura," I said, trying to calm her down. "What are you talking about?"

"Now you want to play dumb, huh? I will tell you, you little bitch. You asked him to divorce Salma, didn't you?"

"No, I did not! My relationship with you and your son ended a long time ago. Please stop calling and yelling at me. I don't care what he does or what you think. Your pathetic son has done what you wanted. You got exactly what you wanted. So go make him be married to that bitch of yours. And don't you dare call me again!" I yelled back at her. I had finally grown a spine.

"How dare you talk to me like that," she said. "I knew you would show your true colors one day. I will show you! My son will never divorce Salma. He would never choose a woman like you. Get the hell out of our lives, and leave my family alone. You don't deserve to be loved. No wonder God made you alone in this world."

I must tell the truth. Her final insult hurt the most. Of everything Nura had said, this was more than I could take.

I worked to control my voice, though I wanted to scream. "I have done nothing to you and your family but help you. If I wanted your son, trust me, I could have had him in a snap. But unlike you, I have some dignity. I know how to curse, and I know how to show you your place. I respected you like my mother, which I now know is a respect you don't deserve. What are you scared of? That I will tell people that you were a beggar? That I had met you when you knocked at our door begging for food? Fuck you, and fuck your son. Don't ever call me again." I hung up on her, and my hands were shaking.

I called Nasteho.

"Oh my God, Nasteho, I just cursed the shit out of Nura. Someone please shoot me! It feels so bad, yet so good!"

"You what? *Bravo!* You finally grew a spine. She deserves it. That witch had it coming. I can't believe it, though. What happened?" Nasteho asked, surprised.

"She called me and started cussing me out. I lost it when she said I'd deserved to lose my family. May God forgive me, I can't believe I said such foul words to her," I said, covering my eyes with embarrassment.

"Good job," Nasteho said. "I am so proud of you. Don't worry, she had it coming. She had been pushing you for years. What a miracle! Why was she yelling at you?"

"Awale divorced Salma. I won't lie. That made me a little happy. I guess karma finally came around!"

"Wow! Today is a miraculous day. He grew some balls, and you grew a spine. Thank you, my Lord. What are you going to do if he asks you to take him back?" Nasteho asked.

"I don't know. I guess I will see what happens."

"Come on, Ayan, we both know you love him more than anything. You worked two jobs to support yourself, to support him and his family, and to save enough to bring him to the US. Seriously, I know you love him more than your own life. Just put everything else aside for once and think about yourself. Think of yourself and what makes you happy. If I were you, I would get back with him without a second thought. At least give him a chance," Nasteho advised.

"I do love him, and he is the only family I have now. That's why I couldn't bring myself to get a divorce."

"The first step to recovery is acceptance. If he comes back to you, it's good. If he doesn't, you have nothing to lose. At least you will be able to move on with your life."

It was getting late, and I told Nasteho that I needed to go to sleep. I went to bed, but I couldn't sleep. Around three in the morning, my phone rang. It was Awale.

"Hello," I said anxiously. "Are you all right?"

"I am in front of your place. Could you please open the door for me?" he whispered. I was feeling happy inside, but I had to hide it for the moment. I jumped from my bed and ran to open the door for him.

"It's three in the morning. What are you doing here?" I asked.

"I am basically homeless. I drove around for hours until I finally mustered enough courage to call you. Could I please stay here until I find a place?" he asked while looking into my eyes.

"Yeah, sure, you can sleep on the sofa." I brought out a pillow and blanket and put them on the sofa for him.

"I haven't eaten any food all day," he said. "I am starving."

"Now you want food too? Okay, I will make something for you."

I brought the food to the living room and found him standing before me without his shirt. I had forgotten how good his body looked.

"Please, put on some clothes." I blushed and turned away.

"I don't have anything else to wear. Am I turning you on? Enjoy it while it lasts," he teased me and sat on the table.

"More like turned off. I don't find married men attractive. Here, wear this." I threw a bedsheet and a large T-shirt at him.

"Why are you blushing? Would you like to touch my guns? I am still your husband," he said, smiling.

"Stop saying those useless words. Do you want to go to jail? It's illegal to be married to two women in this country. Seriously, how many times do I have to tell you that?"

"You are my only wife. I finalized my divorce with Salma, and I also told Mom today," he said.

"Oh, sorry to hear that," I said.

"No, you are not. I know you are very happy because I am getting back together with you."

"With me? When did I say I want to get back with you?"

"I will keep trying. I will wait for you and try to convince you. I hope that you will give me a chance before it's too late. I have waited for you for almost a decade. How long does a man have to wait to prove his love?" he asked, sipping the tea.

"You haven't exactly waited for me," I said and turned toward my room. "I am going to sleep now. Good night."

"I love you," he said. It struck me like lightning, but I kept walking as if I hadn't heard him.

That night, I kept remembering all the times that Awale had stood by me. I remembered how he used to wake up at three in the morning to help me do the house chores when I was their maid. I remembered how he'd bought me books and given me back the hope that I had lost. I remembered how he'd convinced Nura to let me go to school while I worked for them as a maid. I remembered how he'd protected me and encouraged me to go after my dreams. I remembered how he'd built up my confidence, the confidence that I had lost along with my family. I remembered how he'd made me feel that I was not lacking anything.

That whole night, my brain played and replayed the memories of all the things that he had done for me.

Ayan, people make mistakes. He made one mistake—he believed his mother's lies. He is human, and we all make mistakes. You also played a role by giving his mom the opportunity to come between the two of you. A misunderstanding shouldn't cost you everything. He is the only family that you have. He has done so much for you and supported you when you had no one. Is the mistake he made worth forgetting all the good in him and all the good that he has done for you? My brain bombarded me with question after question. I didn't sleep much that night.

By the time the sun rose, my heart and my brain were finally on the same page. I had a decision to make.

The next morning, I woke extra early to look beautiful for him. I brushed my hair and let it down. I wore a beautiful black traditional dress, which is called a *dirac*. I went to the living room, where he was sleeping peacefully on the sofa. The blanket had fallen to the floor. I grabbed it and pulled it over him. I stared at his innocent face. He opened his eyes, and we made eye contact. His gaze shook me to the bone.

"What I wouldn't give just to see your face every morning," he said. "You still love me and care so much about me. Why don't you give us one more chance? I promise you, I will not let you down again."

"I am not the same wife you married all those years ago," I said and sat on the floor beside the sofa. I was so close to him that I could feel his body heat.

"No one stays the same," he said. "People grow and change. But I know you feel the same way about me. You look at me the same way you did on our wedding night."

"I might look at you the same way, but I won't wake up before you in the morning to cook for you," I said.

"That's all right. I am a great cook. I will cook for us." He smiled.

"You? Cooking? I don't know if I can trust you with my food," I teased.

"Tell me what else you want me to do," he said.

"I don't want to have kids until I finish medical school," I said.

"Who wants kids anyway? They are so annoying. We will have kids when you are ready. Plus, I also want to get my MBA. I still want to open that hospital with you." He held my hand and kissed it. I pulled my hand back from him and stood up.

"You are so cheesy," I said.

"May I please sleep on your bed? This sofa is hard to sleep on. I didn't sleep much last night."

"It's a little small," I said. "It will be too crowded."

"We will make it work. Do you still kick and snore in your sleep?" he asked, smiling.

"What! I don't snore or kick!" I laughed.

He stood up and kissed me on the forehead.

"Go get ready for morning prayer," I said.

"I am so happy to have met you and to have married you. I thank God for blessing me with you, and I pray to him to help me get back together with you. I have always loved you, I still love you, and I will always love you, Ayan. I hope you can find it in your heart to forgive me and allow me back into your life." He looked at me just like the day he'd proposed to me.

Suddenly, a thought occurred to me. "You are not homeless, are you?" I asked, laughing.

"Of course not! I just had to get a chance to talk to you. You know there are hotels in Minneapolis, right?"

"You!" I started chasing him around the living room.

My heart had won.

We prayed together like a family, and then we went back to sleep.

As I slept in his arms, I dreamed again that I was trapped inside a glass sphere, cut off from all of the world. But the dream had a different feeling this time.

As I stood in the glass sphere and gazed down at my MD certificate, I looked up and saw that I was standing before a crowd. And there he was—Awale, standing tall and smiling at me. He extended his had to me, but I couldn't reach through the glass that surrounded me.

A tear escaped from my eye, and as it landed on the floor, the glass shattered like ice on a shallow puddle. I reached out my hand for Awale, and we walked toward each other, not breaking eye contact until our hands were united. I held his hand and walked through the crowd with my chin held up high this time. I had love, I had a home, and I had a family of my own.

I walked gracefully through the crowd with Awale by my side. I finally belonged to someone, and someone belonged to me.

"Ayan, look!" Awale said.

I looked up and saw the blue butterfly flying with its lover. Her wing had healed. She danced in the air with her lover, and their light lit up the world. I woke up from my dream.

That evening, I took out my journal so I could write to Uncle Ali and update him on my progress.

Dear Uncle Ali,

I am getting closer to getting into medical school. I still have the necklace you gave me, and I cannot wait to wear it once I officially become a doctor. I just wish you were here to see me and see how hard I am working to get into medical school. I know you would be very proud of me.

I work in a research lab, which will give me good experience before I go to medical school. I am also taking classes to prepare me for medical school.

I am studying for the MCAT, which I will take in about four months. I want to stay in Minnesota, which limits my options a little, but we have a great Somali community here, and I want to contribute to my community. I volunteer at the local community center and tutor high school students so they can get into good colleges and universities. I also teach math, science, and Islamic studies on weekends at a mosque in a Minneapolis. You and Aunt Zainaba were great role models to me, and I hope to follow your footsteps in doing my part in my community.

Getting into medical school in the US is very difficult and expensive, but I am grateful to have Awale by my side. I am sure you would have loved him had you met him. Wait, you did meet him, and you liked him. Remember Nura, the lady who came to our house during Ramadan right before Eid? You helped her and her kids. Well, Awale is her oldest son. He reminds me of you. He is very loving and caring. Awale supports us financially, and I save every penny I make for medical school.

Yours, Ayan

On the day I graduated from medical school, I was no longer alone. Some people had to squat, and others had to sit down to fit us all into one picture. I had finally found it. I found my family, love, happiness, dreams, and the better life that I had been searching for. I found my home.

Just like my mother said, I had lost pieces of myself along the way to finding a better me. I remembered my mom telling me that we are like snakes, that we also have to shed our old skin so we can be newer and better versions of ourselves. She always said that we shed our skin through hardship and pain, that we lose parts of ourselves and sometimes lose the things closest to our hearts.

My graduation celebration was held at Mom's house. Yes, I am talking about Nura. She eventually came around, and she is sweet as pie now, but I'm not sure I totally trust her yet. Nura has been trying very hard to have a good relationship with me, but it will take me some time to get over what she did to me and Awale. Nura helped me a lot while I was in medical school—she babysat our children and helped us around the house a lot. She is a wonderful grandmother to our children.

That evening, when I got home from the celebration, I prayed to God to thank him for all the blessings. And then I took out my journal and wrote a letter to my family.

Salaam, my dear family,

How are you? I have been praying for you a lot. I hope that God has accepted my prayers and that you are enjoying the sight and smell of heaven. It breaks my heart every time I realize that you are no longer on this earth with me. I have missed you terribly, but I won't be selfish and wish that you were still here, as I know that you are in a better place. I won't lie: I did wish you were here with me many times, but I have finally developed my third eye and become a little less selfish.

Uncle Ali, guess what? I wore the necklace you gave me today. I have finally become a doctor. Thank you for giving me a dream, a hope, and a future. You have been an inspiration to me, and your words have guided me through the darkest of times. It would have been good if you were here to see the woman I have become, but that's all right. God knows what's best for everyone. I have been volunteering and donating a lot to help the less fortunate on your behalf and on behalf of our family; I hope the benefits have reached you. I pray to God to bless you with heaven. I know you will go to heaven, for you were the best person I ever knew, and I promise I will keep doing good deeds on your behalf so we can be reunited in heaven. Thank you, Uncle Ali!

Mom, I know what you meant now. I understand your words, as I have developed both the third and the fourth eye. I have two sons and two daughters, Mom. I became a mother. I named my older daughter after you in the hope that she will become like you. Awale is good to me. I know it's because of your prayers that God has blessed me with so many good things. I want you to know that I am happy and all my dreams have come true. May God bless you with the highest level of heaven!

I haven't forgotten any of you. I can still hear your voices and see your faces. You are engraved deep into my heart. My life has become like half of a rose, beautiful but incomplete without you. Uncle Ali knows what I am talking about. Ask him. I love you, and I miss you a lot. Until we reunite in heaven, rest in peace, my loves.

Yours,

Ayan

I closed my journal and caressed the half rose on the cover. I was able to finally say good-bye to my family. The bright butterfly came through the open window with a cool breeze. I smelled the Minnesota spring flowers, which brought a sense of calmness. The butterfly landed on top of my journal, sprang its wings, and then flew off again. She was finally free, surrounded by her family. She happily danced in the flower garden.

Awale came into our bedroom and saw me crying and smiling at the same time.

"Are you all right, honey?" he asked.

"I was writing a letter to my family," I said as I put my journal away.

He wiped my tears and kissed my forehead. He then hugged me tightly.

"I have found home again," I said. "I have found the life I was searching for all those years. I have found my home."

My kids came into the room and saw the tears in my eyes.

"Are you okay, Mommy?" my son Ali asked as he wiped my tears.

"I am all right, baby! Mommy is crying because she is very happy." Tears filled my eyes, and I kissed Ali on the forehead as I hugged my family.

27

About a year into my residency at a nonprofit hospital in Minneapolis, I saw a man running toward me in the lobby.

He was yelling, "Abaayo, abaayo, sister, sister, sister!"

He hugged me so tightly that I could barely breathe or move my arms. I thought he was one of the psychiatric patients at the hospital. He started crying and would not speak or let go of me.

My coworker called security, but I gestured to the security guard to let him be. I stood there, letting him hold me, and I patted his back in reassurance. Something about him felt comforting and familiar, as if my heart and muscles recognized him before my mind could.

After holding me for a good minute, he finally let go of me, and I saw his face. Even through the tears and time, I could see the uncanny resemblance to Uncle Ali. The same eyes, the same smile, the same beard.

I started sobbing with him in the middle of the lobby as my colleagues watched us in wonder.

Fadumo Yusuf (better known by her nickname, Derbi), is a Somali-American author, engineer, and cultural-identity advocate. She was born in the Somali region of Ethiopia to Somali parents and immigrated with her family to Minneapolis, Minnesota, when she was a teenager. *Ayan, of the Lucky,* is her first novel.